Fleeing from Light

E. Michael Mettille

TMR Books
PO Box 510886
Milwaukee, WI 53203
www.themikereynolds.com

All images provided provided by Deposit Photos and Adobe Stock

Cover Artwork – © 2025 L.J. Anderson of Mayhem Cover Creations – www.mayhemcovercreations.com

Published by TMR Books 4/1/2025

ISBN 979-8-9927832-1-6

DEDICATION

For Tim, the smartest guy I've ever known, who would undoubtedly hate this story at least as much as he's hated everything else I have ever written. Thank you for always offering honest and helpful criticism. It makes me better.

CHAPTER 1

THE MARK

POTENTIALITY 0

Lots of folks who have suffered a near death experience—whether they end up crossing that line into clinical death or just come very close to it—talk about seeing a light. For some, this light fills them with joy and hope for what's to come. It reaffirms their beliefs in a hereafter, whatever those beliefs might be. Others are filled with dread. Regardless of how they come away feeling about the situation, some of them aren't ready to go. They are free to continue along on their mundane and useless journeys through this physical existence. Some are ready to go, and they know it. Those poor souls are tormented. Guilt weighs on them like a boulder crushing their spirit into the soft earth. Some think it's demons or ghosts hunting them down to drag them off to hell or heaven or whatever thing they believe in. That part's all in their heads. They are hunted, but it ain't by any spiritual beings.

Bale Lance was a hunter. Millions of realities running alongside one another fell under his jurisdiction, and they all had an equal number of myths and beliefs, gods they worshipped or feared. None of those were real in the sense that the particular entity existed in the way they were described in those stories. All those various supreme beings were nothing more than failed attempts at describing Bale's boss, Orwell Durr. Those souls belonged to him, and it was Bale's job to collect them.

One of those wayward souls was the reason Bale found himself standing beneath the weight of an unseasonably warm, late April sky on a crumbling street in the bowels of Hell's Kitchen. There wasn't a cloud in the sky, but the air was so wet it seemed droplets of rain could form right out of the nothing. It covered his skin like a damp towel. The street surrounding him was littered with trash and empty except for the rodents scurrying about the refuse and searching for unfinished morsels to chow on. The entire place smelled like someone forgot to flush after unloading the chili from the night before that just hadn't agreed with them.

Bale stood in the center of it all, soaking up the despair and letting it beat him down to a dark place inside himself, a hollow pit of desolation where he felt desperate enough to sentence some poor slob to oblivion. He hated his job, but Orwell didn't give him a choice. As he gazed at his prey through a window cloudy with dust from years of neglect, he thought he should be getting hazard pay. For two weeks he'd been chasing this one through the sweaty streets, wet from the heat and humidity and saturated with the smell. He had finally caught up to his mark. It was time to tag his bounty and move on to the next thing.

Bale dragged his palm across his forehead attempting to clear away the sweat beading up above his brow. It didn't help. The soaking air just left it glistening again. He kept his dark hair clipped short. That normally helped keep the sweat off his neck, but it was just as wet as the rest of him. On the plus side, Bale kept himself fit. Having his thick arms glistening when he walked up to his mark certainly wouldn't hurt. Intimidating his prey into believing they couldn't win if they tried had helped him avoid plenty of unnecessary scuffles in his long career. That was good. His favorite kind of fight was the one he could avoid. The folks he hunted typically weren't horrible people. They didn't deserve to be hurt. It was just their time.

Ceasar's Ghost was a shithole of a bar that was probably something fifty years ago, the kind of place where uppity fellows with too much money and too much time could get together to sip bourbon and argue about things nobody else cared about. The name was apropos. The place was just like a ghost haunting a street so littered with trash and sleeping homeless it looked more like a war zone than the vital avenue in the heart of a thriving metropolis that it desperately wanted to be. The unlit neon sign bolted to the front of the building wasn't how Bale knew the crumbling establishment had possibly the most perfectly descriptive name for a place that ever was. That thing was missing enough letters that the ones remaining didn't spell any word in any language. Two weeks of hunting, chasing, and researching a poor slob who knew somebody was after him but couldn't figure out who had led to the perfect spot to hide out for someone who doesn't want to be found.

When Bale finally yanked the heavy wooden door of the joint open and strolled inside, it was like walking into a time warp. He could picture the place packed with a pretentious crowd pontificating over elegant snifters—each filled with two fingers of bourbon that cost more than some folks make in year—about why one philosopher's ideas were preferable to another's. There was no crowd haunting Caesar's Ghost on this night. It was just before last call, and the dingy space was empty except for three other souls besides him. The one on the end of the bar looked like he'd been sleeping for hours under a pile of matted and dirty gray hair. He wouldn't be a problem. The youngster behind the bar had the tools to be a scrapper, but his smooth cheeks and all the product in his hair suggested he'd rather chase tail than trouble. And then there was the fat, sweaty reason Bale had to subject himself to one of the most desperate-looking shit holes he'd seen in his life.

Billy Cross slouched over a big splash of cheap whiskey in a tumbler that looked like it was plucked right out of Aunt May's kitchen. Everything about the guy was sloppy. His dark, sweat-streaked hair stuck to his forehead in spots and straight up in others. The button-down shirt he wore was probably perfect for an office when cleaned and pressed. Instead, the wrinkly, gray thing, that had most definitely been white at some point in its history, looked like armpit stink. The frumpy, brown trousers didn't look any better.

Bale took one more glance around the room before taking a seat on the wobbly barstool next to Billy. Cracks in the plaster spider webbing all along the walls and ceiling looked like veins under thin skin. The back bar was probably glorious during the place's heyday. Now it was cracked and discolored from too many years of neglect. The bar looked the same, a ghost of architectural perfection, faded mahogany scratched with graffiti.

"It's last call. If you want a drink it's got to be a quick one," the pretty boy behind the bar quietly said without much conviction in his tone as he scrolled through his phone, probably deciding whether to swipe right or left.

Bale offered a menacing, back off smile with his response, "Don't worry, kid. We'll be leaving soon." Then he turned toward Billy, grabbed the man's glass of whiskey, slammed it down, and said, "Billy Crass, you died at 10:34 p.m. on Monday, April 1st, in the year of our Lord, 2024. You were supposed to go into the light, but you know that. Why didn't you? Was that your idea of an April Fools' Day prank?"

"Hey, buddy, I don't want any trouble here. Order a drink or step off," the bartender's smoky voice cracked a bit as he held up his phone and added, "I'll call the cops."

There was a reason Bale wore his t-shirts tight. His swollen shoulders looked like they might rip right out of them. He flexed those bulging shoulders slightly as he leaned onto the bar and brought his face closer to pretty boy's. The smile he'd been wearing shifted to something closer to a sneer as he quietly said, "Look, I don't want to hurt you. I have a job to do. Put your fucking phone away, or I'm going to shove it up your tight, little turd squirter."

Billy split. He nearly tripped over the stool he'd been sitting on as it crashed to the floor, and he stumbled toward the exit. The door groaned loudly before slamming shut behind him.

Bale didn't pay any attention to Billy as he fled. Instead, he stared at pretty boy's eyes and let his face tighten into a hard scowl. He sat there in silence like that for an uncomfortable few moments breathing deeply like he was counting backwards from ten in his mind to keep from exploding. He wasn't, but if he were, he'd have only made it to seven before the bartender slipped his phone back into his pocket.

Bale let the smile slip back onto his face as he said, "Thanks, jackass. Now I've got to chase him."

Chase was probably a bit strong a word for all the pursuit would amount to. Bale knew exactly where Billy was heading. The destination was a dumb one. If Bale were trying to run from someone who found him hiding out in a random dive bar he'd never been to before, the last place he'd go would be home. That's the first place most folks who want to find other folks would start, their homes. Luckily, Bale had no doubt that the chubby sonofabitch was on a dead sprint along the four-block route that would take him to his shitty apartment. Bale would be there long before he arrived.

He grabbed a thin, rectangular device out of his pocket. It was about the same dimensions as a smart phone, not the shitty, small ones but the big ultra kind. Bale didn't have one of those. There wasn't anybody he really wanted to talk to that badly, and he wasn't a fan of any media, especially the social kind. He spun a couple dials on the thing and was just about to push the button that would transport him to his next destination without any running necessary when he felt the bartender staring at him.

Pretty boy's quickly morphing expression gave away how hard he was thinking about the next words that would dribble out of his mouth. "Are you going to pay for that guy's drinks since you chased him off?" he asked so quietly it was just a hair louder than a whisper.

"Why would I pay a dead man's debt?" Bale chuckled and then hit the button on his device.

A moment later, he materialized on the top of a six story, red brick building across the alley from an identical red brick where Billy lived on the fifth floor in apartment 508. Both were equally dilapidated. Bricks were missing here and there. The windows that weren't covered in rusty, metal cages were boarded up or missing altogether. Corroded fire escapes looked like the only thing they could help one escape from was life, and graffiti covered the buildings far higher than a human should want to scale a crumbling structure.

The sky was much better to look at than the sweaty hell languishing around the alley below. The moon was big and full that night, and there wasn't a cloud in the sky to hinder its brilliant light in the least. Bale loved the moon, full or a sliver didn't matter. It was one of the only things that brought him any joy anymore. The city lights hid the brilliance of all but the most ambitious stars and planets, but the ones he could see added just a little more magic to the quiet darkness. It looked so peaceful. He'd love to step right off the edge of the building and float off into the nothing, sail off into space and forget everything. He could never do that. There was someone depending on him.

"Where the fuck did you come from?" a voice asked from the shadows behind him, interrupting his little moment of Zen.

Bale spun quickly to get a bead on the owner of the raspy voice who had ruined his peaceful moment. It took a minute to place the fellow. He was buried in newspapers and other random trash. All the exposed parts of him were covered in so much soot, he blended perfectly into the darkness.

Once Bale had identified that the man wasn't a threat, he smiled wide and answered, "Ceasar's Ghost."

"You ain't no ghost," the dirty fellow responded.

"No, I'm not a ghost. I was at the bar named Ceasar's Ghost, and now I'm here," he chuckled a bit as he replied.

"Yeah, but how did you get there?" the man grew a bit agitated as he spoke, "One second there was nothing there, and the next second, you're standing there looking at the sky. How did you get there?"

Bale knew what the guy meant, but he had a few minutes to kill. He had no idea what it looked like to anyone who saw him *arrive*—or *depart* for that matter. That's what he called it when he used his device, arriving and departing. He didn't really understand how it worked, but it was a great tool for his line of work, which was basically hunting people. He plugged in the potentiality, longitude, and latitude coordinates, and hit the button. Then he vanished from where he was and showed up where he wanted to be. It was like a bionic GPS.

"That's exactly how it happened," he finally said. "First I was at the bar, and then, just like that, I was here."

"Bullshit," the guy groaned at him.

"May Athena strike me down if I'm lying," he held his hand up as if it might add some validity to the statement in the skeptical man's mind. Then he scratched his chin and asked, "What did it look like?"

"Static," the man replied quickly, "The air got all shaky, and then it looked like tiny blocks were being put together so fast you could hardly see them. Then you were there, gazing at the moon like a jackass."

Bale thought about the description. The fellow's explanation of what he saw lined up with how it felt to travel. Departing did feel a bit like being torn apart, deconstructed into the most basic atoms to travel through space and time like waves of light or sound, and then put back together on arrival. The process hurt, but the pain was brief. He could never forget the first time he'd done it. It was an instant of terror the moment he hit the button. It felt like a thousand knives sliced into every part of his body all the way into the bone, but the pain ended before the mind-numbing fear could take hold. Then he was standing somewhere else no worse for the wear.

The man's raspy voice dragged Bale away from the brief reflection as he asked, "Well, how did you do that, just show up like that out of nowhere? Is it some kind of trick? Are you one of them YouTube guys that goes around tricking people and fucking with them and making them look stupid. I ain't got no place to go, but I ain't stupid."

It would be a solid minute and a half before Billy made the alley. Plenty of time to humor a guy who probably didn't have much joy in his life. Bale finally smiled and said, "No, you obviously have your wits about you, and I am not some kind of Internet magician or anything like that. I hunt souls. I have a device that can transport me any place in any dimension at any point in their history."

"Bullshit," the man scoffed as he struggled to his feet, "Let me see it then."

Bale tensed as the man approached. There was no reason to hurt the guy. Hopefully, the man wouldn't give him one. "What are you doing?" Bale asked with a bit of authority stiffening his words.

"Relax," the guy groaned as he shuffled closer, "What's a scrawny fucker like me going to do to a tank like you? What are you, like six-two, six-three? You look like a pro wrestler. Steroids?"

"No steroids," Bale chuckled, "I have a pretty strict training regimen. None of the marks carrying around the souls I need to collect want to give them up, and some of them are pretty tough customers. I need to keep myself fit."

The man posed no threat. Even wrapped up in a dingy, old blanket, that much was obvious. There was something sad about the curiosity in the man's bright eyes as they sparkled from the soot caked upon his sunken cheeks. He probably had a good life at some point. Bale thought of asking but didn't. Billy's big ass would be slowly running as fast as he could down the alley any minute, and it would be time to split.

Bale slid the device out of his pocket and waved the man closer, "Here, look at this."

That was a mistake. The man was about a foot away from him when Bale caught a whiff. The guy looked like he spent his days swimming in sewage. He smelled even worse. Bale did his best not to grimace, but the odor was breathtaking.

Bale held the device out from his body to stop the man's advance and struggled through his explanation, "Your reality is potentiality zero. There are millions, maybe billions, of potentialities very similar to this one but different enough that you wouldn't recognize them all running in straight lines next to each other, each a mere vibration from the next. These are like different dimensions, slices of reality running from, based on the beliefs of this reality, we'll say Heaven and Hell. This is the potentiality I come from. Anyone can travel from one to another, but it ain't easy. It requires focus and manipulation of elements. This device does all that extra nonsense for me. I plug in the potentiality I'm traveling to along with coordinates, latitude, longitude, altitude, etcetera, and hit go."

Bale clicked the button as soon as he finished his explanation. That instant of pain wasn't the least bit frightening anymore. He knew it would be over quickly. His awareness spread apart, stretching, thinning, and expanding like a cloud. He could feel that he was moving, but it wasn't like walking or driving, or anything of the sort. It was almost like floating. An instant later he was standing ten feet from the man, holding up his device and flashing a friendly smile.

"Holy shit," the man gasped, dumbfounded.

"Holy shit, indeed," Bale laughed. Then he shrugged, and said, "It's been a slice, but I need to split."

As if on cue, the sound of heavy footsteps and labored breaths echoing off the bricks of the buildings stretching up from the alley below filled the air. Billy had finally made the alley. Bale wondered if the poor soul had enough gas to make it the last half a block to the back entry of his building.

"Is that the guy you're hunting?" the man standing on the roof with him asked, and then followed up with, "You're some kind of alien or something, aren't you? That technology, all that talk about dimensions. You're from a different world."

"I'm not," Bale shook his head as he walked toward the edge of the roof, "I'm from a long time ago in this world."

"Fuck that," the man snapped. His voice gained volume as he grew more and more agitated, "You're an alien. You're trying to steal that guy, so you can experiment on him."

"Dude, calm the fuck down," Bale whispered, "I don't want to hurt you, but I will."

The man dropped his blanket and charged. Luckily, he kept his mouth shut. The last thing Bale needed was for Billy to get spooked and skip his apartment for parts unknown. The scrubby guy just grunted with his first step, lowering his head like he was going to attempt a takedown. It was a short elbow Bale threw at the guy, fast and stiff. It connected right at the back of his jawbone. He dropped like a rock, out cold.

"Dumb ass," Bale sighed as he turned his attention to the alley six stories below. He felt bad about hitting the guy. He'd be alright. He'd be out for a few minutes, and his jaw would be sore for a couple days. Beyond that, all he'd take away from the altercation was a great story about how he fought with an alien to share with anyone who'd listen. It wasn't personal. If the guy hadn't caught him in the middle of a case, he would have enjoyed chatting with him for a while. As it was, Bale had work to do. His target was huffing and puffing six stories below him.

The alley was dark, a wasteland of trash and unfortunate souls hiding among it. There was only one light along the entire block. Halfway from one end to the other. It hummed loudly as it cast a dim glow on a steel security door with more dents on it than a newborn's cranium. Billy was about ten feet from that circle of dim, yellow light struggling to finish the last leg of his journey. His feet hammered heavily into the pavement with each labored step he took, splashing water up from random puddles, potholes filled up from recent rains.

Billy was a mess. His shirt had come untucked, unleashing his sloppy belly to flop in all its hairy glory from his knees to nearly his chin with every slow stride. He fell just before the stoop in front of the door bathed in the glow from that one working streetlight in the entire alley. He crawled up the three steps and pulled himself to his feet on a rusty, old railing that barely held his weight.

"Don't have a fucking heart attack," Bale whispered. It would wipe out his payday if the jerk died before he could deliver him to Orwell.

Billy fumbled with the lock for nearly a minute before finally getting the thing unlocked and flopping onto the stairway on the other side of it. Hopefully, the poor slob would survive the five flights of steps he'd need to climb to make it to his floor. The door swung shut, and Bale turned a couple dials on his device to set the proper coordinates that would land him in Billy's living room. Then he clicked the big button in the middle.

The rooftop around him melted away. After a whisper of darkness, four dingy beige walls materialized around him. He was in Billy's living room with his ass planted in an easy chair which accounted for a full quarter of the furniture in the room. Nothing matched anything else in the room aside from it all being at equal levels of disrepair. The chair he sat in was leather and was probably gorgeous thirty years ago. Now, the material was worn, and both heavily cushioned arms were shredded and losing stuffing. The end table next to him had at one time been stained a light oak. At this point in its life, it was full of scratches and the finish was mostly bare wood. It housed a small lamp that belonged on a child's desk rather than in a living room. The sofa next to that looked even older than the easy chair Bale sat on. It was an awful brown and tan pattern that was difficult to make out amid all the stains and tears in the fabric. Against the wall across from it all was a giant, flat screen TV. At least Billy had his priorities straight.

A solid five minutes passed before Bale heard keys jingling in the hallway. There were no less than four deadbolts keeping the door secure. It took another two minutes for Billy to unlock them all and bust into the kitchen. He didn't even glance in Bale's direction. Instead, he headed straight for the kitchen. The smell of spoiled eggs wafted all the way to the living room when he opened the fridge. Billy's back was to Bale when he cracked a beer and downed it, *twist, fizz, chug*. Then he tossed the bottle into the sink and grabbed another.

Bale let Billy get about halfway through his second beer before he said, "You know, if you ran everywhere that fast, you might not be carrying around the ninety extra pounds that gave you that heart attack in the first place."

Crash! The bottle slipped from Billy's trembling hands and smashed to bits against the floor.

"Who the fuck are you?" Billy stammered without turning around.

"I'm a collector," Bale replied quietly, "You died, but you didn't stay dead. Some folks who almost die, aren't ready yet. You're not one of those. It was your time. You were due in the City of Gold two weeks ago. I need to take you there."

Billy didn't respond. He just stood there, tense and looking like he might try bolting again at any moment.

"Look, I'm sorry, but I have a job to do," Bale's tone was matter of fact as he continued, "You've got no place to go, and you can't have any gas left in your tank. It's over. Don't try to run…"

Billy bolted toward the door.

"Damn it. Now I've got to chase…" Bale said as he thumbed his device and vanished, reappearing in the hallway right outside Billy's door. The stickers on the flimsy thing read *50*, but that was only because the *8* had fallen off.

When Billy busted through the door into the hallway, Bale finished his statement, "…you," as he threw a right hook and dropped him where he stood. Then he looked down at Billy's unconscious body and asked, "Why the fuck do they always run?"

CHAPTER 2

THE RIP OFF

CITY OF GOLD

Orwell Durr was an insufferable cunt. Bale preferred to avoid that particular word, but in all the years he knew the vile thing, a better descriptor hadn't presented itself. On the surface, Orwell was the picture of perfection. His eyes were bright and keen like a fox's. He wore a crisp, white suit that seemed impervious to wrinkles or any form of blemish. It was the same suit he'd been wearing since Bale met him. Of course, it couldn't have been the same exact suit. He must have had hundreds of thousands of them, and they all looked the same. His hair and perfectly trimmed goatee were as white and bright as his clothing. Neither made him look elderly. His skin was youthful and taut, like a twenty-something who'd witnessed a thing so utterly terrifying it shocked the color from his hair.

Beneath that flawless façade dwelled the vilest, most conniving scum to ever tarnish the face of reality. His heart, if he had one, must have been the blackest, deadest thing to ever rot inside a carcass. He was absent even the minutest speck of patience and housed equal amounts of compassion and empathy. He was a void who cared only for perfection at any cost.

Orwell's office echoed his personality. The glossy, mahogany desk he reclined behind was flanked by bookshelves of the same deep, rich finish. Everything was tidy and perfectly in line. There were no ragged edges or oddities which seemed out of place. Everything was precise despite appearing like nineteen-thirty sat on its face and dribbled its goodness all over its chin. Orwell was like that though. He had particular eras he was fond of, and he lived like they never ended. Every meeting was like a scene from some black and white noir film, and he was the big boss behind whatever scheme was happening.

Bale unhappily played the muscle in Orwell's fantasies. He carried Billy's heavy ass over his shoulder all the way up to Orwell's desk and dropped it in front of it in a fat, sweaty pile of unconsciousness.

"Sloppy as usual, Mr. Lance," Orwell droned like an annoyed schoolteacher.

Bale always planned to be polite, to play the game, but he could never stick the landing. As soon as Orwell opened his mouth, Bale became a defiant child battling against the rules. "Sorry, Or," he shrugged, "Fucker ran. Can't figure why. Just look at him. This cat couldn't outrun a stick of butter. He'd probably eat one though."

Orwell's jaw tightened as he replied, "Would you say I treat you with respect, Mr. Lance?"

"Respect?" Bale chuckled, "That might be a stretch. Polite, I'd say, annoyingly polite."

The tension in Orwell's jaw remained as he asked, "Then why do you refuse me the same?" He cleared his throat dramatically before continuing, "Mr. Durr, Orwell, either of those would be fine. When you call me Or, it sounds as if you'd like to reduce me to a common conjunction. Do I appear common to you, Mr. Lance?"

"Of course not, boss," Bale grinned, "There is nothing common about you." He nodded toward the pile lying on the floor next to him before asking, "This fat shit's fifty, right?"

Orwell casually examined his fingernails as he replied, "Twenty-five."

"It was fifty when I took the job," Bale grunted in disgust.

"Clean marks are fifty. You always bring them to me stressed. How we do things is equally important as the things we choose to do," Orwell's tone dripped with boredom.

It was the same as always with this cocksucker. The price offered was never the price paid. As much as he liked to pimp the idea that everyone was dying to get into heaven, or at least their perception of it, nobody gave a shit about Orwell or the City of Gold anymore. If they did, that tightwad wouldn't need to chase these losers down.

Bale sighed deep as he finally replied, "A soul's a soul, and this one was a pain in the ass."

Orwell shrugged and offered a smug smile as he replied, "Oh well, you did succeed where others failed, and he was a slippery one. Probably heavy too, by the looks of him. I'll give you thirty-five."

"Come on, Or," Bale groaned, "You've given me thirty-five for coma patients." He scratched his head, scowled at Billy still lying unconscious on the floor, and pointed several times at Orwell before adding, "Fine. I want to see her then."

The dramatic and slow laugh Orwell offered before responding was as obnoxious as it was infuriating. He loved this shit. When he finally finished his patronizing chuckle, all he offered was more bullshit, "Do I look like a negotiator? Your next visit is in two weeks. You should be satisfied I allow you to see her at all."

"Come on, five minutes. I've brought you eight solid marks since my last visit. Just let me pop in and let her know I'm still around." Bale pled his case sweetening his voice up as much as he was able around the foul taste he always got in the back of his throat when he had to deal with this pretentious twat.

Orwell's smile turned devious as he leaned forward into his desk, rubbed his hands together briskly, and said, "Fine, let's negotiate then. You can have ten minutes, but then you only get ten for the mark."

Bale clenched his fists like he might jump across Orwell's desk and knock the condescending grin off his pompous face. Instead of making that grave mistake, he nearly shouted, "Ten years? That's some bottom-feeder bullshit, and you know it!"

"Your mouth, Mr. Lance! Do not forget who owns whom here. If you want to see her, it is ten. If you would prefer thirty-five, you walk out of here," the smile fled from Orwell's face as his voice effortlessly rose to a volume almost loud enough to make ears bleed.

Bale cringed. Covering his ears failed to keep them from feeling like they might explode at any minute. He knew how to push Orwell across the line. Luckily, he had learned long ago when to stop pushing. The defiance dancing all about his expression fled as he sighed and said, "Please, Mr. Durr. Can we make it twenty-five and ten minutes?"

"That is better," Orwell replied as the smug, satisfied smile slipped back onto face. Then he nonchalantly added, "Now, I have given you two clear options. All you need do is choose."

Bale bit his tongue and choked down all the venom pounding on the back of his teeth that wanted desperately to spew out all over Orwell's desk. None of the words he would assault the boss with would make a damn bit of difference, so he stuffed them deep into his gut to fester until the day he finally decided to take the old man on. He drew in a deep breath, let his body deflate with a big sigh, and said, "Negotiation, my ass. Fine. I'll take ten and ten."

Orwell signaled he was finished with the conversation by shifting his attention to something on his desk. The something didn't matter. It was all an act, just another thing he did to make sure everyone knew how small and insignificant they were. He casually waved his hand and said, "Very good, Mr. Lance. Go ahead then. You know the way."

It wasn't easy to yank his stare away from that vile thing. There was so much more he wanted to say, so much more he wanted to do. But it was done. Nothing he could say or do would make a difference. It would feel good in the moment, but Orwell could erase him with a thought. That wouldn't do. He had more work to get done.

He let the rage radiate off him as he walked toward a decoratively carved, wooden door, finished in the same rich mahogany as everything else in the perfect room. The handle was gold and resembled a solar cross with intricate patterns carved into it. The pattern was allegedly a phrase written in the language of angels. Michael had told him once that it said, "Eternity lies beyond this door." Bale never believed it actually said anything. Michael was full of shit most of the time.

The door didn't lead to any room. When he opened it, it looked like dark water with slight circular ripples slowly radiating out from its center until they terminated at the edges of the doorway. Bright, light-blue beams that were almost white shimmered from those ripples like static racing around those circles. He stepped through.

It felt just like departing. There was that brief moment of terror when his body felt like it was being ripped apart in a split second of excruciating pain followed by an instant of sheer bliss, like floating in a cloud, and then he was put back together in the most beautiful place in any reality he'd ever visited. It was paradise. Too bad it was just a beautiful prison for the only thing he cared about, the only reason he woke up every morning.

Everything around him was just a little bit more. The leaves on the trees were greener. The grass spreading out in every direction was greener and lusher than any lawn, no matter how well kept, in any of the billions of potentialities. Lilacs were the most vibrant purple, elegantly outlined in the purest white. It seemed a prettier flower could never exist until one beheld the irises almost glowing in their own purple hues. The dahlias almost outshined them both. Every flower of every type boasted the deepest yet somehow brightest colors that ever were. It was almost too much. The sky above was the same. The blue of that sky almost seemed fake in its perfection. The water of the small pond she sat next to on a large but perfectly smooth boulder pulling petals from a bright, white daisy and tossing them into the drink reflected the perfection of that pristine sky.

Bale just stood there watching for a moment. The time was short, but something about her innocence always left him yearning for simpler times. Angel Cakes is what he'd called her for the last who knows how many years. He had named her Eirini when she was born, but he hadn't called her that in ages. It had been so long she probably wouldn't even remember. Her perfect, dark-brown hair curled in ringlets that rested gently against her porcelain skin. She looked like a doll.

"He loves me," she finally shouted as she yanked the last petal from her flower and tossed it triumphantly into the air.

The truest joy he'd ever felt was marred by sadness knowing he could never give her the life she deserved, but it still managed to bring a dopey smile to his hard face. It fled far too quickly as he glanced at the two stooges keeping watch. They looked like identical twins except for their long and flowing hair. Michael's was blonde, and Gabriel's was fire-red. They both wore impeccable white suits just like Orwell, and they both looked equally pretentious.

Bale offered the two angels a brief scowl before turning his attention back to his reason to exist and shouting, "Angel Cakes!"

He loved the way her eyes lit up when she saw him. The visits were too short and too infrequent, but she never let on how let down she must have been. She jumped down from the rock she'd been sitting on, dropped her petal-less flower, and ran to him with her arms wide and her perfect curls bouncing all about her head.

She jumped into his arms and stared up at him with wide eyes like two bright blue moons as she nearly shouted, "Daddy! The flower said you love me, and you came. You finally came!"

He planted a smooch on her cheek and said, "Of course, I did. Giant dragons couldn't keep me away from the most beautiful, little angel in five galaxies."

"Giant, fire-breathing dragons?" she asked with a skeptical squint.

"Oh yeah," he nodded his head dramatically as he continued,

"giant, fire-breathing dragons with three heads and a hundred arms!"

Bale spun her around until they were both dizzy. Then he tossed her high up into the air, hugged her tight, and spun her around again. They were both laughing like idiots when they fell to the soft grass.

Angel Cakes curled up against his chest and said, "I miss you, daddy. When can I come home with you."

His eyes filled up as he laid there on the perfect, soft grass gazing up into a flawless blue sky. This was the worst part of every visit, the heartbreak. No tear would fall from his eye. She had to believe the lie he was about to tell her. He wasn't sure who hated it worse as he replied, "Soon. Daddy's trying, Angel. I've got a lot to do, lots of bad people to catch."

"How many?" her tone gained an almost scolding quality as she asked the same question she asked him every time he came to visit.

"Too many to count on your fingers," he replied quietly.

"And my toes?" she was such a trooper. This was the game. It was like she knew he would break her heart again, but she played along knowing how bad it hurt him too.

"And my fingers and toes," his breathing grew steady as he lost ground against the tears desperately waiting to rain down his cheeks.

She cuddled in closer to his chest as he shot a deadly glare at those two bastard angels chuckling at their sorrow. "These bums playing nice?" he asked.

She sat up, gave him the most serious look he'd ever seen, and said, "No. They don't play, or talk, or anything. They just stand there."

He pulled his scowl away from the guards as a smile washed over his face. "Do they still scare you?" he asked while gently mussing her hair.

"No," she scoffed as if it were the most ridiculous question she'd ever been asked, "They're just dumb and don't ever want to play anything."

He laughed as he sat up and asked, "Did you tell them what I told you last time?"

"Yes," she rolled her eyes and giggled. Her bright face could melt the hardest heart. Then she slapped her knee, laughed some more and added, "They didn't think it was funny at all."

He pulled her close again and kissed the top of her head before asking, "What did you tell them?"

A devious grin slipped between her slightly pudgy cheeks as she shrugged and said, "I told them they are big, dopey asshats."

They both fell back to the ground as they laughed together. Someday, this would be every day. Sadly, it wasn't this day. He let the idea slip away as he let the laughter take him away, chuckling like a fool in the grass with his favorite person in the world.

Once he gained enough control of himself to speak, he looked over at Michael and said, "Hear that, asshat? You bums are as big and dopey as she says."

"Time's up, Bale," Michael scowled.

Bale continued chuckling as he replied, "Calm down, Mikey. I just got here, and Or gave me ten."

Gabriel's smile looked like cold death when he said, "Imagine how easy she'd break."

Michael's smile was equally cold and dead when he added, "Like a porcelain doll."

Bale gave Angel Cakes a quick squeeze and a wide smile as he told her, "Give me a second, sweetie. I need to have a chat with the asshats."

By the time Bale got to his feet, any remnants of joy had fled from his expression. His jaw grew tighter, and his scowl deepened as he stalked toward the two angels like death with a wicked hangover.

He put his face close to Gabriel's ear as he quietly growled, "Once my debt is paid, I'm coming for you. One out of place hair on her head, and I'm going to make it hurt."

Gabriel's smile faltered the slightest bit as he replied, "All you are is words."

Bale hadn't noticed Angel Cakes follow him over until she peeked out from behind his legs and added, "Asshat."

The kid was right. He never got a chance to tell her. A swirling circle of blue light spun up out of nothing right next to him. It was the same light blue, almost white light that pulsed in the doorway he used to get to the place. But this time it sucked him right in. He barely heard Angel call him. "Daddy!" she shouted, but he was already being torn apart.

CHAPTER 3

DROWNING

POTENTIALITY 6

C lub Despair wasn't nearly as bleak as the name might suggest. Sure, it was a dive bar complete with crumbling brick and dated décor, but it was clean, full of bright, neon lights, and boasted the best, damn sound system in any potentiality Bale had visited. It also happened to be his favorite place to lick his wounds and drown his sorrows.

Horton wasn't much of a town. Club Despair was the only real establishment of note. Folks came from miles around to disco down to the odd, gothic rhythms pounding out of the speakers. Vampires were into some weird shit. Bale couldn't tell one song from another. They all had the same porn soundtrack drumbeat desperately trying to add some kind of structure to the slow, eerie, violin melodies layered over their top. Whatever the pale, room temp bodies on the dance floor were doing didn't look like dancing to Bale, but they seemed to enjoy it.

Potentiality 6 was a mere six vibrations left of Bale's reality. It was nearly identical on the surface, especially at night. Horton could be any tiny speck on the map back home, but it was more than that. The atmosphere was thicker in this reality. UV light couldn't penetrate. That meant vampires had nothing to fear from the sun. They had nothing to fear from humans either. Bale was well versed in their history. It was exceptionally brutal. The humans in this place tried to eradicate their only competition at the top of the food chain and failed miserably. Potentiality 6's history, like most histories, was written by the victors. They called it the meat war. It wasn't really a war at all. It was a slaughter. All the humans who remained were kept as slaves or livestock. Despite all that, Bale liked it there.

He was well on his way to an epic drunk that would undoubtedly melt into a wicked hangover once he slept it off, but he didn't care. He slouched heavily against a tattered bar nursing a tumbler of this green liquid he always drank when visiting the joint. He had no idea what the stuff was called, but it was stronger than anything he could get back home. Whatever it was, it was the same stuff they used to subdue the humans in the place.

The best damn bartender in all the land and the owner of the joint, who also happened to be the only soul in any reality Bale counted as a friend, leaned against the bar across from him and topped off his glass. The cat's name was Mark Castillo, but Bale always called him Fangs. It didn't really matter to Bale that the dude was a vampire. He was the most down to earth guy he'd ever met in his life, and he'd been alive a long time.

Mark capped the bottle of green shit, set it back on the bar next to Bale's glass and sighed, "You know I love you, man, but you've got to stop coming in here. Everybody's staring."

"Screw them, let them stare," Bale slurred. Then he looked around and added, "Besides, nobody's even looking over here. The one's that aren't grinding all over somebody to this horrid song are lapping blood off one of their familiars."

"Right," Mark shook his head, "Screw them. That works for you. I live here, and these, *pasty carcasses* as you so lovingly refer to them, are my customers."

Bale grabbed his glass, tilted his head back, and drained it. Then he slammed it back down on the bar, pointed at it dramatically, and laughed, "Fill me up, Fangs."

Mark obliged, filling the glass back up. His smile fled as he said, "I hate it when you call me that."

"I'm sorry, Mark," Bale shrugged. When the smile didn't immediately return to Mark's face, he added, "Come on, man. Cheer up. You're the only friend I've got. Besides, what are you worried about? This is the only place to drink in town. Where else are they going to go?"

"You know what I'm worried about," Mark's expression remained joyless as he continued, "Every time you come in here, I lose some regulars. Some are friends."

Bale slammed his drink again and motioned for another before shaking his head and saying, "Not my fault. I mind my own business, drink this green, date rape shit you feed me, and they push, and they push, and they push."

"Bullshit," Mark nearly scowled, "You get drunk, piss everybody in the place off, and then kill a bunch of them."

Bale laughed at Mark as he poured him another drink. "Then it's your fault," he finally said once he gained enough control of himself to speak, "You never cut me off."

"I can't. You're the only one who drinks that shit," Mark lost quite possibly the smallest chuckle that had ever been before his expression grew as stern as it had been, and he added, "Everybody else in here drinks…"

"O fucking negative!" Bale shouted the interruption as he slapped his hand on the bar and nearly fell off his barstool.

Bale's antics attracted what most in a similar situation would consider unwanted attention from a rather large, long-haired vampire sitting at the edge of the bar. Bale's state of mind just then was far from a place where he wanted to avoid confrontation. In fact, right at that moment, he welcomed it. He had lots of pent-up aggression to unload, and he didn't really care too much about who he gave it to.

"Fuck you looking at, room temp?" Bale slurred at the big vampire who offered only a cocky grin in response.

"Bale…" Mark touched Bale's shoulder as he started.

Bale pushed Mark's hand away and grunted, "Don't. Crowns here has something to say."

"Did you just refer to me as Crowns?" the vampire said while brushing his flowing, blonde waves back as he stood up from his stool and laughed at Bale.

He was even bigger than he looked when seated, but he was too damned pretty for Bale to take him seriously. The guy kind of looked like someone plopped Fabio's head on Hadi Choopan's body. The dude was like beauty and the beast all wrapped together.

"Bale, please, let it go," Mark begged, "Come on, man. Drinks are on me."

Bale could feel the guy approaching as he glanced over at Mark and said, "See, Fangs, I try to mind my own business, but they just keep pushing." Then he glanced up at the vampire towering over him and said, "Have you got something to say, or are you just going to stare at me like you want to suck more than just my neck?"

Crowns was obviously not the least bit intimidated. That much was clear when he chuckled down at Bale and replied, "I'm just wondering how long it would take to drain somebody your size, meat-sack. I know you. We all do. You might be something where you come from. Here, you're just food."

"Bale, come on, man. Let it go," Mark begged again.

Bale glanced back at Mark, grinned something devilish at him, and said, "This big fucker is looming over me, trying to intimidate me, Fangs. That's a challenge. This cocksucker is challenging my manhood. How can I just let that go?" He paused, pointed up at Crowns, and added, "I mean, look at him. This big, dumb..."

He lost the thought right there. Too much of the green shit had his mind moving way too slowly. He leaned back across the bar toward Mark and attempted to whisper, "Help me out here, brother. You've got me all fucked up. I'm not firing on all cylinders. Give me a good noun for this big fucker."

"You're the clever one, Bale," Mark sighed, "Why don't you just sit back, enjoy your drink, and forget about it?"

"But he's standing right there," Bale complained. Then he had it or at least he thought he did. He chuckled at Mark before looking back up at Crowns and laughing, "Ha! Maybe I'll suck your blood."

"That's not clever. It's not even a little bit funny," Mark sighed again.

Crowns shook his head, looked over at Mark, and asked, "This is the guy you can't shut up about?"

"Hey," Bale nearly shouted, "Don't talk about me like I'm not fucking here. I can hear you. Blah, blah, blah, blah... Fuck you."

Crowns didn't even look at him when he said, "That's it. I'm going to drain him and make him my bitch."

Crowns had a hell of a grip. Bale's shirt dug into his throat as the big vampire yanked him up off his stool. The room spun a bit. That green shit was really getting to his head. Luckily, his instincts didn't require him to see straight. He grabbed a firm hold of the wrist attached to the hand that was still twisting up his collar and drove his knee into Crowns' gut.

Bale's next move happened so fast that he barely had time to think about it. He had no intention of killing the guy. Yet, the glimmering knife he slipped out of his belt and slashed across Crowns' throat could result in nothing less. On some level, he knew that. That knowledge didn't keep him from executing the vampire.

The expression on Crowns' face was a twisted conglomeration of fear, anger, and confusion. It was a UV blade Bale had gotten from a smith in Potentiality 4,612 where the inhabitants' medieval lifestyles were juxtaposed against some of the most advanced technology in any dimension. Humans ruled that place. They had all manner of monsters, oddities, and nightmare creatures roaming around, but they had developed the weaponry to subdue and destroy them. The UV knife was forged with literal sunrays. Its only purpose was to kill vampires.

The gash in Crowns' throat sizzled only slightly at first. Bale watched that sizzle expand into flames as his regret expanded with it. The music stopped, and a crowd gathered as those flames grew into a proper blaze. Fire danced across Crowns' skin as the poor vampire roared in pain for only a handful of moments. Then he was ash.

There was a lot of grumbling from the crowd. None of it was clear enough that Bale could pick out individual threats, but they were there laced among the noise. He couldn't show any fear, or they'd consume him. Instead, he held the blade up high for all to see and said, "UV, bitches, from a dimension where they hunt things like you for sport. It looks like I've got me a pocket full of sunshine."

The throng of angry vampires was ready to explode like a volcano that had been building pressure for a thousand years. Eyes grew red as fangs dripping with the anticipation of spilling fresh blood glistened white in the bright glow of strobe lights that had suddenly begun rapidly flashing to the thunderous and quick kickdrums of the beat pumping through the speakers. Bale brought his hands up waiting for the flood, but Mark leapt over the bar and put himself in between the group that would either be his murderers or victims.

"Fuck it," Bale shouted at Mark's back, "Let them come."

Mark glanced back at him, briefly flashed his fangs, and hissed, "Damn it, Bale. That's enough." Then he shifted his attention back to the crowd and begged, "Stop, please. I owe him a debt. We all do. He's low right now, and he gets stupid when he drinks. But you all know we'd be dead right now if it weren't for him. Our world wouldn't even exist."

A voice from the mob shouted back, "Get him out of here, or he's food."

Another voice answered, "Forget that. He's not leaving this place alive."

"Get out of the way, Mark, or you can die with him," still another voice shouted.

"Fuck this," Bale grunted as he shoved Mark out of the way and slashed twice with his knife, once forehand and once back, gashing three throats wide open with the first swipe and three more with the second. A moment later, the six sorry souls at the front of the mob crumbled to ash. Their remnants were caught up in the breeze of a ceiling fan and scattered about the rest of the crowd.

Then everything went dark. Mark must have hit him in the head with something. It was heavy. It made an odd, almost hollow sound like a coconut being dropped on cement. He was briefly aware of being hefted up onto Mark's shoulder, and then he was out.

CHAPTER 4

THE FARM

POTENTIALITY 6

A pale, blue sunrise blazing in through sheer, white curtains less than gently tugged Bale's eyelids open. It was like staring into a flood light. He winced as he cradled his throbbing forehead. He adjusted to press his face against the cool leather of the sofa. He knew he was in Mark's apartment, but he had no recollection of arriving there. Neither could he recall much about the prior evening.

It was obvious Mark had no intention of letting him race quickly back to sleep when he loudly stated, "It lives. I can't believe it. I thought you might have finally succeeded in killing yourself."

Bale ignored the jibe and whispered, "I had them."

Mark offered a dry chuckle before responding, "You did. That's why I stopped it. I didn't want you to vaporize everyone in the place. You should really think about therapy…or meditation…something. You've got some real anger issues, and you never point your rage in the right direction."

Bale didn't want to hear the lecture. He rolled over so he was facing the back of the sofa, pulled a crocheted blanket over his head that had too many holes in the pattern to effectively block the light and mumbled, "They started it."

"No," Mark fired back quickly though his tone was absent the disgust such a swift rebuttal might suggest, "You started it. You always start it. Luckily, I dragged you out of there before you could finish it."

"Bullshit. Crowns was a big dickhead. He had it coming," Bale groaned as he tried to burrow deeper into the thick, overstuffed cushions of Mark's sofa.

Though Bale couldn't see Mark's expression while buried beneath the throw, he could sense the disappointment it was wearing in the tone of his voice as he solemnly replied, "I like you so much better when you're sober, and Drew was not a bad guy. You're a bad guy when you drink."

It was obvious Mark had a bunch more to say, but Bale was quickly checking back out to never-never land. His only friend in the world quietly droned on and on as he drifted back to sleep.

Hours must have passed by the time Bale woke again. The sky outside the window was as dark as night gets. The room around him was just as dark. That was a blessing. His head still throbbed from all the drinking he'd done the night before. Bright lights would have been bad just then.

His throat was dry as a southern county in the bible belt, and his tongue was firmly stuck to the roof of his mouth. There was a lingering taste, familiar and unsettling, like he'd been drinking raw sewage the night before. He needed something wet with a flavor strong enough to kill the aftertaste of the prior night's shenanigans.

The room spun violently as he raised himself too quickly to his feet. It made his stomach churn. Mark would be pissed if he puked all over his living room carpet. He paused for a moment there in the darkness until the urge to spew whatever might be left in his belly all over the room.

One step was all he made before stubbing his toe on Mark's coffee table. It was the pinky. He hit it hard too. It felt like he ripped the damned thing right off his foot as pain flared like an instantly hot blaze. "Shit," he shouted as he lifted his leg and grabbed for the injured digit. The quick movement ruined his balance. He stumbled awkwardly for three steps until flopping onto the floor.

"Fangs, where the fuck are you?" he hollered into the darkness, but the place was quiet.

After a few moments of listening for a response, he checked his watch. Everything was still a bit blurry, but he gleaned enough to realize it was just before dawn. That meant Mark would already be down at the barn feeding his flock. "Shit," he muttered quietly. He hated the farm.

He laid there long enough that the rancid taste in his mouth pushed the dull throbbing in his head and the burning in his poor pinky toe aside to become the main object of his focus. It took a few moments to get back to his feet and stumble the last few steps into Mark's kitchen. He didn't rush it. Everything from his head to his gut was still a bit squishy, and his balance had mostly checked out.

The cool blast of air that hit him when he opened the fridge was a blessing. The contents of the thing were a curse to his dry throat. There was nothing in there but bags of blood. Bale's stomach grumbled loudly as bile crept up the back of his throat. He clamped his lips together tightly and covered them with his fist until the urge to vomit passed once again.

At least water was the same in most every potentiality. He turned the faucet to cold and let the water run until it was almost icy. Then he leaned his head down to sip gingerly from the cold stream. It helped the dryness, but it didn't do much to quell the wicked aftertaste still clinging to his cheeks. He needed something with some flavor. As much as he hated the idea, he'd have to walk down to the farm to find Mark. He usually had something good stashed somewhere.

Mark called the building the barn, but it didn't look like Bale's idea of a barn. It was more like a lab. Bright lights glared off stainless steel walls in one massive room. The floor was shiny, white tile. A bank of glass-doored coolers occupied the back corner. They were filled with tubes, vials, and containers. Bale knew from previous visits that they were antibiotics, reality warping agents, and super concentrated vitamins. To say Mark was a bit of a chemist was a massive understatement. That guy had a concoction for any occasion.

None of those things was the reason Bale hated the place. The cages were what really got him. From one wall to the other, were row after row of animal cages stacked three high, but they weren't filled with animals. Each one was occupied by a human being. As dirty and mangy as they were, they looked like animals, but they were people with dreams and desires that would forever remain unfulfilled. They all had tubes connected to their necks slowly draining blood into massive stainless-steel vats that constantly mixed them to keep the precious blood from coagulating. The thought made Bale want to vomit again.

Bale finally spotted Mark. He was pushing a cart nearly overflowing with raw meat and tossing slabs into each cage. Each of the people in those cages devoured their hunk of meat like a ravenous beast. It made them seem even more like animals.

"Yum, yum, yum," Mark sung the words to a tune Bale had only ever heard leave his friend's mouth, "Eat it up."

The idea of farming human beings sent a shiver shimmying down Bale's spine. A small one caught his attention. It was a child, a young boy. He couldn't have been more than ten years old. He got so excited as Mark approached his cage that he seemed more like a puppy happy to see his master at the end of the day than a person. The kid pushed his wide smile as far through the cage as he could while gripping the bars and bouncing gleefully on crouched legs.

Mark gave that one a larger hunk of meat than the rest. He scratched the boy's head as he handed it to him. His voice was about three octaves higher than normal as he continued scratching the boy's head and excitedly said, "Hey boy, you hungry? Yes, you are. Who's a good boy? That's daddy's good boy."

There was something oddly sweet about the repulsive exchange, but Bale had seen enough. "You have got to be kidding me," he finally said with just a tinge of disgust coloring his tone as he stood in the doorway unsure if he wanted to venture any further into the place.

"Oh, come on in. I didn't see you there," Mark nonchalantly replied.

"I hate this place. These are people, man," Bale nearly grunted his response.

Mark's expression echoed how silly the idea seemed to him as he shrugged and said, "Maybe to you. To me they're just food. That's why we farm."

Bale shivered again, gagging slightly as he glanced about the room watching people devour raw chunks of meat. "Disgusting," he muttered quietly.

"Why?" Mark shrugged, "I don't see how this is any different than what the folks in your dimension do with cows, pigs, or chickens."

Bale shook his head and said, "It's totally…" Then he paused for a moment and digested the idea. Mark had a point. "Okay," he finally continued, "You've got me there. It isn't really different at all. But somehow, this seems worse. I mean, they have souls."

"I'm not interested in those. That's your department," Mark chuckled before adding, "Hell, this should make you happy. If any of these suckers decide not to walk into the light, you won't have to chase them down. Caged and ready."

"Good point," Bale made a face as he responded, but he couldn't disagree.

"So, now that you're sober, what are you doing here this time? Did you see her?" Mark asked as he continued pushing his cart and tossing hunks of meat to hungry prisoners.

Bale deflated slightly as he replied, "Yep."

"That explains last night," Mark nodded, "We only get to see you at your worst anymore. Maybe come by sometime when you don't feel like killing everything in sight."

Mark was right. He typically was. He knew more about Bale than anyone in any dimension except maybe for Orwell. What was it about bartenders that made folks want to open their souls and share all their problems? They were like psychologists with their ability to listen to any bullshit anyone was going through and offer useful, sometimes life-changing advice, and they could fix you a drink.

Bale was about to say as much when the world before him started to shimmer. It was like a thin cloud of bright light vibrating in the shape of a door. Then even brighter light shined like an outline surrounding that wavy shimmer. Bale could see Mark still pushing his cart within it until the scenery before him opened toward him like a door, and the row of cages Mark pushed his cart down was pushed to the side while Orwell stepped out. When the door—that hole in reality—closed behind him, Mark was still there in the background pushing his cart like nothing had happened.

Bale's jaw hung slack as he asked, "What in Zeus' veiny thunderbolt are you doing out of your office? You slumming?"

Orwell's expression tightened into the same disappointed look he typically wore when Bale spoke to him as he replied indignantly, "Must you always act like a child? I need to speak with you immediately."

Bale sighed and let the edge smooth off his defiant attitude. He didn't have the energy to give Orwell his typical act. He just sighed again and said, "Okay. I'm listening."

Orwell shuddered and looked like he'd just tasted something foul as he replied, "Not here. This place is filthy. And that smell..."

Bale looked over Orwell's shoulder at Mark—who had stopped pushing his cart and turned to see what the commotion was about—and said, "Get this guy. Are you going to let him talk down your farm like that?"

Mark waved over his shoulder, resumed pushing his cart, and said, "That is one list I'd prefer not to wind up on. He can say whatever he likes."

Orwell flashed his typical patronizing smile as he said, "Let us adjourn to my bar, Mr. Lance. I have an offer I am certain you will want to hear."

Bale just nodded his agreement. His headache had dimmed, but he had still failed to achieve enough clarity to trade barbs with his boss. On top of that, the City of Gold had the best of everything in all creation. That included bourbon. A little hair of the dog might be just what the doctor ordered.

CHAPTER 5

I HATE WOLVES

CITY OF GOLD

The fellow on the roof in Hell's Kitchen had it right when he'd said it looked like static. It felt like that to travel. Orwell was with him this time. Bale wondered if it felt the same for him. It was like being torn apart and put back together, but in that brief transition from one to another there was so much more happening. His kinesthetic sense checked out completely. Every part of his body felt big and bloated but lighter than air. It was like he became a massive balloon stretched until it was so thin it became invisible. But it wasn't quite that. A stretched balloon remained connected. This was different. It really did feel like his body had exploded and each atom raced away from every other, and yet, they all somehow remained connected even if they weren't in the correct places. His arm might feel like it sat where his head was supposed to be, or his foot felt like it was sitting in the middle of his face. Despite all that, everything kept moving, racing, piercing space like a dagger traveling faster than thought. It all happened in an instant.

Then he was stepping through a doorway into another time warp. Bale had no idea why Orwell had such an affinity for the US of Potentiality 0 in the 1930s, but everything about the aesthetic of every area the guy occupied echoed the bygone era. It made sense. He conducted himself like a mob boss. It was elegance juxtaposed against the gritty reality of a grimy street where threats of pain or death were the tools for maintaining order. He thought of asking him more than a few times why he pretended anyone in his orbit had any kind of control over their own decisions. The guy created reality, every reality. He could bend it and shape it at will. Why give anyone a choice? Ultimately, he never asked. That might give Orwell the idea he gave a shit. Mostly, he didn't.

The place was quiet except for a jazz trio softly laying down Rudy Vallee's version of *The Thrill is Gone*. They were good. They had better be. Orwell would probably blast them to oblivion if they missed a note. They were also always there. Every time Bale entered the place, they were laying down some smoky jazz standard. The place was mostly empty besides the band who played on a small stage in the corner. It was a shame. The room was cozy, but everything was the picture of elegant indulgence. There should at least be a small crowd to enjoy it. Like everything else, it all existed for Orwell's pleasure.

Rich, mahogany railings separated two rows of tables with booths on either side, but these booths weren't your common, run of the mill diner booths. Soft, plush leather piled high on hand-carved wood etched with ancient symbols from cultures and belief systems far older than Bale from various potentialities across reality. Orwell was by far the most complex being Bale had ever encountered, but he was somehow simple at the same time in some regards. He liked what he liked, and that was that. For example, the massive and gaudy crystal chandeliers above each booth belonged in a ballroom not a bar, but Orwell obviously enjoyed them.

Bale couldn't blame Orwell for his fondness of the exquisite light fixtures that were wholly unnecessary in the small space. They were magnificent, and as out of place as they were, they seemed to fit just right. He felt the same way about the carvings in the booths. They belonged painted on a cave wall somewhere, but they were perfect right where they were.

From the booths to the stage where the trio played were nine cocktail tables which seemed randomly placed. They were equal in construction and finish to every other piece of furniture or art in the room, but their positioning made them appear to not belong. Bale asked about it the first time he visited the bar, why the seemingly random chaos existed in the middle of Orwell's orderly perfection.

Orwell hadn't given him a straight answer. Instead, he flashed his customary, condescending smile and said, "You're a smart boy, Mr. Bale. Figure it out." What a dick. On the other hand, it did motivate Bale to learn the placement of those tables wasn't random or chaotic at all. It was very precise. It took Bale just over one hundred years and several more visits to the room and various libraries across a number of different potentialities to find out that they represented the planetary alignment in earth of Potentiality 0's solar system at a specific date in history. As far as Bale could tell, it was Orwell's favorite day. The end of the ice age when the earth mostly flooded and almost wiped humanity out. Lots of souls came home that day.

The bar was on the other side of the row of booths in the middle. It was a massive work of art. The rich, deep stain matched the rest of the wood in the room perfectly, and it was also covered in images etched in such impeccable detail they looked like they might leap right off the thing. The wall behind it was the same, but it was packed with shelves of the most exquisite bourbons from all across reality. There were only two from Potentiality 0. They were all in matching decanters, so Bale had no idea where they were distilled or for how long they were aged. It was another thing he had asked about and Orwell had told him to figure it out on his own. He never bothered with this one. They were all fantastic. All he ever asked for was the usual.

Raziel was there behind the bar as usual. It was the only place Bale ever saw him. He looked identical to all Orwell's other angels. They were more like henchmen, but they looked sharp. Flawless hair, flawless skin, and eyes that glistened with all the mysteries of the universe, they were perfect. Bale winked at Raziel who offered a solemn nod in response as he continued to wipe the same not dirty chalice he always wiped when not filling a snifter with more bourbon than a sophisticated man should drink all at once.

Bale would never think of ordering anything directly from Raziel after his first visit. That time he made a beeline for the bar and said, "Hey fella', I'm all kinds of parched here. How about you fix me up with two fingers of the best stuff you've got back there." He couldn't breathe for a solid five minutes after those words left his mouth while Orwell scolded him for being a petulant buffoon. The boss had literally sucked the air out of his lungs. It was one of the many lessons Orwell had given him about how to behave respectfully while in the City of Gold. The lesson was far from lost, Orwell had certainly fixed his wagon, but the words he used could have been the random mumblings of a child just learning to mimic the sounds the folks around him make. It no doubt would have boiled down to him being a naughty child and that he should never do that again. He didn't. Instead, he waited until he was seated at a table with Orwell who would smile, share some pleasantries, and then finally nod at Raziel who would pour and deliver the drinks.

The booth in the back was the spot they always ended up in, but it was usually empty. This time it wasn't. Michael and Gabriel were both there looking like the perfect, dopey jackasses they were wearing the same smug, bullshit expressions their boss always wore.

Bale faked a smile and said, "Mikey, Gabe! You asshats finally got out of prison." Then he turned to Orwell and asked, "What the fuck are these clowns doing here?"

"You should be more pleasant to us," Michael smiled.

"Indeed," Gabriel added with an equally warm smile, "Never forget how much time we spend alone with your precious, little doll."

"Enough! All of you," Orwell rarely raised his voice, but when he did, even the air shook.

Michael and Gabriel both dropped their gazes to the table in front of them. Bale just nodded, rubbed his ears, and slid into the booth. It seemed the two asshats were on the same page with him. Orwell wasn't in a mood to be trifled with, and he'd been pushed as far as any of them should push.

Once Orwell had finished sliding into the booth beside Bale, Bale turned his head toward him and said, "Okay, boss, what have you got. It must be something big if you called me here," he paused to glance across the table at Michael and Gabriel before finishing, "and even brought back up."

"Relax, Mr. Lance," Orwell replied in a much more pleasant tone, "You are always in such a hurry. Slow down. Be in the moment."

This was the only place Orwell wanted anybody to slow down or be in any moment. Normally, he was rushing through everything to get the current case done and the next one opened like a hobo rifling through trash looking for any unfinished morsel.

Bale managed to keep himself quiet despite a long list of wonderfully troubling barbs he wanted to throw at the asshats across the table from him. The effort paid off. After a few moments of silence, Orwell waved at Raziel to bring the drinks.

No one said anything. Michael and Gabriel were like well trained dogs sitting at Orwell's feet waiting for a command, and Bale had learned many lessons. Most of which, he ignored, but things seemed more serious this time than most. Whatever the boss had cooking had to be huge.

Raziel took forever. The guy was meticulous. Pouring two bourbons—Orwell would never share with any of his servants—should have taken a few seconds. As one minute stretched into another and another, it took every ounce of self-control to suppress a sigh and several stupid things Bale wanted to shout over at the methodical barkeep angel who may as well have been concocting twenty complicated cocktails.

It was the same each time Orwell had invited him to the bar. Raziel had a whole ceremony he performed when pouring. He'd bow his head solemnly in response to Orwell's nod. Then he'd pause and stare at the band as if Orwell's drink order might somehow be laced among the notes they artfully crafted together. Once the imaginary message had registered, the angel would turn toward the massive bank of bourbons and bow his head again. Bale always wondered what was going through that clown's head when he performed the odd, booze ceremony. He'd just stand there for at least a minute or two like he was praying to the god of distilled spirits. Then his head would snap up dramatically, like the best idea in the history of ideas just blew its wad all over his mind, and his hand would shoot out to grab whichever bottle the universe had told him to grab. The smile on his face as he held the bottle high was like the insane facial contortions a mad scientist might go through after stumbling on the solution to bringing his lost love back from the dead. Then, after a few moments of silently praising the glorious booze, he'd finally pour the damn drinks. The cat was weird.

The bourbon was glorious, perhaps even worthy of worship. Bale wasn't much of a sipper when it came to booze, but the stuff on Orwell's shelves was to be savored. This one was as magnificent as the last one he'd had. Sweet oak and spices slithered around an assembly of flavors that spun together to embody the smoothest booze perfection he had ever tasted. Carmel wrestled with vanilla while tussling about with just a hint of dried fruit in a battle that was epic and satisfying. It beat the hell out of that green crap Mark was always feeding him.

"I have a job for you, Mr. Lance," Orwell finally said after enjoying a generous sip.

"I didn't think you dragged me in here because you love my company," Bale quipped offering the smirk he typically had for the boss, "What have got for me, Or?"

Orwell rolled his eyes as he replied and handed Bale a manila folder, "More respect than you have ever offered or deserved, and a case. It's a big one, worth one hundred years."

Bale took another healthy sip of his bourbon, grabbed the file and gave it a look. It only took him two seconds to realize he didn't want it. He dropped the folder down on the table, drained the rest of his glass, and waived at Raziel to bring him another before saying, "No way. You know I fucking hate wolves."

"Scared, Bale?" Michael almost purred through his devilish grin.

"Not another word," Orwell pounded his fist on the table as he glared at Michael, "You are a bystander in this conversation, to be seen and not heard." Then he turned his attention to Bale and continued more calmly, "Please refrain from the use of that crass language in my presence, Mr. Lance. You will take this case."

"Forget it," Bale was shaking his head and responding before Orwell even finished, "Rudy Garreau ain't no ordinary werewolf. He knows how to travel. Remember the last time you sent me to Potentiality 7,645?"

"That was an easy case," Orwell shrugged, "The man was in a hospital bed missing both legs."

"Right," Bale pounded the fresh bourbon Raziel had just handed him and pointed at the glass to signify he wanted another before he continued, "That man was missing his legs because Rudy Garreau had torn them off and eaten them. He was the only man out of one hundred who were sent to bring that big bitch in who wasn't completely ripped to shreds."

Orwell took another sip of his bourbon before offering Bale a warm smile and saying, "Mr. Lance, we both know you are better than any one hundred men. Take the case. The price is right, and you will not be going alone."

The trick finally occurred to Bale as he glanced across the table at the two smiling asshats. Orwell planned to get him arguing about not bringing those two clowns with him on the case which would undoubtedly lead to him actually accepting it. Orwell knew him too well. It wasn't going to work this time. "No fucking way," he finally replied before gingerly sipping the fresh bourbon Raziel had just set before him to mock Orwell and then adding, "They aren't joining me on this case, because I'm not taking this case. Let them do it on their own."

Orwell almost chuckled, "Now, Mr. Lance, you know I cannot risk them anymore than I can risk you. You are all immensely important to our operation. They will be obedient, and they will follow your lead."

"They will be a couple of liabilities slowing me down," Bale shook his head and took a healthier drink of his bourbon before continuing, "I'm a tactician. I know how this shit works. That's why you need me. And this isn't just because I don't like them. They may be your best and brightest, the most powerful angels in all the universe, but they don't know the first thing about hunting or tactics, or anything useful in the field for that matter. If you really want this dog, my price is five hundred years off Angel Cake's sentence, and I've got a guy."

Orwell's expression grew suddenly stern as he nearly hissed, "An outsider?"

"A chemist," Bale finished his drink and waived at Raziel for another at the same moment he realized he needed to slow down. Orwell's bourbon was no joke. Maybe that's what had him feeling so bold. That and the fact that Orwell really seemed to have his back against the wall.

Raziel brought the bottle to the table to fill Bale's glass and top Orwell's off as the latter continued in a much more measured tone, "Why would you need a chemist?"

"Listen, Mr. Durr," Bale let all the defiance flee from his tone. He even dropped the smirk as he replied, "If you were sending me to kill this dog, he'd already be gone. That would be easy, but you want me to bring him in. You and I both know he won't come quietly. I'm going to need to subdue him. You don't like me to bring them to you stressed." Bale paused again to sip the fresh bourbon Raziel had just poured him and added, "I need my guy to put him to sleep after I take him down. Everybody wins. You get to collect your wayward soul, and Angel gets 500 years off her sentence."

Orwell took a long drink of his bourbon and a deep breath before gazing up at the ceiling and sighing, "You know I do not negotiate, Mr. Lance, but I want this one to come in clean. Take your outsider, bring me Rudy Garreau clean and alive, and I will take two-hundred and fifty years off of your daughter's sentence." Before Bale could even think about responding, Orwell snapped his head quickly to the right to stare him in the eyes and added, "Before you start complaining about my offer, consider this. I would prefer to give you nothing. You would prefer I give you five hundred. We can split the difference, and you can consider it a successful negotiation."

"Deal," Bale replied the moment Orwell's mouth closed. Deep down he knew he'd have to take the case either way. The fact Orwell had actually negotiated with him somewhat fairly nearly dropped him out of his chair. It was a shit job, but two fifty was nothing to sneeze at.

"Perfect," Orwell smiled, "I leave you to it then. You may go."

"Indeed," Bale smiled at Orwell, slammed the rest of his bourbon, and winked at Michael and Gabriel as he rose from the table and said, "Adios, asshats." He only made three steps before he turned back and added, "One day, we're going to tango, and Mikey, I'm going to shove you up your boyfriend's ass."

"Good day, Mr. Lance," Orwell shouted at Bale who was chuckling his way toward the door.

CHAPTER 6

THE CHEMIST

POTENTIALITY 6

Vampires don't sweat, but the air in Club Despair was moist like it was saturated with heat radiating off all the bodies gyrating together to the strange crap they danced to. It was all in Bale's head. There wasn't heat coming off any of the undead things in the joint. He shouldn't be back there so soon after the ruckus he caused. Regret is a bitch. Unfortunately, the guy he needed was behind the bar.

"What the fuck is he doing here?" a gruff voice called out from the crowd.

"He's meat," another voice answered.

The music stopped. The flashing strobes and disco lights went out as the stark, white main lights came on blazing in all their glory. Bale felt suddenly exposed like a steak under a spotlight surrounded by a mob of starving men. He wasn't looking for trouble, but it found him anyway.

The place seemed to stretch before his eyes like a long corridor packed wall to wall with fangs and hate. The hundred or so vampires closing in on him and shouting various threats describing how they would brutalize or torture him, drain him, or simply rip him to shreds to decorate the walls with his gory and dismembered parts seemed more like thousands. Despite all the shouting, the room seemed oddly quiet. That was bad. Bale's mind always got really quiet right before he lost it. He really didn't want to hurt anybody.

Luckily, one of the shouted threats tickled him just enough to snap him out of kill mode. One voice rose above the collective murmur to shout, "I'm going to wear your nuts as a necktie."

Luckier still, Mark came flying around the corner from the bar, pushing his way through the crowd before Bale could compose himself enough to offer any kind of reply to the strange threat. When Bale got a good look at Mark's face, he thought maybe it wasn't so lucky. His old pal looked at least as angry as every other face hissing at him just then.

"Everybody, back off!" Mark shouted at the crowd as he grabbed Bale by the collar with both hands. Bale couldn't recall ever hearing so much authority in his buddy's voice, or ever really seeing him get angry for that matter. Mark was pissed. The point was made even clearer when he snapped his gaze back to Bale and shouted in his face, "In what fucked up reality did it make sense to you to show your face in here again?"

Normally, Bale wouldn't allow someone to manhandle him like that. Nor would he take someone shouting in his face, but he did his buddy dirty the last time he visited. He let it go. Instead of grabbing Mark's wrists, tossing him into the crowd, and proceeding to pound his way through the throng of room temp bodies pressing in too closely to him, he held Mark's wrists gently and raised his voice only loud enough to be heard when he replied, "I need your help, man."

Mark's expression changed. He was a helper, had been for as long as Bale had known him. It didn't matter what was asked of him. If he had it and you needed it, it was yours. He seemed to gradually deflate like a balloon with a slow leak as his expression softened and he asked, "What do you need?"

"You," Bale shrugged.

The fact that all the dripping fangs flashing from the angry crowd were attached to bodies who loved their barkeep was about as thin a layer of protection as you could get. There wasn't a bloodsucker in the joint who didn't want to rip a big hole in Bale's throat, but Mark's presence was enough to keep the bomb from exploding. Aside from some pushing and shoving—along with a few smacks to the back of Bale's head that were almost enough to make him forget his only friend in the joint owned the place, and he didn't want to make a mess—they made it to the back of the bar unscathed. Thankfully, there weren't any nips or bites. That would have changed things. It was a good thing they jumped on him right when he walked through the door. If he had half a bottle of the green shit in him, it would have been a slaughter.

The music started back up, and the stark, white lights fled in favor of the colorful disco nonsense that had been pulsing along to the beat by the time Mark and Bale made it to the *secret* door behind the bar. It wasn't really a secret at all. Everybody knew about it. It probably had been a secret at some point, but the thing was right there where everybody could see Mark give the blood bag hanging next to the cooler a tug whenever he needed to escape the crowd and the noise. If that wasn't enough of a giveaway, the entire cooler sliding backward and then behind the wall of shelves next to it certainly was. The lack of secrecy didn't matter. Nobody would mess with the VooDoo Lounge. That's what Mark called his office. It was his private space.

Mark led Bale down a hallway that was almost completely dark except for long tubes of neon lights that ran along the ceiling alternating between blue, pink, purple, red, and green. Bale had made the mistake of taking him on a tour of Potentiality 0 once. They hit New York, Vegas, L.A., and that was just in the states. Mark dug all the over the top shit. If he had his way, they'd never play that eerie violin crap in his bar, but his customers just couldn't warm up to anything with any soul. Once in a while he'd sneak in some techno, but somebody would always complain, and the D.J. would give him that *you hired me to make the playlists* look. All of that fun stuff was relegated to the not so quiet sanctity of the VooDoo Lounge.

At the end of the hall there was another door. This one didn't require pulling some kind of lever. It had a retinal scanner. Mark didn't mess around when it came to his lair. Somebody would have to pluck his eye right out of his skull if they wanted to gain entrance. Bale shook his head slightly as Mark put his eye in front of the scanner. It beeped a few times, the light on it turned from blue to green, and the door popped open.

Something about the place reminded Bale of Orwell's bar in the City of Gold. Not that the two places bore any resemblance at all to each other. That wasn't it. It was how well the two places echoed the personalities and interests of their owners and designers. If you boiled Mark down to his fundamental parts, they would look exactly like the VooDoo Lounge. The centerpiece of the entire space was a massive, flat screen television. That wouldn't seem terribly strange in a man-cave, but the VooDoo Lounge wasn't really a man-cave. It was more like a vampire cave. Visual Arts wasn't a thing in Potentiality 6. Aside from the music, all their entertainment was live. The venues were gaudy and the sets extravagant. The only thing they really had in common with entertainment in Potentiality 0 was the pomposity of the entertainers. Those were overdramatic, self-absorbed twats, but they did put on some solid shows.

Mark had snuck Bale into a play once. It was an outdoor venue, midnight show, the story was a modern rendition of *The Birth of the First*, the myth of the first vampire. It was kind of a weird twist on the whole Adam and Eve story. Not that either actually influenced the other, but there were some similarities. Instead of some crusty, old dude shaping a tiny worshipper from clay and breathing life into his lungs, a giant bat fucks a wolf, and they both turn into smoke when they climax. After all that sex smoke dissipates, a wet little baby with fangs is just lying there in the dirt looking for something to drain. The story gets weirder after that, but it was a great show. Bale even shed a tear or two. Vampires were dramatic, if nothing else.

None of those shows were anything Mark could watch on the giant television mounted to the back wall of the VooDoo Lounge. Anything Mark could watch on the giant screen surrounded by muted lights that changed colors based on Mark's mood were things Bale had brought him from his dimension, all the classics from every era, everything from *Nosferatu* to *The Lost Boys* and everything in between. Mark wasn't just into the vampire stuff. He liked all the movies, but he loved watching the vampire flicks and complaining about how wrong they got everything. "The humans in your dimension just make shit up," he'd complain. Bale would tell him it was creative license, and Mark would tell him it was bullshit. He was right. It was all bullshit.

Games were the other thing. Bale had an acquaintance in Potentiality 1,654,247 who'd helped him out with some tech a couple of times. That cat had come up with a device that could send a signal from one dimension to another. It was mind blowing and life changing technology, the ability to communicate with beings from other dimensions, like a bionic radio. Mark used it for gaming.

A message popped up on the big screen as Bale followed Mark to his desk. It read, "Wanna' die again pussy?"

Mark's demeaner completely changed when he noticed it. He stiffened up almost like he was standing at attention. He looked like a soldier getting ready to march off to war as he quietly said, "That little motherfucker dies today." Then he plopped on a headset, grabbed his controller, flopped down into a leather recliner he'd modified into the ultimate gaming chair, and went to work.

It was tr0Gmortem69. The way Mark spoke about the guy, you'd think he was a massive and ominous threat to society. He might be that someday. However, at twelve years old, he was probably only a threat to middle aged men—or vampires—who had the dire misfortune of crossing paths with him in the free for all mode of *World Killer 6: The Battle for New America*. It was a post-apocalyptic, first-person shooter that Mark had fallen for hard the first time he played it. Everything went really well for a long time. Vampires' reflexes are incredibly fast, much faster than a human's. His kill to death ratio was something like 9.62. Then he bumped into tr0Gmortem69, and it all changed.

"Motherfucker," Mark shouted as blood splattered out the back of the head of his character on the big screen in slow motion before the body crumpled and fell off the roof of a four-story building bouncing off the roof of another building and a bench before finally landing in a heap on a street covered in debris. "You're so fucking dead, kid," he added with a grunt as his slayer's character tea-bagged his corpse.

Mark had become obsessed with the kid. He used his dimension penetrating device to triangulate the boy's location, and then searched through all the records he could find on him and his family. The player who used the handle, tr0Gmortem69 was born Elliot Thomas Milner on June 16th, 2013, in Potentiality 0. He was an only child who lived in an uppity, suburban neighborhood in the northern suburbs of Chicago. The little shit even had a nanny who home schooled him. His father was an attorney who had made his boatloads of money chasing ambulances, and his mother was some kind of spiritual healer who ran an overpriced wellness retreat in some shitty, little tourist trap in Wisconsin named Lake Geneva.

Bale couldn't hear what Mark's young nemesis was saying to get him all worked up, but it was obviously working. The vampire's voice got low and ominous as he said, "Thirteen zero four Asbury Avenue. That's your address, isn't it, you little shit? I'm coming, not for you. You can stay with that slut nanny who's raising you while your mom's blowing rich guys up at her lake house. I'm going to drain her and your dad, suck the blood right out of them while you watch. Then I'm tea bagging their corpses for real while you cry and suck your thumb in the corner."

Bale had heard enough. As enjoyable as it was to listen to the calmest, nicest, and most genuinely caring person he'd ever met completely lose his mind over a video game, he had shit to do, shit that required assistance from his frustrated friend. He walked in front of the big television and crossed his arms.

"Damn it, Bale," Mark groaned as he dropped his controller and yanked the headset from his head, "You let the little fucker kill me again."

"You went two to twelve against him in five minutes," Bale smirked, "I'm fairly certain he'd have killed you either way. Besides, what you've got going with this kid isn't healthy. The guy who plays that game ain't you, man."

"I know," Mark finally let the scowl slither off his face in favor of a sly grin, "I don't know why I let this kid get under my skin. He's fucking good. The little fucker toys with me, and he talks shit the entire time."

"I can tell," Bale chuckled.

Mark hung his headset on a hook he'd mounted to the side of his chair before getting up and moving to his desk. Once he was seated, he leaned back in his chair, cracked his knuckles, and said, "Do you know what a trogmortem is?"

Bale shook his head and chuckled through his reply, "I don't, nor do I care much."

"It's Latin," Mark fired back quickly, "It's the Latin word for death and the beginning of troglodyte smashed together."

"So…a dead cave dweller?" Bale shrugged.

"No," Mark shook his head, "It's from some stupid book the kid read. It's a death troll. This little asshole calls himself death troll. Do you believe that shit?"

"Why do you care?" Bale shrugged again.

"I don't know. The kid just really gets to me." Mark nearly shouted before melting into near maniacal laughter. Once he finally composed himself, he said, "Alright, buddy, let's forget about that vile, little, shit-talking twat, Elliot for now. What can I do for you?"

"Finally," Bale sighed, rubbed the back of his neck, and squinted uncomfortably as if anticipating a negative response while continuing, "I've got a case. It's a tough one, and I need you to come with me."

Mark shook his head as he scoffed, "What? I'm not coming along for one of your hunting trips. I've got too much to do. Who's going to mind the bar?"

"Kate. She runs the bar anyway. You really just hang out here, because you have nothing better to do," Bale fired back quickly as if it were a canned response. He'd anticipated all Mark's excuses on the way over.

"That might be true," Mark replied as he raised one eyebrow and shrugged. Then he asked, "But, what about the farm?"

"Kate's a gem, Mark. I'm sure you could convince her to swing by the barn on her way home and throw meat at your blood bags," Bale's reply was just as quick.

"Yeah, she probably would," Mark sighed as his face twisted through several expressions which echoed his search for an excuse Bale couldn't easily shoot down. After a few moments of searching, he finally gave up and asked, "What do you need me for?"

This was the part Bale had been dreading. His entire face squinted up this time as he quietly said, "The mark lives in Potentiality 7,645."

"That doesn't mean anything to me," Mark shrugged, "The only other dimension I've ever been to is yours, and I only know that is Potentiality 0, because you told me it was."

"Right," Bale paused nearly long enough for Mark to prod him before finally blurting, "It's a wolf."

"Fuck that," Mark shook his head violently before adding, "I fucking hate wolves. They smell like shit, and they're completely unsophisticated, sloppy killers. No way. Count me out."

"Come on, man. I can't take him alive on my own, and you owe me," Bale's voice earned a pleading quality that was foreign even to his own ears.

"Are you ever going to stop throwing that in my face?" Mark nearly whined.

"I'm sorry, man," Bale shrugged again, "but you and I both know your kind would have been completely obliterated if it wasn't for me. That UV bomb would have decimated your kind, completely wiped you out."

"I still don't understand why you need me. You and I both know you're not human. You like to think you are, but you're too strong. Your reflexes are too quick for a common meat sack. You can take down a wolf on your own," Mark pretended to be distracted by a half-torn note on his desk as he replied.

"Sure, I could kill him, but he's no good to me dead. I need his soul in his body when I bring it to the boss," Bale's tone grew matter of fact as he continued, "That's where you come in. You're the best chemist I know. I need something with enough silver in it to subdue him but not kill him."

"So, you want me to come up with a silver-laced poison and the antidote. Is that it?" Mark seemed to deflate a little bit with each word while his voice shrunk at the same rate, "I can make you something that fits the bill."

"And…you can join me to administer it after I take the fucker down?" Bale prompted.

The office grew quieter than Bale had ever heard it as Mark continued to examine the half-torn note Bale knew he wasn't really reading. It was a big ask. Wolves were brutal and violent killers. Mark had always assured him that vampires were faster, stronger, and more efficient killers than any werewolf, but Bale wasn't sure whether or not his buddy actually believed those words. It seemed more like bravado than a strongly held belief.

Minutes passed before Mark finally broke the silence and said, "Alright, I'll do this thing, but then my debt to you is paid in full. No more favors, and you quit hanging that shit over my head."

"That hurts," Bale sounded almost vulnerable as he replied, "but I get it. I won't ask for anything else."

"And…" Mark began.

"There's more?" Bale interrupted.

"Yep," Mark smiled. "You need to do something for me."

Bale cringed at the evil grin decorating Mark's face before tentatively saying, "Name your price."

"When this mission is complete, you take me on another trip to your reality," wickedness flashed in Mark's eyes and smile.

"Elliot?" Bale nearly chuckled.

"I have a promise to keep," the devious smile never left Mark's face as he nodded.

CHAPTER 7

THE WOLF

POTENTIALITY 7,645

The earth of Potentiality 7,645 had eight moons. At least one of them was full on any given day. That worked out well for the werewolves who inhabited the place. They could change at will, even during the day. On paper, their war with the humans of that potentiality should have seen a similar end to the meat wars of Potentiality 6, but they hadn't. Wolves were physically superior to humans in every way. They were stronger, faster, and all their senses were one hundred times keener than even the fittest human, but they lacked any kind of central leadership or planning. If you got any more than forty wolves together in a group, they'd start puffing out their chests and turning on each other. They were way too territorial to cooperate on anything bigger than a hunt. And that's not even considering all the lone wolves who couldn't play nice with anybody. Rudy Garreau was one of those.

If you read the humans' history books, you would come away believing they won a convincing victory over the wolves of Potentiality 7,645. In a sense, they did. However, they failed to eradicate or control their adversaries in any sort of meaningful way. And they effectively gave up their freedom to freely roam about the countryside. They built massive walls around their cities made from an alloy similar to steel, but it was infused with enough silver to keep the wolves away. If that didn't work, every bit of ammunition for every single weapon they made was laced with silver. Even their latest monument to destruction—a laser that could incinerate meat within milliseconds of contact with an effective range of several miles—fired a beam that was infused with enough silver molecules to get the job done. With all those fortifications and firepower, the humans were safe within their cities, but they could never leave them.

That left most of the planet to the wolves, and the land was wild and pristine. Lakes and streams were fresh and cool. You could stoop right down and take a drink without worrying if someone's toilet was draining into your creek, and fresh food grew everywhere. All that glorious nature was enough to draw the growing number of humans who resented all the safeguards that had been put in place to protect them out into the wild to try their luck. Most of those ended up as food for some pack of wolves, but most didn't end up in Rudy's belly. He'd only eat the humans in his backyard if they came looking for him. He had other places to hunt, like Potentiality 0.

Religion existed in every potentiality, and it wasn't just the humans who based their lives and decisions on fables and fairy tales. It seemed like every sentient creature needed some all-powerful being to grovel before and worship. That was the bitch about the ability to reason. Instincts trigger you to satisfy your most primal desires, but the ability to reason makes you think they're wrong. That's guilt, and that sends a mind searching for some kind of relief or forgiveness for all the wickedness it has imagined or done. Bale knew it was all bullshit. None of the folks he hunted really knew anything until they croaked, and then they couldn't tell anybody any different. But Bale had seen it. Those streets of gold were a horrible lie.

Bale knew Rudy was religious. Wolves had a belief system at least as fucked up as any other group of beings in any potentiality he'd ever visited. It tasted a lot like Voodoo, but it smelled kind of Pagan. The first wolf roamed the never-ending expanse, galloping across chaos. After a time, the first moon, Luna Primis imagined herself out of that same chaos. The wolf was dazzled by her light and enamored with her form. He tried to mount her, but she refused to allow it. He had no name. She bade him accept the name she gave him, and then she would allow him to lie beneath her. Though he was wild and refused to be tethered, his desire for her was too great to ignore. He accepted the name she gave him, UR-BAR-RA, and she showered her glory upon him for one hundred years. The result of their coupling was the sun, followed by seven moons, each one larger than the prior, and finally the earth. The earth was born beautiful and teaming with life. Such was her beauty, she was the only one of Luna Primis' offspring to be given a proper name, KI-LA-LA. Her siblings—only ever known as the seven moons—were jealous of the glory bestowed upon her by their mother. Yet, they were drawn to her, trapped by her beauty and unable to turn their gazes from her glory. Thus, they shined their magnificent light down on her and would forevermore.

Wolves came first among the creatures born to crawl about the earth, and they were free to roam where they would and eat whatever they wanted. Yet, they remained unsatisfied. The hunts were too easy. They needed a challenge. UR-BAR-RA was unmoved by their grumbling, but Luna Primis was sympathetic to their desires. She loved them above all else in her creation, even more than KI-LA-LA. She pled UR-BAR-RA to grant her favored souls their desire. He finally submitted to her glory and lay with her again. The result of that coupling was human, and the rest of the story gets closer and closer to reality until it rolls right from the realm of mythology into the realm of history.

Rudy lived in a rundown shack smack in the middle of the bayou surrounded by nothing but water, trees, swamps, and bugs. The latter seemed the same no matter what potentiality a soul found itself in. Biting flies, mosquitos, and all manner of tiny pests to annoy and antagonize any warm-blooded creature who happened to stumble into their midst. When Bale and Mark arrived just outside Rudy's cabin, everything was quiet except the damn bugs.

"Shit," Bale whispered loudly as he smacked his left shoulder.

"What?" Mark whispered back.

"A fucking mosquito bit me," Bale continued whispering as he aggressively scratched his shoulder.

"Here," Mark chuckled quietly as he jabbed Bale in the ass with a needle without giving him any warning the poke was coming. "This will keep the bugs off."

Bale stopped scratching and grabbed for the spot where Mark had poked him, "Ouch. What was that?"

"You said you needed a chemist, but as usual, you were only focused on the prize not the journey," a smile seemed to dance about Mark's whispered tone as he chided Bale, "That will taint your pheromones a bit, and your sweat. You won't smell it. The bugs will, and they won't like it one bit. The itchy lump that bite will become is the only souvenir you'll take home from this shitty swamp."

"It's not a swamp. It's a bayou," Bale fired back.

"Same fucking thing," Mark shrugged as his face twisted up like he desperately wanted to add, 'duh,' to the end of the statement.

"It isn't," Bale shook his head slowly, "The vegetation is denser in swamps. It's subtle, but if you know, you know. And the water is stagnant which makes it appear murky. The water around us is moving. It's slow, but it's moving."

"Okay, Jungle Joe. They sound like close kin to me," Mark replied before offering a bemused chuckle. Then he asked. "Who cares?"

Bale grew suddenly serious, "Listen, I know you think I'm a drunk who doesn't give a shit about anything. Mostly, you're right, but not about the hunt. Besides Angel Cakes, the hunt is the only thing in my life that really matters. I have to hunt if she's ever going to be free. That means I have to get it right every time. I need to know where I'm hunting. This a bayou, not a swamp."

"Okay, this is the bayou not the swamp," Mark held his hands up in front of him. Then he glanced around the darkness and asked, "So where the hell is our prey?"

Bale's keen eyes pierced the darkness as he replied, "He's probably hunting. That means he has more than likely split this dimension to head to mine or one like it where the humans have no real competition at the top of the food chain. They're more relaxed in places like that, less apt to be suspicious of a tall, dark, and handsome dude sniffing a bit too close."

"How does he get out?" Mark asked.

"The same way fuckers from your dimension do," Bale shrugged, "The same way you could if you wanted, by using the elements. Earth, air, fire, or water, any combination of them will do the trick. Rudy thinks it's a spiritual experience. It isn't. It's just science, understanding the rules enough to use them to get what you want."

"Firewalkers," Mark's stare went blank as he said the word.

"Those fuckers are crazy," Bale nodded, "Of all the ways a vampire can die in your potentiality, fire has got to be the worst. You guys turn into ash immediately. It's like you explode."

Mark kept staring into nothing as his voice grew even quieter, "Yeah, it's fucked up. You'll never catch me walking the flame."

"But you could, if you believed," Bale winked.

The deadness finally left Mark's stare as his words vibrated into the world on a laugh that was almost too loud, "In the all-consuming flame of the great bat? It's too bad I don't. I'd be a crispy critter for sure."

"It is pretty crazy," Bale agreed before correcting Mark, "But it isn't belief that makes it work. It is a series of calculated steps which need to be taken in a particular order to crack the barrier between dimensions. Your kind uses air and flame. Rudy uses water and earth."

"So…mud," Mark grunted in disgust. "I fucking hate wolves."

"Me too," Bale nodded.

"Wait a minute," Mark's tone suggested he'd just had an epiphany. "He's not even in there is he?"

The same moment that Mark birthed the idea into the air, there was movement in the darkness beneath Rudy's cabin. The thing was on low stilts, more than likely to account for rising water levels during wetter seasons. The space beneath the weathered structure was nearly pitch, but Bale caught the subtle shift in the darkness. A dim light confirmed he hadn't imagined it. Rudy was the dark shape slipping out of the muck beneath the cabin and up into it through a hatch under its belly.

Bale pulled his GPS device out of the holster he kept it in while hunting and whispered quietly, "It's go time. I'm not giving him a chance to get comfortable. Give me two minutes to get him under control, and then get in there. Make sure you're ready to inject him with that silver shit as soon as you're inside. He's going to be hard to hang onto."

Bale estimated the distance from where he was sitting in the darkness to the hut and added five feet. Then he set the height. The floor of the place sat about four feet above the muck below. He added a foot to account for joists and floorboards. That should put him right in the center of Rudy's living room. He slipped the device back in its holster, took a deep breath, glanced over at Mark and said, "Two minutes," as he hit the button.

A brief moment of pain swirled out from his chest. It felt like his form was stretching, but not intact. Like each cell in his body forgot to cling to the cells they normally would to maintain the shape of a body and all the stuff inside. It was like being torn apart. Then, for an instant which inexplicably seemed both minute and eternal at the same time, he felt the sensation of traveling, but not as one whole being. It wasn't like walking where you can feel each of your limbs moving through time and space. It was like each cell moved on its own, like they all knew where they needed to go on some subatomic level. Each bit felt everything each other bit felt, sharing each experience with the whole, separate, but still connected on some strange, spiritual level which Bale didn't quite understand.

Then, just as quickly as he'd been ripped apart, he was put back together. Arriving didn't feel all that different from departing. The pain was the same. It was just in reverse. As much as he liked to pretend the pain didn't bother him, like he'd grown accustomed to it or something, it hurt every time. At least it was quick.

This time wasn't any different than any other time he'd arrived somewhere. It seemed as if the new scenery he'd traveled to materialized around him. It was almost as if he hadn't moved, but the old scene broke apart so the new one could be built. Though his senses suggested as much to his mind, he knew it wasn't that. He was deconstructed and reconstructed rather than the scenery doing the same.

Once all Bale's bits were back in their proper place, he was ready. He had a plan. Rudy would be surprised at his sudden presence right smack dab in the middle of his domicile. Bale would use his victim's moment of shock to incapacitate him. Despite how strong wolves were, their knees were just as fragile as any other being's. Driving a heel into the side of one of those knees would take the fight right out of the biggest of them and leave them in a heap on the floor. Once Bale had Rudy on the ground with a busted knee, gaining control and choking him out would be easy. Then Mark could swoop in and inject him with the silver juice. Target acquired. That isn't at all how it went.

The cabin was quiet when Bale materialized in the center of a dimly lit great room. Great room might have been a stretch. The entire place was one big room, but there wasn't anything great about it. The floor was dusty, worn planks. The walls were the same. Oddities were hung randomly about the walls: parts of animals or humans, feathers all twisted together like some kind of macabre art, and all manner of dried vegetation that looked like it might crumble to dust at any moment. Bale assumed all of it was used in some kind of oddball ceremony or another.

The kitchen sat to Bale's right beneath a loft accessible by a makeshift ladder constructed of rough-cut branches tied together with twine. There were three cabinets, a metal wash bin that probably didn't get much use, and a weathered table with one chair. There were three mason jars on the table. One was half-filled with some murky green liquid that somewhat resembled swamp water, while the other two housed powders, pink and a light brown that was almost the color of dirt respectively. There was a simple shelf with eight more jars. Some contained similar stuff to those on the table. Others housed dried herbs and other plant life. It was all probably stuff Rudy used for some spell, curse, or some other superstitious nonsense.

The area to Bale's left looked like it wanted to be a living room or den or something of the sort. It didn't quite fit the bill. There was a dirty animal skin that was old and worn enough to completely fail at resembling what it was when it lived and breathed. A simple wooden chair that was at least as old and worn sat in the middle of it. Comfort obviously hadn't been on the carpenter's mind when the thing was crafted. Bale could almost hear it creaking as he examined it. The small table next to that chair matched it almost exactly. An old book rested on it. Bale wondered what kind of tale a werewolf might read.

There was a fireplace built into the wall beyond the sparse furnishings. It was constructed of random, odd-shaped stones. It had probably been nice at some point in its history, but the years had apparently been cruel to it. The mortar in between the stones was cracked and crumbling. It was amazing the thing managed to stand. The hearth at its base was so blackened with soot, the inside of it appeared like a yawning abyss, like it could drag a soul right out of the living world all the way to hell.

The idea sent a shiver down Bale's spine and returned his mind to his current predicament. Where the hell was Rudy? The cabin seemed suddenly cold. Bale knew it was all in his head. The temperature hadn't changed at all since he arrived. It took him a moment to place the sensation tightening up his joints and causing his heart to pound so loudly he could hear it in his head. It was fear. The wolf wouldn't have had time to escape. That meant he had to be there hiding somewhere in the dim light, but there didn't seem to be any place to hide.

"I wasn't expecting company," a low, almost seductive voice slithered across the stale air of the cabin, "Who be this scared, little sheep who's stumbled into my den?"

The voice taunting Bale had an accent that almost sounded like the Cajun dialect of Potentiality 0. That made sense. The area surrounding the cabin reminded him of rural Louisiana. It was an oddity he couldn't quite explain nor understand. In the thousands of potentialities he'd visited, the inhabitants all seemed quite similar to their counterparts in other potentialities, any differences subtle enough to be barely noticeable. The oddness of those similarities wasn't what caused the hair on the nape of Bale's neck to stand. It was the fact that he couldn't place the origin of that voice carrying those words in the familiar dialect that somehow made the room feel much colder than when he arrived only a moment earlier. Rudy obviously had a bead on him. There would be no surprise busted knees. Bale did his best to hide his concern as he nonchalantly responded, "Rudy Garreau, you died exactly six minutes before the howling hour on the fifteenth day of the 3rd cycle in the three-hundred and twenty-fourth year of the war age. You know you were supposed to go into the light. That soul doesn't belong to you anymore."

"Oh, mon pote, I ain't quite done with it yet. I've got more to do, haven't the time to be dealing with no soul collectors," Rudy's reply sounded almost like a chuckle. He paused for a few moments before adding, "Today must be your lucky day. Normally, someone so rude as to disturb the serenity of my domicile would have had their throat ripped clean out by this point, but, you know, I just returned from a very productive trip. I'm feeling quite full and tired. What say you skitter on back from wherever the hell you came from, and I'll let you keep all your sloppy bits inside your skin?"

Bale had keyed in on the origin of the sound while Rudy droned on. At the same time, his instincts and combat training had managed to chase out that brief moment of strength-stealing fear which had grabbed hold of him when he'd first arrived. He was the hunter, and Rudy was his prey. It wasn't the other way around. His quarry was standing in the darkness of the far corner of the kitchen. Covered in wet muck from the soft earth beneath the cabin, it was a perfect hiding spot. It was his teeth that gave him away, a couple quick flashes of dim white while he spoke. Bale had him.

"Believe me, buddy, I'd much prefer not to have to do this, but my boss ain't the type who takes no for an answer. It would be best if you came quietly. It won't hurt as bad," Bale replied, keeping a sharp edge on his tone.

It was a good ten feet Rudy covered as he launched himself at Bale from the darkness and pounded into his chest with two fists. He looked like a dirty glob of slime as he closed the distance. Once he connected, Bale caught a whiff of him. He smelled like sewage that had been festering in sweltering heat for days. As much as Bale didn't want to touch the sloppy mess of werewolf attacking him, he didn't have a choice. His hands slipped a bit as he grabbed hold of Rudy's wrists the moment his fists connected with his chest. Then he let the momentum carry him onto his back rolling with the assault as he pulled his knees in tight and thrusted them into Rudy's gut. The blow sent the wolf sailing upside down into the wall. Planks cracked when his big body hit. Bale was back on his feet by the time Rudy had slid down the cracked planks to land on his head.

Bale didn't waste any time. He cleared the distance between him and Rudy in two steps, dropping a knee into the wolf's gut just before dropping a couple heavy right hands against his left cheek. It wasn't until the slimy wolf was wriggling out from under him and blasting him in the side of his head with a sloppy, wet elbow that Bale realized Rudy hadn't turned yet. The idea was troublesome. Rudy was as fast as a gazelle and as strong as a bear in his human form. He'd be downright devastating once he turned. There was no time to worry about it. He rolled with the attack using the wall to steady himself as he regained his feet.

Rudy had only made about three steps toward the window before Bale was on him again, tackling him around the waste, spinning and tossing him against the wall again. As soon as the wolf was back on his feet, Bale stepped toward him and fired a front kick at his sternum. It was a solid blow that launched Rudy right back into the wall.

As Bale ducked beneath a wild haymaker the wolf tossed at him after bouncing off the wall, it occurred to him that Rudy didn't have any form of combat training. He was all muscle and emotion, rage and mayhem. Bale calculated his movements and fired a short, left hook to Rudy's ribcage. The blow nearly doubled the wolf over as he winced in pain. It also ruined the trajectory of his next attack, a roundhouse that sailed high over Bale's head instead of blasting him in the temple. Bale used the opening to deliver a right uppercut that snapped Rudy's head back and sent him tumbling back against the wall. Bale stayed right on top of him as he finished the combo with a left hook followed immediately by an overhand right. The first snapped Rudy's head to the left just before the follow-up bounced the back of his head off the wall. That's when the wolf began to turn. At least, that's when Bale noticed it.

It was difficult to see the change on Rudy's face or his form as covered in muck as both were. The thing that gave it away was the howl that accompanied his counter to Bale's last attack. No human being could make a sound like that. On top of that, the steadily growing claws on the hand sailing toward Bale's cheek were moving at least one hundred times faster than any of the previous assaults he had easily avoided. Getting out of the way of this one left him rolling end over end away from his prey. He hadn't even settled onto his ass when he heard the window break. By the time he was back on his feet, the wolf was gone, out the window and racing into darkness.

"Shit," Bale muttered under his breath as he charged out the window after him.

The bayou felt quiet as Mark sat in darkness hiding behind some form of bush he couldn't identify—it kind of resembled a southern magnolia, but it was a bush not a tree. It wasn't really quiet at all though. The nocturnal beasts of the bush sang out a symphony around him. He recognized some of the sounds. There were definitely bullfrogs croaking out their bassy notes while at least one owl added a deep, soft, and stuttering rhythm of hoots. Some other bird whose song Mark couldn't recognize chirped out a melody that was joined by the random barking of some critter he also couldn't place. Even with the symphony blaring out around him, something about the darkness seemed quiet, almost still, like death.

He checked his watch carefully covering up the dim glow of the tiny light that illuminated its face so as not to be spotted by any eyes which might be prying in the darkness. The silliness of checking the time on a device geared to track seconds, hours, and minutes from his own reality set in. A minute is a minute everywhere, but they aren't precisely the same amount of time. Bale told him to wait two minutes. He had no idea what two minutes represented in Potentiality 7,645. He did know that two minutes in Potentiality 0, where Bale was born, represented almost three minutes in his own potentiality, two minutes and fifty-six point three seconds to be exact. Only forty-five seconds had passed on Mark's watch since Bale pulled his odd, disappearing trick and left him alone in the sweaty darkness.

As he sat there in the loud quiet of a dark bayou which didn't seem all that different from a swamp, he contemplated going up against a wolf for a guy who had never been a good friend. Well, he was that, a good friend, but he didn't act like one. All he ever brought with him when he'd come for a visit was a bad attitude and the kind of mayhem you can't imagine until you witness it unfurling before your eyes. The guy was like a headache manifest into a human being. Yet, he could never say no to him. It was probably guilt. He'd listened to the poor slob sobbing out his sad laments about his daughter at least a million times. On top of that, he had inadvertently thwarted a terrorist attack from Potentiality 23,596, some holy crusader who'd learned that his reality was only one of potentially millions that existed just a single vibration from those adjacent to it. A vampire had killed his son, and this righteous crusader devised a weapon that could wipe out this dark place which could spawn something so heinous as a nightmare creature who lived off the blood of men. Bale described it as a nuclear bomb but with the power of the sun. His explanation of what that was sounded like a massive fusion reaction the likes of which no vampire or human had ever contemplated in Potentiality 6. Lucky for Mark's reality, Bale had arrived at the exact same moment as this supposed destroyer. He hadn't been able to explain how he knew this man had a nefarious purpose, but he used his device to drag the poor sucker to space and left him there to die while his UV bomb exploded harmlessly in that dark vacuum.

The bottom line for Mark was the same as it always was when his mind would get traveling down the path of trying to understand why he'd never cut Bale off. He owed him a debt. More than that, his entire reality owed the man a debt. It was a debt none of them could ever repay. As much as just once he'd love to look in Bale's eyes and say, "Not this time, fucker. You're on your own," he knew he never would.

He checked the watch again. Only thirty more seconds had passed. The loud crash of breaking glass assured him he wouldn't have to wait the other forty-five seconds Bale had asked of him. Things must have gone sideways.

Mark's heart sunk into his gut as he glimpsed the shape stumbling as fast as it could into the darkness. It was difficult to get a clear look, but he saw enough to know it was Bale's bounty, and that bounty was transforming from a human who could be easily subdued by the likes of Bale Lance into a wolf that could give that guy one hell of a run for his money.

"Son of a bitch," he muttered quietly as he saw Bale come flying out that same window to give chase.

Mark wasn't like Bale. Bale lived for the hunt. He'd been correct when he suggested Mark saw him as nothing more than an aimless drunk. Anyone who didn't know him would fail to see anything more than that. It was a far cry from the truth though. Bale was a unique combination of stealth, intelligence, and brutality that Mark had never seen in any individual he'd ever met. The guy was one of a kind. He was a hunter. Mark wasn't that at all. He was comfortable. He ran his bar and the farm. Between the two, he had everything he needed. Vampires hadn't needed to hunt for centuries. The war that erased that need ended generations before Mark was born.

The night suddenly seemed even darker as Mark sat there trying to will his legs to straighten him up, so he could chase his quarry deeper into that murky abyss. The air even seemed heavier as he stood up from a crouch and sighed something that sounded like quiet defeat to his own ears. As he gazed out into the blackness of the dense forest beyond Rudy's cabin, failing to will his legs further to carry him into that yawning cavern of uncertainty, he realized that everything seemed more than it had been. It wasn't just the deepening darkness or the weight of the air upon his shoulders. The symphony of forest critters hooting, chirping, croaking, and barking their melodies out into the world seemed to twist into a cacophony of terror, a macabre blend of sounds which shouldn't occur in nature while the mellow odors of a slow-moving brook, fragrant flowers, and decomposing leaves melted from something that smelled like fresh, country air into something that stank like festering death. Mark knew it was all in his head, but that didn't make it any less real.

It was a few long moments before he could wrangle his trepidation enough to keep it from boiling into mind-numbing terror, but he took that first step toward the path Bale had chased Rudy down. His pace quickened after a few slow steps. Duty was finally winning. Bale was a loner. He had never really asked for any help outside of an ear to hear all his sad stories. The idea that this human who wasn't afraid of anything, a guy who always knew he was going to win, had obviously admitted to himself that he needed help sparked some primal thing in Mark that had been buried beneath years of comfort and normalcy. Of all the souls Bale knew across all the realities he'd visited Mark was the one he came to for help.

It was an odd sensation; a feeling he couldn't quite define. It was something like purpose but more than that. Whatever this foreign thing was, it had his legs churning ever faster into darkness that no longer seemed like an unconquerable abyss but an obstacle to his goal.

On top of that, like all vampires, his eyes were built for the dark. All the inky and terrifying blackness was in his head.

The deafening chorus of creatures hidden about the bush slowly morphed from the overbearing horror it had become into something that felt more like a triumphant charge to greatness. Mark's heart pounded in his chest as hard and as fast as his feet pounded against the trail. He felt like a soldier, fearless and mighty, charging off to battle in honor of some great purpose. His friend needed him. What greater purpose was there than that?

A loud crack off the trail to Mark's right assured him that Bale had caught up to his quarry, or that quarry had ambushed him. Either option meant stealth no longer mattered and speed was paramount. His mind shifted. It was something all vampires could do. It wasn't quite a trance, but it felt like it. Mark allowed his mind and reason to get out of the way of his senses. All of them were as keen as any nocturnal hunter. His ears latched on to that loud sound that must have been a branch—far too thick for any man to break—snapping under extreme weight. His body continued in that direction without his mind commanding it to do so. His eyes locked onto targets, spots on trees with clear paths to launch to and from. His legs bent and extended propelling him at least one hundred feet with each powerful leap. He sailed through the darkness as if he were flying beneath the canopy, slicing the still forest air.

Mark had only taken two of those mighty leaps before he smelled both hunter and hunted. By this point he wasn't sure which was which. Bale's smell was familiar. He was an impeccably clean man, but he hated perfumes and colognes. No human would notice, but vampires didn't just smell things like humans. They had organs and chemicals in their nasal passages which could sense and interpret chemicals emitted by other creatures. Because of this, Bale smelled kind of musty to Mark, like sweat or an old shirt ready for the laundry. Also because of this, Rudy smelled like rotten meat and feces festering in the hot desert sun. Wolves smelled like shit. It was the anal glands. They were constantly seeping nastiness into the air.

After one more leap, he could hear the two combatants battling in the darkness. Claws made a distinct sound when they sliced the air. It was almost a whistle but thicker than that like they pushed more air than they cut. Rudy's claws were moving fast. The wolf must have finished his transformation as he was furiously slashing at Bale who must have been doing all he could to keep from being gored to death. That would explain all the grunting and tumbling Mark heard.

Mark leapt twice more before pausing. He could finally see them. Bale was on the defensive. He ducked, tumbled, and jumped out of the way of wild, roundhouse attacks that came faster than a human should be able to avoid or even see. Bale was special though. Everything about him was human, but there was something more, something Mark had never been able to place or identify. He could do things humans simply should not be able to do, like go toe to toe with an exceptionally brutal werewolf and hold his own.

Mark fished a small pouch out of his pocket as he clung to the tree with just his feet. Then he fished a syringe out of the pouch. The fluid inside the thing shimmered even in the dim light that was barely a breath from total darkness. He waited there in silence watching for the perfect moment to strike. As fast as he was, his target was moving just as quickly. His timing and his movements had to be precise. He tracked Rudy's attack patterns, logging every move the wolf made in his mind. There appeared to be three distinct combinations. The pause between them was barely noticeable, but these three patterns had distinct beginnings and ends. The first and most common attack the wolf employed was only three moves, all wild haymakers. It was a horizontal slash with his left hand, then one with his right, and it ended with a strange vertical slash with his left that resembled an uppercut with no technique. The second started with a bite toward the face which was followed by two short slashes with his right hand that were followed by three short, quick slashes with his left. It ended with a downward slash of his right hand. The last one started with something that almost looked like a jab. The wolf would fire his left arm straight out and flick at his target with his claw once fully extended. It wouldn't produce a deep gash, but it would slice flesh. That was followed by an odd, spinning back-handed slash with his right hand which he probably only used to confuse an opponent to set up a flurry of left and right horizontal slashes that came faster than any of his other attacks, five with the left and five with the right. The last one would present the perfect time to strike. Mark would spring his attack right after Rudy began his spin into the backhand. He would launch himself through the air and stab his syringe right into the vein throbbing beneath the thick fur of the wolf's neck.

A foreign tingle danced about the base of Mark's neck as he

watched Bale battle the wolf and waited for his opening to attack. It stood the hair on his head on end and had his scalp tingling and tightening just the same. It was the moment. It swept him up like a helpless leaf yanked from a tree by a furious gale. He was excited about the fight. As he watched his friend block and duck, dive and counter the wolf's relentless attacks, he wished it were him battling the beast in the darkness. He had almost lost himself in a waking dream when his moment came and shocked him back to reality.

Rudy fired out the strange looking jab with the quick claw flick at the end of it. That would flow right into the spinning backhand. Mark leaned deep into his crouch as time seemed to slow. As soon as Rudy slipped into his spin, Mark launched himself into the damp, night air. And then Bale ruined everything.

Right at the moment Mark fired himself toward the wolf, Bale threw a counter to Rudy's jab. The soul hunter brought his heel down in something that almost looked like a quick stomp right on the side of Rudy's ankle. The beast howled as he stumbled through the rest of a spin that Bale wouldn't let him finish. Instead, he grabbed the thick fur on the wolf's back and used the momentum of the spin to toss him into a thick tree trunk. Bale had barely released his grip on Rudy's fur when Mark slammed into him, sending them both tumbling into the brush and dropping his needle in the process.

"What the fuck?" Bale groaned as he slipped on wet leaves while failing an attempt to scramble back to his feet.

Mark had the wind knocked out of him, but he managed to reply, "I had an opening, and you fucked it up."

"Well, where the fuck is…" Bale's voice trailed off as Rudy crashed into him carrying him deeper into the brush.

Mark couldn't tell who was hitting whom as the two combatants battled in the darkness. It sounded like someone pounding a steak into submission with a meat tenderizer. Hopefully, it wasn't Bale being beaten into the sloppy muck.

Mark needed to get off his ass and find that syringe. It couldn't have gone far. He crawled about the bushes sweeping the ground with his hands. "Shit, shit, shit," he muttered quietly as he searched adding, "Come on, come on, come on. Where is it?"

A wave of relief washed over him as his right hand rolled over the top of it. This time he wouldn't wait for the perfect moment. He'd just dive into the melee and poke the first part of that grizzly beast that got close enough to him.

He had only taken two triumphant steps toward the loud scuffle when he heard another howl. This one wasn't the familiar howl of a wolf crying out at the moon. This was the howl of a man in pain, and it was followed by Bale's deep growl, "Motherfucker, bit me."

The loud proclamation quickened Mark's step even further. If Rudy didn't kill Bale, Bale would turn. Then Mark would have two wolves to deal with.

The two were in a clearing when Mark finally caught up to them. Bale had definitely been bitten. A big chunk of his shoulder was missing, and his ripped-up shirt was covered in blood. Despite all the gore, he was holding his own. He drove his head into Rudy's snout just as Mark was charging toward them. The move presented him with another chance to find his mark.

As Bale stepped back to collect himself for his next attack, Rudy stumbled a few steps in the other direction reeling a bit from the blow. Mark dropped his head down and launched his shoulder in the wolf's stretched belly. They tumbled end over end a few times, but Mark maintained his grip on the beast's fur. Mark was on top when they finally settled, but Rudy bucked wildly to wriggle out from under him before he could jab him in the throat with the needle. Then he felt the burn. It wasn't deep enough to really tear up any meat, but he felt each of the wolf's four claws as they cut into his flesh and gashed him across his chest. He only spared a moment of lament to how out of shape he was for the kind of fight he was in before instinct yanked control back from his brain. He wasn't losing to a fucking wolf.

Had his mind not been completely checked out, the hiss that poured out of his mouth from somewhere deep in his gut might have surprised him. The slash which followed the beastly sound would have shocked him all the more. It felt different when your own claws cut deep into soft skin than it did when the meat being sliced was your own. He ducked before he even saw the next attack flying at his face. He was too fast for the wolf. His left hand shot out like a bullet as he rose from the deep crouch and grabbed hold of Rudy's skull. The sound that left him as he felt the wolf's skull crack beneath his claws was foreign to his ears. A moment later, his right thumb was pressing the plunger on his syringe to deliver the sleepy time serum he'd concocted to subdue the beast right into Rudy's carotid artery.

Rudy began transforming back into a man almost immediately as

Mark watched the fruits of his efforts with equal parts relief and disappointment. The rush of battle was like a drug, a high he never wanted to end. He had just fought a werewolf. He only knew one other vampire who had ever even encountered a werewolf—wolves weren't native to Potentiality 6—and that wolf was just trying to get home. He must have taken a wrong turn at Albuquerque. Thanks for all the DVDs, Bale. Whatever landed him in the wrong place at the wrong time, that vampire didn't want to fight anybody. Mark hadn't wanted to fight anybody either, but once he was in it, he was in it all the way.

By the time Rudy finished his transformation back into a man, he was completely unconscious. A moment prior, he had looked like an unstoppable, abominable beast. Lying there naked and vulnerable, he looked like something completely different. Mark almost felt bad for him. The idea the poor slob was already supposed to be dead almost made it worse. His time was over.

Mark didn't get too far down the trail to Pityville before Bale's hoarse voice dragged him back into the moment. "Fucker bit me," he grunted in a tone that didn't sound like his old friend.

The empty syringe in his hand sent a loud thought roaring through his mind. He should have brought more than one dose. "Listen closely," he said as he spun quickly toward his soon to be mindless, werewolf friend, "You're turning. It is going to happen quickly. Grab your bounty and use your device to get both you clowns back to Orwell. If he's everything you say he is, he should be able to bring you back."

A part of him knew it before he even began talking, but it became obvious it was too late when Bale growled something that sounded like a pack of wolves being shredded alive in a giant meat grinder. It was a horrid song that harkened to pain, hollow sadness, and bitter lament all rolled into one grizzly note. And then Bale was a goddamned wolf. Mark dropped the syringe, sighed the deepest sigh he could remember ever leaving his body, and prepared to defend himself.

"Come on, Bale. Think about your kid. There must be something of you left inside that cranium. Pull it together," Mark pled.

Bale just growled and lunged at him. His black fur fluttered as his large form sliced through the forest air. His jaws were wide; white, hungry fangs dripping saliva and desperate to tear into tender flesh. The growl roaring from those open jaws should have been impossible as wide as they were stretched. It seemed the plan in that suddenly beastly mind was to pop Mark's head off in one bite. That wouldn't do.

Mark gave up on the idea of reasoning with Bale. He had obviously checked out. The idea of checking out himself and foregoing logic and thought to go full beast himself fluttered through his mind quickly enough that it barely earned a thought. He didn't want to kill his old friend. If he went that route, one of them would surely be dead when all was said and done. The plan came together quickly as the mass of muscle, claws, fur, and fangs ate up the distance between them.

Bale's clothes had ripped off him as his body morphed from its natural, human form into the new beast he had become. His muscles had swollen as his bones stretched and changed shape until he was far taller and larger than the human he'd been. That was good. Though Mark couldn't see the shredded clothes, he could smell them. He could hear the weak vibration of the device Bale used to skip from place to place and dimension to dimension. Allowing his senses to triangulate the location based on both the scent of the clothes and the sound of the device, assured him that the most important piece of his quickly developing plan was still in the pocket where Bale kept it. That was a blessing.

Once all the minute details were in place, and clear enough they wouldn't be lost when he submitted control of his body to his instincts, he let go. Bale was a mere step from him when Mark lashed out with both hands and grabbed hold of the fur on the sides of the wolf's head. Then he stepped to the side and allowed the beast's momentum to carry him into the trunk of a tree thick enough that it was surprising the thing fell after a loud crack and an explosion of splintered wood.

Mark had barely let go of Bale's fur when he turned and launched himself toward the smell of Bale's clothes. After a few moments of rummaging around, he gripped Bale's device, his only chance to get out of the situation he was in without dying or killing his old friend.

Despite the fact that Bale had given him a tour of the device some years prior, logic had mostly fled. The lights and dials staring back at him meant very little. Luckily, he recalled enough to know the small, red button on the right side of the thing was a kind of home button, a reset, a way to get back to the source, back to Orwell. That little red button was the key to getting out alive. The only thing left was to get Bale intertwined enough with Rudy's comatose form that both would make the journey.

Mark crouched deep to launch himself toward Rudy, but he wasn't able to extend his legs and complete the journey before Bale was on him again. The wolf slammed into his chest sending them tumbling end over end through rough brambles. Mark barely noticed the thorns scratching his skin as Bale's jaws snapped again and again. All his attention was intensely focused on not getting bitten. That would be the worst possible outcome. Mixing wolf and vampire blood resulted in abominations that should never exist in any reality. He had only heard of one, and the thing was a mindless, destructive beast. Eliminating it took a coalition of wolves and vampires, many of whom lost their lives to the effort. That was a thing he didn't want to be.

Bale's jaws snapped again and again. It took every bit of Mark's speed and agility to avoid the dripping fangs those jaws would punch into his flesh to infect him with the tainted saliva. His efforts to fight back were mostly futile while he clung desperately to the device that would send his opponent back to Orwell. It was like fighting with one arm tied behind his back. All he could do was push Bale's limbs and head off course to keep from earning a scratch or bite.

As they continued to tumble, Mark managed to pull his knee up to his chest. Then, on the next go round, he extended his legs abruptly as soon as Bale's back connected with the ground. The move propelled him up and away from his attacker as well as getting him closer to Rudy. As soon as his feet hit the ground, he crouched deep and jumped again, this time directly toward where Rudy lay beneath a tree. Based on his trajectory, he'd land right on top of him. He almost succeeded in doing just that. The next few moments were a blur.

Bale slammed into his back. He must have given chase immediately after Mark had leapt off him. The added momentum would have pushed them both well past Rudy, but Mark managed to reach out his free hand just in time to grab the sleeping form by the arm. As soon as his fingers were wrapped around Rudy's bicep, he clicked that magical, red button with his other hand. Time seemed to stop as soon as he did.

Though he could still feel Rudy's arm gripped within his fist and Bale on his back as they tumbled together sans control, it felt like every cell in his body exploded in separate directions. It suddenly seemed his brain was receiving impulses from more nerves than just his own. It was as if his essence somehow melded with both Bale's and Rudy's while still maintaining the slightest hint of its individuality. It was like pain tripled. At the same time, his senses were overloaded with every type of experience he could imagine, and even more he couldn't before they happened. Every color he'd ever witnessed exploded before his eyes before melting together in some kind of demented kaleidoscope that burned to look at. Closing his eyes did nothing to quell the pain. It was obvious his eyes weren't witnessing the colors his mind experienced.

Those colors would have been enough on their own to force him to tears if he could find his eyes to shed any, but they weren't alone in the assault on his senses. Joining them was a cacophony of what seemed to be every sound that ever was at volumes that should be impossible battering ear drums as scattered as his eyes. It was an unholy symphony of terror exploding across the cosmos.

At the same time, it tasted like putrid garbage festered on his tongue. Every flavor imaginable melting together into the most horrible taste that ever was. It was worse than gargling with garlic, or at least what that idea tasted like in his imagination. The burning sensation accompanying the pain was worse than what he imagined it would feel like.

As stretched and scattered as his skin must have been, each individual cell burned like tiny, hot needles repeatedly stabbed into them. While pains he could only imagine as aches more massive than a whole moon throbbed about the rest of his discombobulated form. There was no pause in the mounting assault, not even the briefest relief, as the pain continued to mount toward some grand crescendo or explosion that might finally end it, but it didn't come. Each speck of a moment seemed a twisted agony that must be the top, that must have been the most pitiable and dire pain ever felt in any reality, until the next moment proved it wasn't.

Then it all finally ended. The twisted and ghastly colors, the screeching and booming sounds, the putrid and vomitous odors and tastes, and even the searing pain like blazing needles piercing every bit of his skin, it all ceased abruptly. Then it felt like he was being smashed back together, as if he'd been stretched out like a rubber band just to the point it might break and then released to snap back into shape.

For a moment, how long or brief was impossible to know, it was like a limbo, like his senses had checked out and he was simply nothing. Of course, that could not be the case. He was still aware. Being aware you were nothing would be something. Could you ever truly be nothing if you knew you were? The question lived in Mark's awareness for the unknowable duration of that moment, right up until he felt the hard floor against his left shoulder. A faint but musky hint of mahogany delicately drifting about the air around his head pleased his sinuses when he finally took a breath. It was a delicious contradiction to the putrescence that had invaded his olfaction while traveling to this unknown place.

Mark wasn't terribly far down the path to comfort when the stark realization of where his body rested inelegantly on a polished, wooden floor occurred to him. He was somewhere in the City of Gold. If Orwell was even the faintest shadow of the horrible creature Bale had described to him during so many drunken rants, the rapid and shallow breaths he was suddenly taking as panic began squeezing his heart would probably be his last.

"What is this disrespect?" The clarity and beauty of the tone carrying the question into the world were undeniable despite the obvious rage boiling off the statement. That had to be Orwell's voice, terrifying despite its perfection.

The words in the back of Mark's throat that would undoubtedly amount to an insufficient answer never made it past his mouth as the furry lump beside him first stirred, then roared something that sounded like a confused threat. Mark instinctively rolled away from the mass narrowly avoiding the stony claws that would have punctured his gut before gashing it open. Instead, those powerful things glinted like obsidian in the perfect light as they carved ragged cuts into the glossy sheen of the polished floor.

As Mark slid further away from his recently wolfy friend, he finally saw the angels Bale had described to him in one or another of his drunken rants. Sometimes they would look like walking dragons. Other times, they would present themselves as the winged and glorious host glowing with god's glory as described in so many religious texts and myths of humans across so many realities. In this moment, they looked like well-dressed muscle, beautiful lackeys clad in impeccable, white suits with light pouring off them as if they were stars shining in the heavens. Beholding them was almost painful, yet the simple act of it filled Mark with such complete joy, he almost forgot to be afraid of what Orwell would do to him for coming to this place with Bale.

The consequence of Mark's actions would obviously have to wait as Orwell shouted to his angels after Bale howled and flipped the table where they sat, ripping it from the rail it was nailed to, "Do not simply sit there like dull idiots while this beast mars the perfection of my temple. Subdue him, you fools."

Before either of them could move, the fire-haired Gabriel was sailing toward the bar off a backhand Bale had blasted him with. Mark watched as the perfect angel flew helplessly through the air. He was perfect, a stark contrast to the vile thing Bale had described to him. Everything was perfect in this place. Perhaps that was the illusion. Bale's understanding of Orwell and his angels was vast and fueled by millennia of experience interacting with them but seeing it for himself made all those stories seem like fiction. Everything about them was flawless.

Golden-haired Michael was flying through the air toward the bar a moment before Gabriel slammed into the shelves behind it and smashed at least half of the bottles housed there. Bale had kicked him in the chest and sent the angel sailing.

Then the air vibrated with the glorious and horrible sound of Orwell's voice. "Enough," he shouted at the ceiling before looking back at Bale and adding, "You are not a wolf."

The proclamation sounded like a command. Perhaps it was. As soon as the words were born from Orwell's perfect lips, Bale stopped in his tracks. His body trembled hard enough to cause his fur to shake violently as if whipped about by howling winds.

That was all Mark saw of the City of Gold. While Bale convulsed, Orwell turned his attention to Mark and spoke in more measured tones that were, though quieter, no less glorious, "You should not be here. However, I appreciate your effort in returning what is mine. You will live. Go home now."

And the world was suddenly dark for Mark.

CHAPTER 8

THE MOTHER OF ALL MARKS

CITY OF GOLD

It was obvious the space surrounding Bale was Orwell's office when he woke up. The sheer perfection of every minute detail feeding an experience that no other room in any reality could ever hope to even mimic left no question. However, there was something muted about it, as if he were looking at it through filthy glass. A few quick blinks cleared it up and allowed it to shine in all its usual glory.

Bale sat in a chair he'd never occupied prior. It was next to the one he always sat in whenever he had occasion to sit in Orwell's office. It was an exact match to that one as well, but he had never sat in it. The idea held his attention for longer than the thought probably deserved. Was he such a creature of habit that he couldn't bear to sit in a different spot? He didn't think so but faced with the reality of it there seemed no other logical explanation. He had a chair he always sat in, and somehow, he'd ended up in a different chair. The idea troubled him enough to prove he was as much a creature of habit as one might think of someone who would be bothered by occupying a seat which wasn't his.

He had no real memory of arriving in the wrong seat, just flashes of recollections that were more like raw, malformed feelings than actual memories. Colors, odors, and sounds that might help add some definition to a thought if presented in even close proximity to anything he'd experienced concurrently with them might assist in forming some kind of memory. They didn't come like that though. They were separate, standalone sensations which carried very little meaning on their own. About the only thing he could deduce from all of it was the fact it was a miracle he still lived.

A horrible, sucking sound dragged his attention from the non-memories battering his consciousness. It sounded like a starving beast furiously slurping at a scavenged bone in an attempt to draw just a bit more marrow from it after all had been spent.

He'd witnessed Orwell feeding before. It never got easier. The sounds were probably the worst. The sight of a soul leaving a body wasn't as gruesome as one might think. It looked like swirls of light emanating from the forehead and chest of the body it was leaving with tiny balls of brighter light flashing about among them. The violent convulsions of the host giving up their essence and identity as if they were hopelessly battling to cling to their ego was troubling but not really any worse than watching a creature die. Bale had seen that enough times that its effect had dulled enough to hardly be a bother. The expression Orwell wore while he consumed a soul was troubling, almost as bad as the sounds he made. It was like watching someone torture a thing and revel in its anguish while leaching the most immense pleasure from its pitiable pain. The few times he'd witnessed it always left him wanting to vomit.

Bale stretched a bit of stiffness out that had settled between his shoulder blades as Orwell finished up his meal and dropped the meat sack that used to be Rudy Garreau to the floor. That shell hadn't rested for more than two seconds before a couple of imps scurried in to drag the body away. Those had always troubled Bale. Orwell had scolded him for referring to them as imps when he'd asked about them, but he couldn't see them as anything else. They were equally perfect to every other creature Bale had ever seen in Orwell's sphere, but they were tiny, like toddlers without the pudgy cuteness. Orwell had explained the hierarchy to him once, but he'd been uninterested. Whether they were cherubim or seraphim or whatever other branch of Orwell's angelic host they might have been, he didn't care. They creeped him out.

"I see you remain troubled by my," Orwell began after licking his lips and wiping his mouth in satisfied fashion. He paused long enough to suggest he may never finish the statement before finally adding, "...*imps*, as you so callously refer to them."

Despite the overly dramatic tone dancing about Orwell's statement, he had an odd pep in his step. There was an uncustomary glee skipping across his expression. The typically morose boss of all existence seemed happy. It was enough to make Bale forget himself long enough to comment, "Something big must have happened. The last time I saw you this happy, you had just slaughtered every first-born child of an entire species."

Bale cringed after letting the thought escape his lips, but Orwell was unaffected by the jab. Instead, he grinned slyly before casually replying, "I am going to miss that wit when I finally allow you to perish, but you are correct. Something big has happened."

Bale slumped further into the rich leather of his chair. Anything big for Orwell could mean nothing less than trouble for him. He didn't want to ask what this big event might be, so he didn't. Instead, he asked, "Why am I still alive? I obviously fucked up pretty bad. I'm not even sure how I got here, but I know Rudy scratched or bit me. I know I turned. That had to be messy. You hate messy."

"I despise messy," Orwell boomed at the ceiling and raised his arms dramatically, before offering Bale a warm and genuine smile. Then he took a deep breath and, in a much more measured tone, added, "Luckily for you, what I learned immediately after returning your dear, vampire friend—who was obviously much less useful on your mission than my angels would have been—to his home, has left me in such a mood that not even your juvenile choice of words succeeds in marring my joy."

Most of Orwell's words dashed right past Bale's awareness. The one bit he latched onto was the fact that Mark had survived. "My friend, he's still alive then?" had he not been so concerned for Mark's well-being, the choppiness of his tone would have bothered him to his core.

"Of course, he is," Orwell seemed almost giddy as he gushed. He sat in his chair and folded his hands before continuing, "Though it is utterly unimportant, I know it is eating at your mind, and I am in such a state at this very moment that I feel compelled to humor you. You indeed did fail miserably on your mission. Lucky for you, your friend behaved bravely and managed to bring all three of you back here using the device you had so carelessly lost. He served his purpose. I know you think me unwavering and completely void of empathy, but that simply isn't true. Mark managed to succeed where you failed and earned his life. Then you made a big mess of my bar, but that wasn't his fault either. I sent him home and then subdued you. And here we are. You with questions about my demeaner, and me with your next case."

There it was. The way Orwell dragged out the words *next case* could only mean it was the kind of work Bale wasn't looking for. He grimaced slightly when he finally replied, "Rudy was a tough sonofabitch. He turned me into a werewolf for fuck's sake. I'm not feeling quite myself yet."

The wide smile never left Orwell's face as he replied, "The incident apparently had no impact on that foul tongue of yours," Then he paused, sighed shallowly, and tapped his index finger against his desk several times before adding, "I appreciate the challenges you have just experienced. Unfortunately, there is no time to wait."

None of it made any sense. What in any reality could color the big guy's cheeks and strap a genuine smile across his timeless face? Bale had never seen anything other than disgust haunting Orwell's perfect countenance. It seemed crazy, but it could only mean there was someone or something in some reality that he truly cared about.

"You will go to Perver City, and I need you to leave immediately," Orwell continued before Bale could find the next question he wanted to ask.

"Perver City?" Bale nearly stammered, "Do you remember when you told me to go to Perver City?"

Orwell's smile faded if only slightly as his brows dipped shallowly toward his nose while he replied, "There was no time when I instructed you to travel to Perver City."

"You did," Bale nodded his head abruptly as he lost control of an incredulous laugh he'd have preferred to stifle. He quickly composed himself and added, "Never. You told me never to go to Perver City. Nobody leaves that place."

"You are correct. I did say that," Orwell acquiesced. That was probably more troubling than his wide smile and odd demeanor. The guy was always right and rarely granted anyone else's thoughts or opinions even the slightest value.

This was big. Bale had asked around about Perver City after Orwell had instructed him to never go to that place. Nobody knew anything about it, not where it was or even what it was, except Michael. Bale had asked him about it during one of their verbal sparring matches. When he asked, "Hey, Mikey. You think you know everything. Tell me about Perver City," he didn't expect to even see a flash of recognition in the angel's eyes. Michael surprised him though. The annoyingly perfect creature didn't miss a beat when he replied, "It's hell, but hell isn't what you think. This place is like what your kind thinks of as heaven, total spiritual bliss. Perver City isn't burning for eternity in a lake of fire. Those are just the stories the boss has passed around to keep the simple folk in line. If they knew what it really was, everybody would want to go there. Nobody cares about feeding their souls anymore. They only care for their indulgences, and that is what they can find in Perver City. It's like your Vegas, but on steroids. There are no rules and no ramifications. You could shoot enough heroin to kill a blue whale and wake up in the morning like nothing had ever happened. It is total physical bliss."

Orwell had obviously noticed the struggle Bale was going through and finally prodded him, "It seems you struggle to find the correct words. Let me help you. The words for which you search sound quite a bit like, thank you for the honor of serving your glory. I shall depart immediately."

"I don't trust myself enough," Bale finally sighed, "I mean, don't get me wrong. The place sounds great, but you and I both know why that won't work for me. I am not the same man you made that deal with so many years ago."

"Half," Orwell's smile faded as his tone grew serious.

"Half of what?" Bale asked.

"Half of what of what you owe on her sentence," Orwell shrugged before adding, "If my calculations are correct, and they always are, that amounts to six-hundred-seventy-two-thousand-three-hundred-twenty-five years. That is a long time."

Bale nearly fell out of the comfortable leather chair so effectively holding his weight. He normally had a pretty solid poker face. It was nowhere to be found. Half was a lot. It was a damn sight more than the ten to thirty years he usually got for a common mark. Hell, it was a damn sight more than the two fifty Orwell owed him for bringing Rudy in. The situation being what it was, he could see Orwell trying to stiff him on that. However, that dopey grin strapped across his face suggested he might actually see the pay day for it.

"Well," Orwell finally prodded, "despite my generous mood, my time is still valuable, Mr. Bale. Please confirm what we both already know. You will be leaving for Perver City immediately."

There were lots of words floating around Bale's mind just then, but none of them managed to coalesce into a cognizant thought that might make it past his lips. He was afraid of Perver City. The fear slithering down his spine and causing his right heel to nervously tap out a steady cadence on the polished floor wasn't for him. It was that little girl with those innocent eyes, the only one who believed in him, and the only reason he kept getting back up every time he was knocked down. He would have swallowed a bullet years ago if it wasn't for her. She needed him. Who knows what kind of sick shit Orwell might do to her if he didn't keep taking jobs.

Bale hadn't noticed the slight twitch in Orwell's left cheek until the big boss broke the silence again. "Could it be? Does Bale Lance actually have nothing to say? In more than two-thousand years, I have never seen you speechless," Orwell said, the slightest hint of condescension sprinkled about his tone.

"I don't," Bale sighed as he shook his head, "On the one hand, that is a long time. On the other hand, that means I've got a long time left to go until my little girl is freed from that perfect, little prison you have her stuck in. And on the other hand..."

"You only have two hands, Mister Bale, and I grow tired of this useless waste of my time," the smile fled from Orwell's face as he interrupted.

"You're right. I do only have two hands," Bale said as he held those two hands up before adding, "That's your fault. Isn't it? You created everything. Maybe you should have given me more hands, because I have lots more to consider. I don't trust myself."

"Oh, come, now," Orwell scoffed, "Your love for your precious little Angel will bring you home, and you can both delight in the massive amount of her sentence that just flitters away."

"Who's the mark?" Bale asked as his gaze shifted toward the floor.

"He likes folks to refer to him as Lou, but I don't like that one bit," Orwell's expression shifted as if the words tasted foul leaving his mouth.

Bale's stare remained locked on the floor as he asked, "Lou, huh? Why is he so special?"

"He is my son," the answer was as matter of fact as any words Bale had ever heard spoken.

"Wait, what? Since when do you have a son?"

Bale's brain nearly melted. What a horrible thing that must be for any creature. Bale could think of very few things worse than knowing that heartless, emotionless, vile, cunt of a thing was your father. There was another reason not to take to the case. If his son needed to be hunted, that kid probably didn't want to be found.

"My spawn is none of your concern," Orwell sneered as his voice lowered, "All you need to know is in this file."

Orwell suddenly held a manila folder in his outstretched hand. It looked like every other file he'd ever handed him. For some reason, Bale thought the file of Orwell's son might be a bit fancier. But that wasn't Orwell's way. He liked things uniform, constant, and perfect.

Bale remained still making no effort to reach for the folder Orwell held out across his desk. After a few moments of silence, he finally said, "I need some time to think about it."

Orwell stretched his arm further across the desk as he replied, "You have no time. Either take the case and wipe away half of your daughter's sentence…half…or remove yourself from my office immediately. I will give it to someone else if you do not want it."

Bale knew it was risky, but he called his bluff, "If you had anyone else to give it to, we wouldn't be talking right now. I need a week."

"Does it trouble you in the slightest what I might do to her if you fail to satisfy my request?" Orwell's tone grew ominously low.

"I think about that all the time," Bale shook his head, "But you would never do anything to her as long as I'm keeping up my end of the bargain. You can't. We have a contract. You like the rules you make too much to break them."

"Two days, Mister Lance," Orwell nearly growled, "You can have two days to work out whatever nonsense is running through your mind. If you fail to return to me when the sun is at its highest in your reality, I will consider our contract breached, and I will do unspeakable things to only thing in any reality that you love."

CHAPTER 9

DAYS GONE BY

POTENTIALITY 824,634

B ale leaned back in a rocking chair he had built more years prior than he could remember in a cabin he had built during the same period. A thick layer of dust covering everything reminded him of how long it had been since he visited the peaceful sanctuary he retired to whenever he needed a quiet place to contemplate or lament.

The room around him blazed in the orange glory of a setting sun shining through the one window on the western wall of the place. Bathed in that glorious light, the aging wooden planks that made up the walls of the small room almost seemed alive, like they were breathing, sentient things that might share a thought at any moment. Of course, they wouldn't share any thoughts. There were no creatures in Potentiality 824,634 who would. None of the species occupying this reality had gained the level of knowledge and function required for speech. The only communication he'd ever heard were howls, growls, grunts, or hoots and the like. Those weren't bothersome at all. There was something beautiful in their simplicity. Rather than detracting from the peacefulness of the place, they added a kind of calm serenity. They belonged with the rush of wind blowing through the crowns of massive trees and rustling through the thick brush below. They bore a stark contrast to the sounds of honking horns, revving engines, and the random shouts of angry people he'd find in other realities.

Bale had found the place by accident. He was aiming for Potentiality 824,635 and plugged the wrong numbers into his device ending up in the very spot where the cabin he resided in now stood. At the time, he had no idea the place was void of intelligent life. He probably should have realized it then. The spot was too perfect. Had men—or any species who'd evolved similarly—existed in the place, the hill would have been overdeveloped and all its pristine beauty destroyed. The fact his first thought upon seeing the spot was to build something on it saddened him slightly, but that is just what he did.

As he sat there contemplating days gone by, he held a picture in his hands. It was the only image he had of Angel. There were no cameras when Orwell had taken her from him. His wife had planned to hire an artist to paint a portrait of her, but their lives were destroyed before that could happen. Orwell had given him the image to remind him why it was wise to follow his direction. It worked.

If only they had lived in a different time or in some other reality, they might have been allowed to grow old and die like everyone else is blessed to do. That had been such a brief moment in his life, barely a blink, and yet those few years represented the only part of his long existence he considered life. Everything after that had been payment, and he had no memory of a time before.

His oldest memory was walking out of a cave and startling an old man who was failing miserably at collecting one of his sheep who'd wandered off. Once the elderly shepherd calmed enough to speak, he introduced himself as Nikolaos and then proceeded to share his entire life story while Bale helped him wrangle his wayward sheep.

"Thank Apollo for sending you in my time of need. You are a blessing from the gods," Nikolaos finally said when he'd finished his story. Then he bowed his head slightly, touched Bale's cheek, and asked, "What do they call you?"

"I am Bale," he replied. At the time, he knew very little else. His cheeks flushed when he had to ask, "Who is Apollo?"

"It is impolite to tease an old man, but denying the gods is something worse," Nikolaos replied, his tone echoed the offense he took to the apparent slight.

Bale hadn't intended to hurt the man's feelings, so he quickly answered, "Please, forgive me. I do not tease. I have no memory of anything before walking from that cave and seeing you. I know nothing of this Apollo nor anything about what these gods you speak of might be."

The honesty of his reply must have echoed in his expression as Nikolaos' suddenly tight jaw loosened. "I am sad for you," the old shepherd finally replied with the kind of smile you might offer someone you'd just learned was dying. Then something sparkled in the old man's eyes as that conciliatory smile morphed into something that resembled true joy, and he quickly added, "I could teach you of Apollo and all the gods. Do you have a place to rest your head?"

"If I do, I do not recall where that place might be," Bale shrugged.

"Stay with me then. I have no sons. The gods saw fit to take my wife as she brought my only daughter into the world. You can help me tend the flock, and I can teach you all I know."

Taking the old man up on his generous offer was the best decision Bale had ever made. The daughter he mentioned was Alexandra. They were taken with each other almost immediately. It was more than a mere physical attraction. There was something calming about the warmth he saw in her eyes when she smiled. It was a strange thing, but he somehow felt safe when she looked at him that way. He loved the way she saw the world and marveled at the wonder that would color her face when she experienced some new thing. Regardless of how simple a thing it might be, it seemed she rejoiced in the new experience, enamored with life and all it had to offer. She would examine things that might seem commonplace or unimportant to Bale, like a pattern in the dust she was about to wipe away. She would look at things like that and wonder why they happened the precise way they happened. Bale loved that about her. She had a curious mind.

By the time Bale had mustered enough courage to ask Nikolaos for Alexandra's hand, the old shepherd had become somewhat of a mentor to him. He taught him how to tend the flock and manage the lands. Both would have been useful skills if things had gone differently.

It wasn't long before Angel came. They named her Eirini, but he'd been calling her Angel Cakes so long the name seemed foreign when he thought about it. She liked Angel Cakes and asked if it could be her name forever. There wasn't much he could give her anymore. Honoring her wishes seemed the least he could do.

He longed for that time, the life they built for themselves. It was simple. They were happy. Looking back, it felt more than he deserved. It was heaven.

Then everything changed. Nikolaos had been teaching him to tend the flock, and they were out moving them from one pasture to another through a rather tight valley between a range of hills separating the two fields. It was a pass they'd used many times prior without incident. This time was different. This time would change his life forever.

"Something is wrong," he had complained to Nikolaus as soon as they entered the tight corridor. He couldn't explain what. It was a squishy feeling in his gut coupled with a voice shouting from the back of his mind to turn back.

"Nothing is wrong," Nikolaos had assured him, "The sky is clear, and the air is cool."

The feeling in his gut intensified while the voice shouting in his head to abandon the journey grew louder as they slowly guided the sheep through the narrow pass. They had almost reached the end when the reason for his seemingly misplaced sense of foreboding came into view as they rounded a sharp bend in the trail. The path was blocked by a wall of boulders piled too perfectly to be an accident.

"I should have listened to you," Nikolaos gasped as the realization of what the artificial barrier must have meant flashed across his wide eyes.

Then they came, armed men who moved and fought like well-trained soldiers. There had to be more than fifty of them. Bale had carried a small sword at the time. He fought to defend the flock and the man he'd grown to see as something of a father, but there were too many of them. He had lost consciousness at some point. When he woke, the flock was gone, and Nikolaos' bloodied and lifeless body was sprawled across some rocks.

As he prayed over Nikolaos' corpse, it occurred to him that he should have been dead too, or at least severely injured. As far as he could tell, he had sustained no injuries in the brief skirmish. He could find no wounds anywhere on his body.

The air next to him suddenly shimmered as if tiny suns sparkled out of the very air to blaze briefly until they flamed out. The sensation lasted only moments before a man with white hair wearing odd clothing stood before him. He knew now that it had been Orwell. At the time, he thought it had to be Apollo, or even Aries, to help him avenge Nikolaos' murder.

He fell to knees before the god and prepared to beg assistance, but fear wrapped itself around his jaw and held his tongue fast. It would be offensive to pray to Apollo if it were in fact Aries or some other god shining in all his glory before him. Instead, he said, "Please forgive the limits of my mind, great lord, but I fail to recognize you in all your dazzling brilliance. Are you Apollo aroused from Mt. Olympus to grant me blessings and heal this man I have grown to know as father? Or perhaps mighty Aries come to grant me strength to avenge him in death?"

"Apollo? Aries?" Orwell had chuckled in that same condescending way to which Bale would eventually grow accustomed, "No. Hades, perhaps. I come with no blessings for you or this man you have been following. I come with an offer."

Bale dared not look up from the ground as he replied, "What has the noble lord of the underworld to offer me?"

"Merely the life of one you hold dear. You failed to defeat your enemy," the god casually responded.

"It would appear so," Bale conceded.

"That does not bode well for those you love," Orwell smiled that same devilish grin he'd used on Bale in all the centuries since.

Had he known who the thing standing before him truly was, he may have rejected the offer right at that moment, but probably not. As it was, he asked, "Why must the gods speak in riddles? What is your offer?"

"Look there," he replied, as he pointed to a spot behind Bale.

The air between the hills sparkled just as the air had before Orwell arrived. The trail suddenly vanished, and he was in his home. Sweet Alexandra lay naked and bloody upon the tile as men clad in the same armor as those who he'd fought rifled through his home and filled sacks with anything of any value. Everything else was tossed about the floor. He saw Eirini hiding in the very spot he would expect her to be. It was her favorite spot when they would play hide and seek. It wasn't the best hiding spot. Eventually, those men would find her.

Bale ran toward the vision but failed to enter the room. It was as if some invisible barrier blocked his way.

He fell to his knees and cried out, "My daughter. My heart. Please, fair Hades, stop them. Save the only thing I have left in this world."

He remembered the sick delight in Orwell's voice as he replied, "I could do that. I could strike those men down and save your daughter from the awful terrors they will undoubtedly inflict upon her, but not for free."

Bale forgot any fear for himself in that moment, crawled over to Orwell, grabbed hold of his leg, and begged, "Do that, please. I will do anything. Name your price."

"The cost of a soul is a soul. Nothing else holds equal value,"

Orwell replied.

"It is done," Bale cried, "Take my soul. Take anything. Just spare my daughter's life."

The memory flittered away as he hugged the picture of Angel close to his chest and sobbed, "I thought it was my soul he wanted. If only I had known the real price."

CHAPTER 10

WHY NOT ALL OF IT?

POTENTIALITY 6

The room was quiet. Bale sunk into Mark's sofa as he leaned his head against the plush backrest. It was quite possibly the most comfortable seat he'd ever occupied. It was like resting on a cloud. Mark had told him the name of the fabric years ago, but it didn't mean much to him. It was some kind of blend of stuff unique to Potentiality 6 that felt like leather all twisted up in silk, and whatever the thing was stuffed with felt like cotton candy if that fluffy, sweet treat could hold your ass up. Every time he sat on the thing, he wanted to fall asleep.

Mark sat across from him in a gothic black chair that almost looked like a throne. He was sipping blood from a decorative crystal chalice. It was the kind of piece most folks would display in a glass cabinet and never use. Not Mark though, he was fancy about that kind of stuff.

Mark had been slowly shaking his head while he sipped and contemplated the story Bale dumped on him when he showed up unannounced. "So, what are you going to do?" he finally asked.

Bale sunk deeper into the sofa as he glanced down at the tumbler full of that green shit Mark always fed him and set it on the end table next to him instead of drinking it. "I don't know," he finally sighed after a long pause. Then he picked the tumbler back up and emptied it into his throat before adding, "Half her sentence is a lot, but hearing it..." He trailed off as his gaze dropped to the floor.

"Hearing it what?" Mark asked.

Bale sighed deeply as he grabbed the bottle Mark had left for him

81

and refilled his glass. After emptying it again, he wiped his mouth with the back of his wrist and said, "It just made me realize she'll never be free."

Mark stopped sipping and drained the rest of his chalice. Then he stood and walked toward the kitchen. He turned back toward Bale as he opened the fridge, offered a sad chuckle, and said, "Buddy, I could have told you that a hundred years ago when you first told me about her and that fucked up deal you made."

Somehow, it hurt worse to hear it in somebody else's voice, but Mark was right. It was a whole contract, and he didn't even read it. There wasn't time. Those soulless assholes would have found her, and who knows what they would have done to her.

"It was a bad deal, but I'd do the same thing again if I had to," he finally said after filling and draining his glass again.

Mark's short stroll back to his chair distracted Bale, slightly. Everything the guy did seemed more elegant than necessary. Vampires were so dramatic. If Baled had walked to the kitchen to grab another drink, he would have either shuffled or stumbled and probably stubbed his toe on the way there. Mark seemed to be dancing as he almost floated from the kitchen back to his gaudy chair.

Once Mark was comfortably resting in his favorite seat, he sipped from his chalice and asked, "How long have you been alive?"

Bale filled his glass again. This time he sipped. The booze was finally starting to kick in. Then he shrugged and said, "I don't know. A couple thousand years or so, give or take thirty or fifty for that whole B.C., A.D. thing they did with the calendar."

Mark failed to suppress a laugh as he replied, "Yeah, you've got some weird beliefs in your dimension."

"Really?" Bale laughed back at him, "You worship a bat who mates with a wolf, and they both turn into smoke."

Mark nodded as he laughed a bit harder and added, "That is a gross oversimplification, but you're right. It is at least as stupid. Anyway, my point is this. How much time have you already burned off that sentence?"

"Not enough," Bale shook his head, "Even if I take this gig, it'll take me another ten thousand years to work the rest off."

Mark set his chalice down and leaned closer to Bale as he said, "It might take a lot less time if you could follow the rules and quit pissing him off."

Bale humphed, slid back deeper into his seat, and sighed, "I know. I just…" his voice trailed off as he drained his glass and filled it again. Once armed with a full splash in his glass, he continued, "Fucking hate that guy. So, do you think I should do it?"

Mark sipped his chalice and set it on the table next to him. Then he ran both his hands down either side of his face from his temples to his chin and said, "I do, but not at what he's offering."

Bale belly laughed at this one. Once he finally composed himself, he said, "He doesn't negotiate."

Mark stood and began pacing back and forth as he spoke, "No doubt. Listening to you rant all these years, I feel like I know him. Do you really think he can send anyone else? I mean, I have my doubts that he actually has anybody else. I think that's just some shit he tells you to keep you in line."

Bale shook his head rapidly as he replied, "No, no, no. He has other agents."

"Fine," Mark stopped pacing, "For the sake of argument, let's say he does have other agents. Do you really believe he would give you any time at all to think about it if he really could send someone else?"

It was a good point. Orwell always threatened to take jobs away and give them to some other agent, but none of those agents had names. They were just nebulous ideas. He'd never worked with anyone, and the only twats he ever saw with Orwell were Mikey, Gabe, and Raziel, except for those creepy little cleaners. Maybe Mark was on to something.

"That's a big gamble," he finally said.

"What have you got to lose?" Mark's frustration seeped into his tone, "You aren't very much going to like what I'm about to say, but it needs to be said. The life you and your daughter have isn't any kind of life, and you were right when you said she'd never be free."

"I know," Bale stared off at nothing while he slowly swirled his glass, "but at least she's alive."

"Brother, she hasn't been alive since you made that deal," defeat slinked about Mark's tone.

Bale knew Mark was right, and he knew what he needed to do.

CHAPTER 11

A NEW DEAL

CITY OF GOLD

Orwell's office was as perfect as always. The air was completely clear. Most rooms with the amount of light shining in so brightly from the bank of floor to ceiling windows across from the boss's desk would be filled with dust particles floating all about. There wasn't so much as a speck of dust on any surface in that room. Everything was pristine. Bale hated it.

He strolled up to the desk doing his best to appear as aloof as possible. It was all an act that Orwell would probably see through as soon as he looked up from the paper he was poring over. The truth was, his heart was racing in his chest, and his hands were clammy enough he could have rung them out like a sopping cloth. Despite that, he took the chair he normally sat in, slumped deeply into it, and stretched his legs out in front of him.

Orwell didn't look up from his paper as he said, "You are early. Well played. I assume you have come to a decision."

"I have," Bale replied nonchalantly.

"Excellent," Orwell set the paper down and clapped his hands as he finally looked up adding, "You should depart straight away."

While Orwell leaned down to open one of the drawers of his desk and retrieve Lou's file, Bale replied, "I think you misunderstand my intentions."

"How so?" Orwell asked as his eyes narrowed, and he held the file across his desk toward Bale.

"I have decided not to take the case," Bale shrugged.

Unbridled rage flashed across Orwell's expression for a moment so brief Bale might have missed it if he wasn't staring intently at it. It fled as quickly as it had come, replaced by a smile that desperately wanted to be genuine. Once the odd smile had settled into what it would be, Orwell attempted to reply calmly, "That isn't like you. No negotiations? No pleas for me to take more time off or let you see her? You sound like a beaten man."

"Take it however you like," Bale scratched absently at the top of his head, "It's really pretty simple, boss. I don't trust myself, too many vices. What if I like it so much there that I never want to leave? I can't take that chance. I fucked up once with her soul. I won't make that mistake again."

"Your love of your daughter isn't strong enough to overcome your urges?" Orwell scoffed.

That was Orwell's game, needle into the nerves he knew were most exposed. Bale didn't bite. He shoved his ego deep into his gut and prepared to respond. The words sailing through his mind that would flop out of his mouth surprised him. They represented his honest feelings. Despite the fact that he was quite aware he was in the middle of a bluff and totally acting, the words he wanted to speak were the truth.

"Maybe," he finally said, "I really don't know. I'd like to think I'm strong enough to turn away from anything for her, but that's a gamble I'm not willing to take. You said it yourself, nobody who goes to Perver City returns."

The rage returned to Orwell's expression like a fire burning up his cheeks. He dropped the folder he'd been holding onto his desk and pounded it with both fists.

The slightest hint of fear settled into the base of Bale's spine. Orwell had almost lost his cool a few times, even shouted once or twice, but the unbridled fury flashing in his eyes was something Bale had never seen before. He had either just hit the nail on the head, or he'd made a horrible mistake. Either way, he wasn't getting a mulligan on this one. He'd have to play it through.

Bale's instincts almost dragged him out of his chair to defend himself as Orwell stood, picked the folder back up, and rounded his desk holding it out. "Take the case, Mr. Lance," the furious god shouted as he nearly shoved the folder into Bale's chest, "There will never be another job to pay this much."

Bale could hear his heart pounding in his ears, but he maintained his cool demeanor as he casually replied, "My mind's made up, boss. What else have you got."

"There are no other cases," Orwell snapped.

Bale hoped the smile puffing out his cheeks didn't look as fake as it felt when he said, "Come on, Or. There's always another case."

The boss almost looked defeated as his chin dropped to his chest and his arms flopped to his sides. Then he sighed deeply and said, "You love to push my buttons, sitting there with your smug, little grin. What if I never gave you another? What if I never let you see her again? What if I consumed her soul?"

"You could do that," Bale nodded, "You could do any of those things."

Orwell perked up as the smile returned to his face. Then he leaned down and held the file in his hand against Bale's chest.

Bale smiled back up at him as he continued, "But you wouldn't. It's like I told you last time I was here, I've known you for a long time. Rules can't be changed. We can't have messes like that in the City of Gold. You made all the rules, boss. You would destroy yourself before you broke them."

Orwell stiffened back up as his tone grew ominous, "I thought you didn't want to gamble with her soul. Whatever game you are playing right now is very risky indeed."

"I call it a safe bet," Bale shrugged.

Orwell leaned his head back and shouted, "Damn it, Bale. Take the fucking case."

It took every ounce of fortitude Bale could muster to keep from cringing, recoiling, or jumping up out of his chair and racing for the exit. It would have been a mistake to do any of those things. He could tell he had Orwell on the ropes. As terrifying as the idea was, he had to take the chance.

"Language, Mr. Durr. Where is your composure?" he chuckled dryly before adding, "Just give it to somebody else."

Orwell dropped the file on Bale's lap, grabbed the arms of his chair, leaned in close, and growled, "Name your price."

"Freedom," Bale wanted to look away as he said the simple word, but he managed to keep eye contact.

"You jest," Orwell's tone remained deep and gravelly, "Do not play games with me."

Bale shook his head, picked up the file in his lap, held it against Orwell's chest, and said, "That's my price. Take it or leave it."

Orwell's expression twisted, shifting quickly through a series of emotions that seemed far too human. He was always in control. Bale never broke eye contact. This fact had him feeling both terrified and ecstatic at the same time. On the one hand, it seemed he might actually have a shot at freeing Angel. On the other hand, Orwell might just suck his soul right out of his body. He'd probably make him watch as he did the same thing to Angel before finally letting him die.

He could have cried when Orwell finally sighed, "Fine. Bring me this mark and consider her debt paid in full."

"Deal," Bale fired the word out quickly. He knew Orwell would be sore after losing, but he had to push just a little bit more. He took a deep breath and added, "I want to see her before I go."

"No more deals, Mr. Lance," Orwell shook his head.

Bale shook his head right back at him as he said, "This is part of the deal. I may never see her again. If I fail, you keep her. I'm not going to lie to you, boss. I'm terrified of going to this place. I need the image of her face in my mind if I want to have any hope of getting out of there."

"Done," Orwell nearly grunted, "You know what I do with the souls you bring me, correct?"

The thought twisted his gut into knots, but he nodded quickly as he replied, "I do."

"Good," Orwell smiled as he brushed imaginary things off Bale's shoulders and added, "If at any point during your mission you feel you may fail, imagine me doing that to your precious Angel Cakes but slowly. I could take eons to consume her. Imagine how she would suffer."

CHAPTER 12

FROM THE MOUTHS OF BABES

CITY OF GOLD

The pond, the trees, and all the fragrant flowers were as breathtaking as always, basking in the glow of a sun that shined almost too perfectly to be real from a sky which shared the quality of being almost too flawless to exist. Everything in the place was like that. It made it impossible not to smile despite whatever heavy dread might be weighing on a soul. The dopey and unintentional grin strapped across Bale's face was a testament to the fact. He couldn't help it.

Angel was there sitting next to the pond on a large, smooth boulder in the same spot she always occupied on the rare occasion he was granted a visit. Small details would change from time to time. Sometimes there would be mountains in the distance. Other times a thick bank of trees lined the opposite shore of the pond that never seemed to be the same size or shape as the last time he'd seen it.

Seeing her there attempting to skip stones across the glassy surface of the pond filled him with a mix of emotions. It was like a battle in his heart. A thorny dread bristling with fear of what would happen to her if he failed teamed up with helpless rage at the lack of control he had over either of their lives to beat back the joy her simple presence brought him.

She held up a perfect stone for skipping. It was thin, flat, and perfectly smooth. She said something he couldn't hear to Michael before she fired it toward the pond snapping her wrist just right when she released it. It was a perfect throw. That stone should have skipped seven or eight times at least, but it didn't. It just plopped through the surface of the water with no ripple or any other visible evidence that it had even hit the water. It was all a façade.

Angel turned to Michael again and said something. It must have been something cheeky. The angel rolled his eyes and shook his head slightly in response.

"Where is the most beautiful little girl in five galaxies?" he finally raised his voice and asked.

The sheer joy on her face when she saw him and jumped off the big rock to run to him gave the joy that had been steadily losing ground against all the darker emotions battling for control over his mood just the boost it needed to shove those other feelings deep into his gut.

She shouted, "Daddy," when she jumped into his arms. The uncontrollable laugh she lost when he spun her around three times and tossed her up into the air was icing on the cake. Then he held her close and hugged her tightly. If only he could stay in that moment forever.

"You're here again already?" she asked before adding, "You never come back so soon."

He set her down and held onto her shoulders as he said, "I am, and I have big news, kiddo. This is it, the last time I ever have to leave you in this place. The next time you see me, we leave together, and we can go wherever you want."

"What? You mean we get to be together all the time?" The incomprehension echoing in her eyes broke his heart. She couldn't even fathom a normal life.

He managed to keep the sadness tingling behind his eyes from leaking out and running down his cheeks when he answered, "Forever."

"Forever and ever?" she still seemed confused by the idea.

"And ever and ever until the end of time," he replied quietly before gently kissing her forehead.

Bale was so wrapped up in the moment that he hadn't noticed Michael and Gabriel saunter over until the two joined in a humorless chuckle. He didn't care what either of them thought about anything, but they always had something to say.

"Your only job for two-thousand-some-odd years has been standing in the same spot watching a six-year-old girl, and you're laughing at me?" Bale shook his head.

A condescending grin and a brief chuckle accompanied Michael's reply, "Not at you, specifically. It's more that glimmering optimism."

"We know where you're going," Gabriel added with an equally annoying chuckle.

"And why," Michael continued before both angels lost themselves to laughter.

The laugh was overly dramatic and lasted longer than it needed, theatrics. A fact proven when Gabriel abruptly stopped laughing to add, "She'll never see you again."

Michael picked up as if he were continuing Gabriel's thought, "And when you're gone…"

Angel's eyes suddenly went wide with terror as she nearly cried, "Are you really never coming back?"

Bale could have choked both of those assholes in that moment. Instead, he offered Angel the warmest smile he could muster and asked, "What do we know about asshats?"

"They never make any sense," she said the words, but her expression betrayed the fact that she didn't feel very confident in them.

"That's right," Bale's smile dipped to a shallow frown, "But this time they aren't totally wrong. Where I'm going is a dangerous place."

The innocence in Angel's eyes broke his heart as she peered up at him and asked, "Are you scared?"

"A little bit," he nodded.

"They're going to eat you alive down there," Gabriel chimed in.

Bale ignored the jibe focusing all his attention on his little girl as he continued, "This is a big risk. I need to know if you think I should do it."

Angel looked around at the place as she began nervously chewing on her thumb. She'd never had to make any kind of decision before. It broke Bale's heart to lay something so heavy on her, but it affected her. It only seemed fair that she had a voice in the matter.

He'd never seen her look so sure of anything when she finally said, "Do it."

"A death sentence spoken from the mouth of a child," Michael chuckled.

Bale continued to ignore both goons looming over them as he looked deeply into Angel's eyes and asked, "Are you sure?"

The steadiness of her expression didn't falter in the least as she replied, "You said nothing could keep you away, not even fire-breathing dragons."

"I meant it," he nodded.

"I believe you," she smiled.

He wished in that moment he could believe in himself as much as she did. Her faith would have to be enough for them both. He shoved the thought deep into a pit in the back of his mind before it could echo across his face. Then he kissed her on the cheek, stood, and shifted his attention to the two cackling idiots.

"Hear that? It's last call. The next time you see me, the rules will have changed," he said, his tone emotionless despite the sneer he offered them. He let the smile slip back into his voice when he turned his attention back to his little girl and said, "I'll see you soon, Angel."

CHAPTER 13

GET YOUR GUNS

PERVER CITY

The night was alive. Throngs of people marched about on missions to their next distractions drowning in neon and flashing strobes. It should have smelled like trash and sweat, but the air was sweet like a forest after fresh rain. Revving engines, gunshots, and laughter filled the night sky. Anything goes.

Bale stood before a storefront amid a bank of similar establishments like some kind of fetish mall. Whatever your kink, you could find exactly what you needed to scratch that itch. He looked up at the neon blazing above him. The script font of the sign read, "Kill 'Em Quick." This was the place.

The case files Orwell gave him were always perfect, containing every minute detail he'd need to close them out. Lou's file was no different, aside from the fact it contained zero details about the target, save the name. Even that was incomplete. There was no last name included, just Lou. Apparently, that wouldn't be a problem. Allegedly, the cat was sufficiently well known that the simple moniker would be enough to find him. Before he could do that, he needed to arm up. Apparently, he wasn't the only one looking for Lou. That's why the gun shop had to be his first stop. He strolled inside.

The entire store was little more than a wide hallway terminating in a small glass counter that sat before rows of automatic rifles mounted on the back wall. Despite how small and simple the place was, it was like a macabre Candyland. Implements of destruction lined the walls on either side. Everything from swords and knives to axes and maces were prominently displayed among other creative killing devices.

Bale knew the guy behind the counter adding more rifles to the collection on the back wall was his first contact without asking his name. Azrael looked identical to Michael or Gabriel despite being grubby and dressed like he slept on the street.

Bale admired the handguns under the glass of the counter for a moment before clearing his throat and saying, "I'm looking for the angel of death."

The undercover angel spun quickly, grabbed a hold of Bale's collar, and whispered loudly, "Have you lost your fucking mind? Don't say that so loud. Nobody knows me here. Do you think I'd look like this if I wasn't under deep cover?" Then he glanced around nervously and asked, "Are you alone?"

Bale gently removed Azrael's hands from his collar, smiled, and replied, "Calm down. I am alone, and you are obviously who I thought you were." Then he looked him over and added, "You're looking pretty rough. That's got to drive you nuts if you're anything like your asshole brothers."

"I am," he sneered, "and it does. Cut me some slack. Like I said, I'm undercover."

"I don't know," Bale cocked his head to side, "You look just like them, but you seem less condescending."

"Yeah, well, I've been here a while. This place will change you." The slightest hint of excitement slipped into the disheveled angel's tone as he raised his eyebrows, lowered his voice, and continued, "So, is it really you? Bale fucking Lance?"

"You have been here a while," Bale almost laughed, "All I get from your brothers is not so thinly veiled threats. Yeah, it's really me."

"Holy shit," Azrael laughed, "I have been waiting a long time for you. So, they finally found him, hey? Nobody tells me anything."

The guy seemed too giddy to be the angel of death, but that's what the file said. Bale had to ask, "And...you are the angel of death?"

"Fuck that," the smile drained from his face, "I hate when he calls me that. My job, my real job before I came here, was to guide souls who go into the light like they should to the hereafter, be that here in Perver City or to..."

"Get eaten by Orwell?" Bale interrupted, adding, "I'd say angel of death fits pretty good."

"Come on, it's spiritual bliss. They become one with god," Azrael shrugged.

"That's not what I hear," Bale shook his head, "Oblivion, limbo, they cease to exist."

A sadness haunted Azrael's eyes as his gaze dropped to the floor, and he replied, "Yeah, well, it makes my job easier when I don't think about it that way. Anyway, I think you already know my name is Azrael, but folks around here only know me as the gunsmith. I'd like to keep it that way. If they ever figured out who I really am…"

"Oblivion?" Bale asked.

"Worse. They're pretty fucking creative down here," Azrael paused long enough to shudder slightly. He'd obviously seen some things. Once he pulled it back together, he added, "Anyway, nothing you see in this room will do you any good in Perver City."

Bale's face twisted up as he asked, "So, what's it for, show?"

"Absolutely not," Azrael's tone shifted to something that sounded like a sales pitch, "I told you, man, this is Perver fucking City. Anything goes. Total physical bliss with no limits. What's your kink? Some like killing fuckers, some like torture. They all come to me."

"Being killed or brutally molested to scratch somebody else's itch doesn't sound all that blissful to me," Bale scoffed.

"That's the beauty of it," Azrael chuckled, "You can do whatever you want here and never pay the bill. Drink enough to kill an elephant and wake with no hangover. Die, you wake up the next day just as right as rain. Torture, with no pain. Unless you're into that kind of thing. I try not to judge. That's Orwell's job."

It all sounded too good to be true. Bale's tone grew skeptical as he asked, "Ever tested that yourself?"

"Oh, hell yeah," the angel smiled, "All the time. I love me some heroin, boatloads and boatloads of it."

"Well, alright. I guess I'll have to take your word for it," Bale laughed. Then he got serious and asked, "If none of the shit you have in here can actually kill anybody, then what am I doing here?"

"Now you're talking," Azrael smiled and pointed at the wall behind him, "I've got my secrets, and I've got some special shit for you. Follow me."

Bale thought the angel might have been confused, or at least a bit eccentric. There didn't appear to be any place to go. It was just a wall with a bunch of guns mounted to it. Then Azrael grabbed the barrel of a pristine Thompson submachine gun and turned back to smile at

Bale while he pulled down on the barrel. A seam down the middle of the wall formed, and two panels opened inward. It was a good trick. That seam had been invisible until Azrael gave the barrel of that tommy gun a yank.

Bale nodded slightly as he worked his way around the counter and followed Azrael through the doorway. The doors began to shut immediately when he walked through them. There was a quiet *click* when they finished closing. It sounded ominous in the sudden darkness. A hint of panic skipped through Bale's mind. A setup didn't make any sense. Orwell wasn't big on theatrics, and he could just erase him with a thought if that was his desire. Unless Azrael was working for the other side. Then it would make total sense. Take him out before he even had a chance to get his bearings. By the time unnecessarily bright light filled the small room, Bale had brought his fists up as if he were getting ready for a boxing match.

Azrael chuckled nervously at the pose and said, "Calm down, big guy. You have nothing to worry about from me. I have too much time invested in this to mess it up, and you're the key to everything."

Bale slowly calmed down as he glanced around the small room. The bright light filling the space radiated from the walls. Mounted to those walls was every kind of hand-held weapon a guy could want. It really was Candyland.

Azrael must have noticed the sparkle in his eye. "This place must be heaven for a guy like you."

"A guy like me?" Bale wasn't sure he appreciated the connotation. What the hell was a guy like him?

"You're a stone-cold, fucking killer, man. Everybody knows it."

Bale shook his head, "I'm just an over-glorified delivery boy."

"Guess we're the same," the angel shrugged.

"Except I have to chase down the ones you lose track of," Bale mumbled as a pair of polished chrome Desert Eagles caught his eye, "I suppose that makes me the cleaning crew."

Azrael chuckled dryly and replied, "Yeah, free will's a bitch."

"It's an illusion," Bale replied offhandedly as he pulled a tactical knife off the wall to test its weight. After working through a few striking techniques, he changed the subject and asked, "Anyway, this shit will do the trick, you know, real death?"

"Limbo, oblivion, call it what you want. You kill something in Perver City with anything in this room, and it stays dead for eternity,"

Azrael nodded with something close to sadness darkening his smile.

It was obvious the poor slob didn't like his job. It would be tough to enjoy a profession that earned you the reputation of being the angel of death. Bale felt a little sad for the guy as he watched him grab a big duffel bag and begin filling it with weapons. A couple grenades went in, a couple knives, and then a bunch of handguns with enough ammo to take down a small army.

The bag was already looking pretty heavy when Azrael turned to Bale and asked, "You want any rifles?"

"No," Bale shook his head, "too conspicuous. I wouldn't say no to something automatic with a high-capacity magazine."

Genuine excitement filled Azrael's eyes as he said, "I'll do you one better."

The suddenly animated angel set the bag on the floor and slid open a long drawer in a cabinet that ran along the wall at roughly waist level. After removing a few random implements of death, he pulled a false bottom out of the drawer and set it on the floor. Then he reached into the drawer again and retrieved two golden pistols that resembled the Desert Eagles Bale had been admiring moments prior.

The guns glimmered in the bright light as the smiling angel held them out to Bale and said, "No magazines required. You could shoot these beauties off consistently for a thousand years and never lose a charge."

"No ammo? How do they work?" Bale's expression squinted up like he'd just sucked a lime after a shot of tequila.

"I didn't say, *no ammo*. I said, *no magazines*," Azrael smiled as he handed the guns over to Bale for inspection, "Imagine condensing the power of a star into a capsule no bigger than your thumb. It's like that. Billions of years of nuclear energy. Talk about oblivion."

"I like the sound of that," Bale replied as he handed the guns back to Azrael. Then he asked, "Can you point me in the direction of Lou?"

"Right, back to business," Azrael nodded and zipped up the bag, "Start at New Eden. Don't talk too much. Lou has a lot of friends. Just listen. He's the talk of the town. Eventually, somebody will say something about some event he's hosting or attending. That's the best you can probably do without attracting the wrong kind of attention."

Bale accepted the bag from Azrael and said, "Thanks for all your help."

"All in a day's work," the angel frowned, "I wish we'd met under different circumstances. I'd love to trade stories with you, share some scars."

"Same," Bale nodded, "With any luck, I'll live long enough that we could meet again sometime, kick back a few drinks and tell some tales."

CHAPTER 14

WELCOM TO NEW EDEN

PERVER CITY

Pink neon lit up the night high above throngs of people milling about waiting to get in. The marquis read, *Paradise. Anything goes and we never close.* The people packed tightly together in something that resembled more of a mob than an orderly queue were a mixed bag of everything. Some were primped and primed and dressed to the nines, others looked like they just crawled out of a dumpster, and everything in between.

Bale stood off to the side of the mess soaking it all in. The constant symphony of sounds that seemed to radiate from every inch of the city had blended to become white noise. Gunshots, revving engines, and random unintelligible shouts all swirled together into a vibrating hum. If he gave them any attention, each could stand alone like a solo. He didn't have time for that. Standing in front of a busy club with a big bag of guns was a bad place to be.

The entrance, two golden doors etched with the kind of symbols decorating Orwell's bar sat wide open like a gaping maw waiting to consume all who might seek whatever mysteries hide inside. A narrow, golden podium sat just to the right of the doors. It looked like a spot where a bouncer might stand, but the space behind it was empty. All of it was cordoned with red, velvet ropes. So much for anything goes.

As Bale inched closer to that gaping maw that might swallow him whole and drop him into the pit of New Eden where he might be digested for all eternity, he noticed a slick cat in leather and shades working his way through the crowd. He seemed to be pumping them up. That had to be the guy who belonged behind the podium.

"What do you want?" the guy leaned his head back and shouted.

"Paradise," the crowd cheered back at him.

"When do you want it?" he leaned back even farther, shouting at the sky.

"Now!" The response was like an explosive report that echoed off the walls to fill the night with the sound of raging desire.

The need for stealth fled as the velvet ropes disintegrated, and the mob rushed the door. Bale slipped into the crowd as they pressed against each other like cattle herded toward their doom. None of the faces melting together in a wild blur around him looked like they were headed toward any kind of doom or terror. They all glimmered with the promise of ecstasy, total physical bliss, whatever that meant for them. It was the opposite for Bale. His gut twisted up in a knot dreading the parade of temptations he knew lie beyond those doors.

The place was massive and already packed. The fact made the line outside seem silly to Bale. Perhaps it only existed to build anticipation. Group after group were held back until they were ready to explode, and then they would be unleashed like an orgasm to do whatever they would do to each other.

It was sensory overload for Bale. The place was a massive, empty warehouse all decorated and dressed up like a disco ballroom. Lights mounted all about the ceiling pulsed colors onto a crowded dance floor filled with bodies gyrating and grinding against one another motivated by electric beats.

Cages hung from various spots in between the lights. Each was filled with some naked creature dancing or displaying their wares for the world to see. Bale shuddered when his gaze fell upon a werewolf in one of the cages. The furry fucker was howling as he jacked himself off into the crowd. It reminded Bale of how little control he had for the bit of time he had spent as a wolf. The memories were sparse, mostly just feelings. He was hungry. He wondered what that would feel like in a place like this where any urge could be satisfied on a whim.

A bar made of solid gold lined the entire wall to Bale's right. That was the spot he was looking for. He didn't want to get lost in the gyrating mass on the dance floor. Or, maybe he did, and that's what he feared. It looked like a place he wanted to be. He had to focus on the mission. Angel needed him.

The bar wasn't any less busy than the dance floor. Luckily, a reptilian guy who looked like an iguana without a tail fell out of his chair after injecting himself with a syringe filled with something that resembled banana pudding. Nobody seemed to care that the poor slob shit all over the floor as his body trembled and foam oozed from his gaping mouth. It didn't look like bliss to Bale, but he didn't judge. Everybody had their kink. He took the guy's chair.

Bale hadn't even managed to wriggle his way into his seat when the massive dude to his left tensed up, leaned his head back, and roared at the ceiling. The two horns protruding from the big guy's skull began glowing in rhythm with the subtle trembles that started working their way through his big body. Bale was about to jump up and prepare to defend himself when he noticed the cause of all the ruckus. It was a little dude wearing nothing but a thong who couldn't have been more than four foot five going to town on the big guy's cock. Bale couldn't tell where that wee fellow was putting the massive, veiny, and throbbing thing, but the big horned dude just kept slamming it in. It looked like the little guy's jaw was just going to snap off at some point, but he didn't seem to mind. Took it like a champ.

The big guy noticed Bale staring once he finished blowing his wad into the little guy's stretched mouth. It was an odd sensation. Bale suddenly felt like he'd been caught spying. He wasn't sure how to react, so he gave the guy a nod and hoped for the best. It must have been a sufficient response, because the big guy gave him a smile and a wink as he thrusted one more time into the little guy's mouth.

Apparently, *anything goes* was more than just a mantra. There were people getting whipped, led around on leashes like dogs, even hanging by their skin from hooks. Every kind of drug imaginable, even some Bale didn't recognize, was being snorted, smoked, or shot into someone's veins. And the ones who weren't shooting, snorting, torturing, or being tortured were fucking, sucking, or rubbing one out.

It was almost too much for Bale, the place, the scene. The only touchpoint to a reality that resembled anything remotely familiar to him was the guy behind the bar. He had salt and pepper hair and a strong jaw. He didn't fit the rest of the place as he stood there wiping a clean glass with a pristine, white cloth. The guy looked like he'd fit better in Orwell's bar, like he was plucked right out of a speakeasy. There was a comforting calmness in his eyes. None of the madness going on around them seemed to faze the guy in the least.

The bar keep must have noticed Bale staring. He leaned in and asked, "First time in New Eden? What can I get for you?"

The guy's smoky tone was a nice touch. It had a calming quality to it. He was probably a big help to first timers who had only recently crossed over. That would probably be a jolt. One moment you're living a normal, boring life in whatever normal, boring dimension you spent your physical existence, and the next moment any creepy desire you've ever had is right there in front of you just waiting for you to reach out and grab it.

"Got whiskey?" Bale finally asked.

"More or less," the bar keep winked as he set the clean glass he'd been wiping in front of Bale, dried his already dry hands on the impeccable towel, fetched a bottle from beneath the bar, and served up a healthy pour.

A loud thud on the bar to Bale's right dragged his attention from the bar keep who had yet to break eye contact. Again, the guy wasn't fazed. Bale nearly jumped out of his seat. He turned to see a blond in a tight, blue sequin dress face down on the bar with her dress pulled up to her lower back. A pale-eyed dude in a zoot suit grabbed a handful of her hair and took her from behind thrusting so hard it seemed he we was trying to hammer her right through the bar.

Bale opened his mouth to ask if she was okay with what appeared to him to be assault. The barkeep shook his head slightly and interrupted the thought. "Anything goes," he said in that damn soothing voice.

"That's what I hear," Bale sighed, shook his head, and took a drink of whatever the barkeep had filled his glass with that was more or less whiskey. It was too smooth to be straight whiskey, but he wasn't complaining. The shit was damned delightful.

After a couple more pulls, Bale decided to try a bit of small talk. Hopefully, it would loosen the barkeep up enough to share some info. "Busy night," Bale commented only loud enough to be heard.

The barkeep just smiled and said, "Welcome to paradise."

Bale's efforts at small talk bore little fruit. The barkeep kept up his end of the conversation, but nothing Bale said seemed to hook him in. He'd probably seen too much to find anything overly interesting, especially small talk. The guy just kept nodding, offering some generic truth, and wiping the replacement glass he had picked up after giving Bale his drink.

After a few more of the almost whiskeys the barkeep continued to generously pour for him, Bale decided the small talk wasn't getting him anywhere and went for it. "Cat named Lou ever come in here?" he asked after draining his glass.

This one got him. The barkeep finally stopped wiping his glass. That strong jaw tightened slightly just before he asked, "Who's asking?"

Bale managed to keep the shit eating grin that wanted to plop right onto his face at bay when he replied, "Just a poor soul passing through who heard he's a good guy to know."

"Not a salesman, are you? I wouldn't give you a fat cent for that story," the guy replied and went back to wiping his glass. Then, without looking back up at Bale, he added, "Do not turn around like an amateur and look, but there is a man in black leather leaning against the wall over your right shoulder. There is another guy dressed exactly the same over your left shoulder. Both are giving you the kind of attention you don't want, and neither will like it at all if they hear you asking silly questions like that."

Bale resisted the urge to be the amateur the barkeep had just instructed him not to be, but it was tough. He didn't know if it was just him or something everyone struggled with, but a statement like that was almost a challenge. Luckily, before he could let on that he knew the cats behind him were scoping him, something terribly intriguing leaned heavy on his shoulder and breathed lightly against his neck.

"Barkeep, fix me a martini before I get nasty," the voice carrying the command past Bale's ear was a sultry purr. After a brief pause, that enticing voice added, "And make it dirty."

"Right away, miss," the barkeep dutifully nodded and got to work.

Bale didn't want to look to see who the owner of that incredible voice leaning on his shoulder might be. It would be a distraction, a wonderful distraction if the mental image that voice had painted on his brain proved to be anything close to reality. Distractions were the exact opposite of what he needed just then, no matter how delightful they might be.

He almost shivered when he felt her finger on the left side of his chin guide his face toward her as she said, "You're new here."

He closed his eyes and replied, "Just passing through."

"This is Perver City, baby. Nobody just passes through." The voice tugged his eyelids open. He couldn't help it. He had to see what kind of creature could generate a tone so perfect. It was a mistake.

It felt like her eyes grabbed hold of his soul. They were green, but that wasn't what got him. They were nice eyes, gorgeous even, but there was something deeper there like a story. Timeless was the word that popped into his head. There might be whole worlds to explore living deep within that gaze. Knowledge, that's what it was. She looked like she knew things but seemed too young to know the things she knew. The soft curves of her face couldn't have seen more than thirty years.

Her hair was a mass of wild curls that bounced with every subtle move she made. Those perfectly chaotic curls danced in the periphery as her eyes held Bale's stare prisoner. He should have just gotten up and walked away.

Bale barely noticed the barkeep delivering his new companion's drink—the martini she needed to keep from getting nasty—as her eyes continued to hold his gaze. The movement of her body jumped to the center of his awareness when she reached out to grab the vessel of mood saving liquid. The skin of her bare arm was flawless. He suddenly wanted to touch it. The small voice in the back of his head shouting about focus and the mission grew increasingly quieter as desire pushed it further and further aside. He couldn't help it. It was more than just the softness of the skin begging to be touched. It was the way she moved like a delicate ballet. The simplest gesture was like art being made before his eyes.

"Got plans for the night?" she asked as she pulled a stick impaled through three olives out of her drink and dragged her tongue seductively over them before slipping them into his mouth.

The correct answer would have been yes, but that isn't what he said. Instead, as he absently chewed olives that tasted better than any olive he had ever eaten, he said, "They're coming together."

The answer surprised him. He wanted to shake his head and correct the erroneous statement, but the smile parting her full lips was something he suddenly wanted to explore. That quiet voice still shouting at him from the back of his mind was completely extinguished when she said, "Let's go. My car is parked outside."

Like a dutiful servant, Bale grabbed his bag and followed her lead. He barely noticed the small entourage of big guys all clad in black leather just like the two the barkeep had warned him about following closely behind. Truly, he barely noticed anything besides his new friend's ass as she strutted in front of him guiding him through the crowd of sweaty bodies living out their every fantasy. Everyone she passed seemed distracted by her as if she floated through a cloud of desire.

The back of the Limo was like a discotheque. Alternating pink and blue lights pulsed along to a loud, fast techno-industrial beat. Bale was in a trance as he watched the elegant stranger who'd stolen his focus move like a snake above him. She was a pro. Every delicate touch, every pinch, and every spot on his flesh she licked vibrated through his entire body like electric shocks. He wanted to grab those perfect breasts as they delicately bounced with each movement or grab a hold of those wonderful hips gyrating on his lap, but he was frozen. She was in charge, still the artist. He was merely the canvas she painted.

Bale's entire body was ready to explode as he trembled violently beneath her. It was like an earthquake shaking through him. It felt like she was hugging his cock— the hypocenter of the tremors—with wet velvet, pulling, dragging, and squeezing with each gyration or thrust of her hips.

She didn't miss a beat as she reached down, grabbed a half-spilled bottle of champagne, and took a swig before emptying the rest down Bale's throat right as he exploded inside of her. She slowed at that moment tensing up as she leaned her head back and howled at the ceiling drenching his cock as she continued to slide slowly up and down it from its base to its tip.

Bale came longer and harder than he ever had in his entire life. It was like she knew how to drag it out, how to keep him cumming until she was done with him. At the very moment a hint of panic that he might die there in bliss beneath this perfect stranger began growing at the back of his mind, she finally showed mercy and allowed his orgasm to end. Her form deflated onto his chest, and he finally held her. He knew it was a silly thought when he embraced her, but it felt like love when she cuddled into his chest.

Bale felt suddenly awkward lying there. As much as he wanted to be in the moment, reveling in it for as long as it lasted, he couldn't keep his mouth shut. For some stupid reason, he needed to say something. "Holy shit. I feel like I should call my priest," he blurted.

"Are you religious?" she asked as she rolled off him and slithered back into her dress.

Bale could have smacked himself in the forehead. Why did he have to open his stupid mouth and ruin the moment of bliss? He felt vulnerable and exposed but mostly disappointed in himself as he mumbled, "I wasn't. Maybe now."

He watched her finish dressing while wishing he was back inside of her when she smiled and said, "A spiritual experience for you, was it?"

"It was something," he sighed, sweating in the blue and pink disco of it all.

She giggled as she casually rolled his clothes up in a ball and tossed them to him. Then she fished around on the floor for another half-spilled bottle of champagne and downed it. "Hurry up and get yourself together," she said after finishing the bottle.

It seemed she was done with him. The brief moment of bliss for him was little more than a distraction for her. He'd helped her scratch an itch, and now she was on to whatever the next thing would be for her.

She leaned up toward the driver and said, "Pull around the corner and park."

Everything was suddenly moving too fast. He'd barely gotten his pants up to his knees when she opened the door and shoved him out of the car, tossing his shirt and shoes out behind him as he flopped to the pavement in a heap.

Her smile was still inviting as she blew him a kiss and said, "Thanks, lover. That was completely adequate." Then she leaned back into the car and said, "Take me home."

Bale watched the door close as the black, stretched limo pulled away. He watched the taillights until they disappeared around the corner. He felt so used while struggling to his feet and pulling his pants the rest of the way up as he went. He'd just been a prop in her night out, and she was probably off to find her next distraction.

"Thanks a lot. I don't even know where the fuck I am," he shouted at the spot where her car had just turned the corner. Then he looked around at the dark street surrounding him and added, "Bitch."

The street and buildings around him were different than the main drag where engines revved, horns honked, and people shouted. It was darker here, like the rusty backlot of a sparkling façade, the dirty underbelly of Perver City, the reality behind the illusion. Bale slipped his feet into his boots and pulled his shirt over his head before starting off around a corner to who knows where when he realized his big bag of guns wasn't among the things his date had returned to him. Great.

CHAPTER 15

SURROUNDED BY IDIOTS

CITY OF GOLD

Orwell sat at his desk surrounded by the impeccable perfection of his office. Though it was precisely as he wanted it to be, nothing in the space brought him any joy. Bale was off hunting for the one thing that could bring him anything close to it, and all he could do was wait.

He didn't need to look up to know the quiet footsteps approaching his desk belonged to Chamuel. Nor did he need his eyes to know the creature resembled every other angel he'd ever perfected closely enough to be a clone of any of them. Truly, the only difference between them was the color of their hair and sometimes their eyes. It was something he thought of very infrequently, but when he did, it occurred to him they all represented his vision of physical perfection, or hers more probably. They were flawless, just as anything he must behold should be.

It might have been boredom, but he ignored the angel for a few moments before acknowledging his presence. The act didn't bring him any more joy than anything else occupying the space with him, but he let Chamuel sit there long enough to feel uncomfortable before finally acknowledging his presence and saying, "I take it you dare interrupt me only because you have something useful to report."

Chamuel bowed when he replied, "Yes, my Lord, God of gods, Creator and Origin of all things, I bring news of Mr. Lance."

"Had he succeeded in his mission, he would be standing before me with my son in tow. Am I safe to assume your report will be unsatisfying?" he grew increasingly tense as he spoke.

Orwell could almost feel Chamuel trembling as the angel replied, "Please forgive me, but yes."

He finally turned his fiery gaze toward the terrified angel and commanded, "End the suspense. Share this unsatisfying news you bring."

"She has found him," Chamuel dropped his gaze to the floor when he answered.

"Kaye? I assumed she would discover him at some point," he shook his head before continuing, "Neither subtle nor precise are words I would use to describe Mr. Lance. However, I did not expect it to happen so quickly. Did he survive?"

Chamuel continued staring at the ground as he answered, "Yes, the collector yet lives. However, he has been disarmed."

"Completely?" the volume of Orwell's voice rose as he asked the question.

"Sadly, he had all of Azrael's gifts together in one container."

"Tell me that damned, pompous imbecile did not carry a bag of weapons into New Eden."

"It appears he did," the angel nearly whispered.

It always had to be something with Bale Lance. The thought of that man executing a mission without unnecessarily placing himself in precarious situations seemed a fancy too fantastic to imagine. He was too brash and confident to believe any creature could get the better of him. If only he knew how wildly unprepared he was for the likes of Kaye. She would eat him alive and spit out whatever she didn't swallow down.

"Where is he now?" he finally asked.

"On the streets of Perver City. Kaye's men are tracking him," Chamuel's tone remained quiet.

"She's toying with him," Orwell shook his head, "Bitch."

He let Chamuel stand there and tremble as he worked through the angel's damning report in his mind. Bale was a brash and unsophisticated barbarian, but he hadn't failed yet. Despite his unorthodox techniques, he had always managed to achieve his goals one way or another. This one was different though. He'd never tangled with an adversary like Kaye. This would be a test. She was conniving, and she had all the tools necessary to drag a dog like Bale off whatever scent he was chasing. At this point, all he could do was hope that his dutiful soldier could hold a strong enough grip on his desire to free his daughter to see through Kaye's charade.

After a few moments of silent contemplation, Orwell finally turned back to Chamuel and said, "Leave me, now. I have much to consider. I want to know immediately of any changes in the situation."

CHAPTER 16

HUNTED

PERVER CITY

The street was alive with activity. Throngs of people hurried to this thing or that while random loners were shooting up and shaking against brightly lit buildings and still others engaged in some of the freakiest shit Bale had ever seen. Some folks would stop to watch someone eating somebody's ass in the middle of the street or some guy fucking some other guy's armpit, but mostly nobody seemed to care what anybody else was doing. There was something oddly satisfying about it. Everybody just left everyone else alone to do what they would.

As brightly lit and bustling as the street was, it all seemed dark and quiet to Bale as he drew deeper into his own head. The bright lights seemed muted somehow, like a thick cloud passing in front of the brilliant white light of a full moon. Honking horns, catcalls, and howls all swirled together and clung to the street like white noise too heavy to make it up to his ears. He was alone, and he was fucked. New Eden was a dead end, and as wonderful as that broad in the red dress had been, she totally screwed him over. It had to be a setup. Those leather clad cats with their dark shades had a bead on him. She must have been working with them. Who was calling the shots? Guns. He needed to get more guns. It was obvious somebody knew he was there.

Bale pulled out his GPS device and began entering the coordinates to drop him directly across the street from *Kill 'Em Quick*. It would be quicker to drop right into the armory, but caution suddenly seemed paramount.

The air changed slightly just as he was about to hit the button. It was subtle, something like intuition. The hair on the back of his neck stood up just as the explosive report of a gunshot rumbled through the night. Instinct dragged him quickly into a doorway as some random passerby vaporized right in front of the spot where he'd been standing. That was real death, a gun like the ones Azrael had gifted him. Now he knew what it looked like, and he didn't like it one bit.

The bright lights of marquis and bar signs lit up the street like some kind of twisted carnival. They also killed any chance Bale might have at a stealthy escape. "You missed," he shouted from the doorway. Then he whispered, "Fuck," to himself. He was exposed.

Bale slowly leaned his head out of the doorway to get a bead on the shooter. Four men clad in leather and dark shades just like the stiffs watching him at New Eden were walking down the middle of the street with guns out and ready to puke real death all over the people milling about who had become a wild, screaming mob terrified of melting into oblivion after the first shot.

The four gunmen were probably demons. It was pretty obvious they'd been expecting him. He hadn't been in town for more than a couple hours, and they were already coming for him. The doorway Bale crouched in was a terrible hiding spot. He poked his head out to find a quick escape. An alley stretching into darkness across the road seemed the perfect destination.

Another shot rang out as soon as he ducked back into the doorway to adjust the settings on his device. The doorframe immediately above his head shattered covering him in shredded wood chips and debris. Time to go.

"Shit," he whispered loudly to himself as he charged out of the doorway to get a running start before thumbing the button on his GPS.

All four gunmen let loose. The barrels of their rifles belched fire lighting up the night as screams rang out from the mob of innocent bystanders. Those poor suckers gave Bale the perfect cover to make his escape as car windows shattered and suddenly sad souls exploded all around him.

Bale was at a dead run when he vanished into the scenery of the brightly lit street and stepped into the safe darkness of the alley he'd targeted. He felt safe for the briefest moment. The feeling fled when a door on the building to his right opened, and he slammed into a body dressed just like the gunmen chasing him. Time seemed to slow in that instant, and he got a good look at the man's face. Aside from the slicked back hair, the guy looked nearly identical to Michael or Gabriel. All these leather clad fuckers were demons, the so called fallen. The only difference between them and their counterparts in the City of Gold was geography.

Time seemed to catch up when the demon pulled a gun from his jacket and brought it up toward Bale's head. Then it sped up like a bullet train rocketing down a track. There was no time for thought, so Bale let his instincts and training take over. He grabbed the guy's wrist pushing the barrel of the gun away from his head and drove his forehead into the guy's nose. It was as soft as any man's as it crunched and shattered under the weight of Bale's cranium. He followed with a right uppercut that connected squarely with the bottom of the demon's chin. Bale ended the assault with an elbow to the side of the guy's jaw. He let the arc of that last blow continue until it terminated with his own hand pulling the gun from his adversary's suddenly weak grip.

BANG! The demon was nothing but sparkling bits that looked like flakes of gold floating on the musty currents slowly swirling through the alley, and Bale had a gun. It felt good in his hand, and he suddenly liked his odds a bit better than he had a moment prior.

The hair on the back of his neck stood up again. Somehow, he knew the four gunmen hunting him down would be rounding the corner as soon as he turned around. As if the universe was letting him know he was onto something, the walls around him began to explode bits of shattered brick into the air amid the roar of gunshots echoing through the darkness. Bale spun and ducked.

He clocked the four henchmen bearing down on him. They were relentless, just kept coming. He raised his gun calmly and squeezed off a shot. And then there were three gunmen walking next to a cloud of glittering gold. Another soul lost to oblivion.

The three remaining gunmen opened fire again lighting up the dark alley. Bale was outgunned and outmatched. He dove into the open doorway the poor sucker who'd given Bale his life and his gun had emerged from. It led to a stairway. Bale slammed the door behind him, locked the deadbolt, and charged up the stairs. After three flights, it occurred to him that there was a firehose on every floor. The fact wouldn't seem odd in any other reality, but in Perver City, they seemed out of place. Of course, any arsonist who found their way to the home of total physical bliss would most likely want to start a fire or two in the afterlife. Hell, it was probably a given. All the other kinks Bale witnessed the population of Perver City delighting in seemed to focus on sex, drugs, torture, or control, or some combination of them. Those weren't the only kinks folks carried with them to the afterlife. There must have been all kinds of depravity lurking in the confines of this twisted place.

The thought fled as Bale reached the top of the fourth flight of stairs. He may have troubled over the idea longer had the door on the landing not busted open with another leather-clad pain in the ass bursting through to pound into his chest and drag him back down all those damned steps he just ran up.

Angels were tough whether they resided in the City of Gold or Perver City. As far as Bale knew, Orwell had only created them to be his perfect soldiers. The rebellion and the war were probably bullshit, but there was some reason a full third of them split the City of Gold and started calling themselves demons, relishing the title of the fallen that Orwell had given them. Bale had never fought one despite how bad he wanted to go a few rounds with Mikey or Gabe, but he had seen their handy work firsthand. Any time Orwell decided a species had strayed too far from the path he'd envisioned for them, he sent in his angels like an elite strike force to wipe any memory of them from the face of whatever world they occupied. All the myths were bullshit. The angels represented Orwell's wrath, brutal and efficient killing machines.

Bale wasn't looking for a test as he rolled end over end with a reject from Orwell's army. At that moment, he was just trying to survive. He didn't give that damned demon a chance. As soon as his back hit the first step, he slammed the butt of his pistol into the guy's temple. Then he did it again and again, pistol whipping the sonofabitch the entire way down the steps.

By the time his feet touched the landing, Bale was feeling a bit woozy from rolling end over end down all those stairs. Based on his adversary's eyes, he wasn't the only one feeling less than fresh in the head. He would have shot the sucker in the chest if his momentum hadn't carried him right into that damned firehose. The glass shattered when his back slammed into it. The jolt was sufficient to jar the gun from his grip and send it skittering down the next stairway. Damn. It looked like it would be a test after all.

The demon drew his gun. Bale could have used a moment to get his bearings back, but there wasn't time. Oblivion was one short trigger pull away. He threw his left hand out like he was blocking a punch and pushed the barrel away from his face just in time. The plaster behind his head exploded a split second after the muzzle belched fire close enough to his cheek that he felt the heat. The loud report left his ear ringing. It was too close. He couldn't give him another shot.

Bale dipped to his left and threw a hard hook to the lower part of the demon's rib cage. He didn't know much about angelic physiology, but he hoped there was a liver hiding in there to damage. He didn't have time to pause and check the results. Instead, he stood quickly and fired a right hook to the demon's jaw. The guy was still reeling when Bale stepped back and fired off a kick to his knee driving his heel into the joint with precision.

The blow brought the demon to his knees, but the bastard wasn't done yet. He was still trying to bring that gun up to fire it at Bale's face. He almost succeeded, but Bale was too quick. He fired another kick right at the guy's hand and sent the gun over the railing to fall harmlessly to the steps below. The sight of the little, oblivion stick sailing over the railing gave him an idea. He reached back and grabbed hold of that firehose. Thank Orwell for arsonists. Then he quickly wrapped it three times around the demon as that relentless sucker was trying to get to his feet. Once it was wrapped tight, he fired a quick front kick to the guy's back and sent him sailing over the railing. The poor slob was gurgling some kind of threat when Bale pulled out his GPS, hit the button, and disappeared into the shattered plaster of the wall.

The dials on his device must have gotten bumped at some point, because he didn't walk out onto the street across from *Kill 'Em Quick*. Instead, he strolled right out of the scenery into a sex shop. He didn't have time to browse. Those damned demons could be anywhere. He was on a dead run toward the back of the store as soon as he materialized inside of it. He raced past walls decorated with the usual stuff one might expect to find in a place like that. There were handcuffs, whips, dongs, jellies, and masks. It all seemed pretty tame until he happened upon an older gentleman bent over a display case sucking his thumb and crying while a thick chick wearing a strap-on and a bad wig was shoving her giant, fake dong in his ass.

The distraction only slowed him slightly as he charged toward the counter at the back of the store. The wide-eyed kid behind the glass display case filled with other odd goodies looked terrified. He had pink hair and more piercings than Bale had ever seen on one human being. Unfortunately, Bale didn't have time to share any calming words that might assure the poor kid that nothing bad would happen to him. Instead, he hopped over the counter, shoved the innocent bystander out of the way, and charged around the corner toward the back door of the place.

Bale gripped the knob of the door and paused. Charging through doors with reckless abandon had proven to be a poor choice. Instead, he slowly turned the knob, opened the door a crack, and peaked into the alley beyond. It was crawling with those leather clad demons. He was trapped like a rat in a cage. There was no place to go.

Then he spotted a door across the alley. It was a risk. There was no way to know what was on the other side. After a few moments of contemplation, he decided it couldn't be any worse than the alley. He quietly closed the door, adjusted the dials on his device, took a step toward the closed door and hit the button.

The next step he took was away from the back door of another shop that looked like a candy store. Luckily, the place was close to empty. He kept his head down and walked toward the front. With all the heat outside, it would probably be a good idea to take a moment and let things cool down.

Bale kept his head down and browsed the shelves. They weren't filled with candy, at least not the kind a child would be interested in. Plastic buckets filled with all manner of pills and powders lined them. They had everything from X to coke to heroin, various amphetamines, and more variations of marijuana than Bale had ever seen. A lot of those edibles looked like candy.

It would be easy to just check out. Anything goes. He could just get high enough to quit caring and drift off to sleep, figure it out tomorrow. He tossed the idea out of his head. He still had a job to do. He couldn't let a little thing like the complete impossibility of success get in the way of his effort.

Bale glanced toward the counter. It was laid out like a pharmacy. The guy behind the counter even wore a white coat. It bore a stark contrast to all his piercings, tattoos, the wild mop of hair sprawling from his head, and the small baggy of powder he held in his outstretched hand. Maybe he'd been a pharmacist during his physical life and got all tweaked out after a few years in Perver City. Bale winced at the idea. You'd have to love your job pretty hard to want to keep it in the afterlife. He was probably just an overambitious dealer.

The pharmacist, or whatever he was, was speaking to a clean-cut businessman with slicked back hair wearing a shiny, silver suit who seemed to be hanging on every word. It must have been an interesting story. Bale listened in.

"I think this is exactly what you're looking for," the stoner pharmacist said wearing a salesman's smile.

"What is it?" the suit with the slicked back hair asked.

Somehow, the pharmacist's smile seemed even more slithery when he replied, "I call it Unicorn Food. Imagine laying in a cloud while angels lick your balls and you ejaculate non-stop for twelve hours, a little bit of heaven sprinkled right up your nose."

"I'll take it," the businessman eagerly replied.

"Make sure you have some food nearby," the salesman winked, "You'll be famished when you come down."

It was an easy sale. Bale decided the suit must have been pretty new to the scene. He was too eager. Maybe he hadn't quite figured out his kink just yet. Based on the looks of him, the shop was filled with things he'd wanted to try during his physical life but never did. Now he was free to sample it all for the rest of eternity. His eyes would lose that innocent shine in time.

Bale continued pretending to shop as the suit happily strolled out of the store with his next high in hand. As he watched the guy leave, it occurred to him that not only had the fellow been great fuel for speculation, he'd also been a perfect distraction. As soon as that distraction was gone, the stoner-pharmacist-salesman turned his attention to Bale.

Bale was pretending to examine a baggie of fine, white powder when the pharmacist looked over at him and said, "Heroin, is that your thing?"

Bale shook his head slightly when he replied, "Just browsing."

"Nobody comes in here just to browse," the pharmacist replied, switching back into salesman mode, "You want to soar to new heights, achieve that unattainable, all-time high."

"Is that what I'm looking for?" Bale asked, "How can you tell?"

The pharmacist shrugged and replied, "Your eyes. They give you away. You've seen too much, done too much. Nothing's shocking anymore. Am I right?"

Bale paused. It was probably just a standard line the guy used on every sucker who walked into the joint, but he hit pretty close to the target. He implied as much when he replied, "Probably not as far off as I might like."

The pharmacist ducked down, fumbled around behind the counter for a few moments, and returned with a baggie of pink powder. "This is what you want," he said, holding out the bag and motioning for Bale to approach.

Bale played along, examining the bag as he neared the counter. "You fucking with me?" he asked.

"Not at all, friend," the pharmacist flashed his snake oil salesman smile, "But I must be sure you're ready for this one. That shit I just handed the newbie is nothing compared to this."

Bale slipped further into character offering a sheepish grin as he replied, "I don't know. Blowing your wad nonstop for twelve hours while angels tongue your sack sounds pretty fucking spectacular."

"No doubt. It's fucking stellar," the pharmacist nodded, "But this is Angel's Embrace."

Bale's brow dipped toward his nose as he asked, "Angel's Embrace, huh? What's it do?"

"Glad you asked. Glad you asked," the salesman kicked into full swing, "You won't just see god, you'll feel like you are god. Picture slipping your cock into wet silk and exploding all over a crowd of adoring fans as you soar above them."

"Rockstar orgasm?" Bale continued to play along, nodding and offering a wide smile, "I'm with you. I'll take it."

The pharmacist pulled the baggie back when Bale reached for it and added, "But wait. There's more."

The salesman's act faltered in that moment as a bead of sweat trickled down his temple. The sonofabitch was trying to keep him talking.

"Motherfucker. You're stalling, aren't you?" Bale dropped his act as the pharmacist dropped the baggie on the table and turned to bolt.

The little shit played his part well, almost an Oscar worthy performance, but the only award Bale had for him was a bruised forehead. He shot his hand out like a snake and grabbed hold of the pharmacist's ratty hair so he couldn't get away. Then he slammed the kid's head into the counter. Out cold.

Bale took two steps toward the front of the place before pausing.

A big bag of drugs might come in handy if things went sideways. He hurried back and grabbed the baggie before entering coordinates on his GPS that would put him a few blocks from all the scrubs hunting him down. He needed a minute to figure things out. He hit the button and vanished.

Jimmy's head was throbbing when he woke up. His limbs were all stuck in awkward positions, and his right hand tingled with pins and needles from being trapped under his head for who knows how long. Things were a bit foggy, but the last thing he remembered was a bright flash after that big dude slammed his head into the counter. Then everything went black.

Judging by the throbbing numbness in his hand, he must have been out for at least fifteen or twenty minutes. Everything was stiff as he used the counter to pull himself back up. It seemed he couldn't stretch any part of his body far enough to work out the kinks.

Jimmy stiffened up even more when he heard the back door fly open and loud footsteps echo from the back hall. They weren't going to be happy that he let Bale Lance get away. A small part of him wanted to run, but he knew that would be worse. They were too fast, and it would just piss them off if they had to chase him. Time to face the music.

Boss Yaaz's crew never gave their names when they came around, and they all looked the same. Three of them came flying around the corner like a pack of hounds running down a scent. They reminded Jimmy of the faceless muscle that used to shake him down before he took that long stroll into the light. The only difference between these bums and the other ones was that these guys didn't care about money or making names for themselves. They ruled the streets of Perver City, and if they found cause to look your way, no amount of money or drugs could save your ass. So much for anything goes. If you ended up on their list, you could kiss your sweet ass good-bye.

"Where the fuck is he?" the apparent leader of the small group shouted.

Jimmy sucked in a deep breath and grimaced when he shrugged and replied, "I don't know. He knocked me out."

It was like a crack of thunder, the sound the gun made when the guy squeezed the trigger. The muzzle flash was like a ball of fire. The slug burned when it pierced the flesh of his forehead. Then everything was kind of cold. He could feel the thing sliding into him like a fat needle. It didn't seem real. He'd been shot before. This felt different.

Everything happened in slow motion. He knew this was the real death he'd heard tweaked out, terrified people ramble on about. Oblivion. His gut was spinning like a tornado bounced around in his belly. Every other part of him felt like it was being ripped apart, like each of his cells were being blasted away from each other until there was nothing left of his form. He felt lighter, a cloud of dust floating on stale currents. His brain must have been microscopic particles by that point, but somehow, he was still aware.

A different voice asked, "What the fuck?"

Another one answered, "He let Bale get away."

"Fucker deserved it," the first voice added, as if getting beat up by a trained killer was truly a crime worthy of death. It wasn't fair, but it didn't matter.

"Yeah, well Miss Yaaz is going to be pissed when she finds out she needs a new pharmacist," the second voice responded.

Jimmy couldn't really see or hear anything after that. He knew the three of them were rifling through his goodies and stuffing their pockets with all they could carry, but it was more like intuition than stimuli from any of his sense organs. Those had long checked out.

Then everything went dark, and Jimmy the pharmacist was aware of nothing more.

CHAPTER 17

CRUCIFIED

PERVER CITY

The alley was quiet when Bale materialized in the middle of it. It had been a good guess. The darkness wrapped around him like a warm blanket. He'd been hustling pretty good when he made the jump. The need for speed seemed to have fled. He took a deep breath and slowed his pace before finally stopping, leaning his back against a wall of damp brick, and running both hands through his sweaty hair. A quiet moment to think was exactly what he needed.

The first thing he needed to do was get back to the armory. Hopefully, Azrael could hook him back up with more guns and point him in the right direction. New Eden was a bust, and those damned demons were swarming the streets for blocks around it. There could be only two possible reasons they focused their attention on New Eden. They were either tracking him, or they knew he was going to be there. The former seemed unlikely. The only thing he had on him was the GPS device from Orwell. It would make no sense for the boss to send him in carrying a method to track his every move. The latter was concerning. Maybe Azrael was a double agent who sold him out. Bale had his doubts about that as well. He could have just killed him in the armory. Either way, he couldn't trust anybody.

As he leaned against the wet brick in quiet darkness, his plan came together. First, he needed a change of clothes, some kind of disguise. They all obviously knew what he looked like. Anything that could give him even an extra few seconds would be an advantage. Then he needed to case *Kill 'Em Quick*. The odds seemed pretty good that the clowns hunting him would have that joint locked down if it was the only place in town to get guns. Finally, he needed to blip himself right into the armory. If Azrael had sold him out, there would be no sense in talking to him again. He could blip into that beautiful closet full of weapons, grab everything he could carry, and blip right back to the alley he was standing in. Then he'd have to figure out where to go next.

The street to Bale's left was busier. He took a deep breath, gathered himself, and jogged to that end of the alley stopping to lean against the building. He counted to three in his head before peeking around the corner. The coast was clear, no leather clad nuts with oblivion cannons to puke slugs of real death all over the place, just a bunch of random souls looking for their next fix. He slipped into the crowd and moved with the swarm.

A wide-brimmed, purple hat with a long, black feather sticking up from it seemed to be floating above the crowd. Bale quickened his pace to catch up. The dude wearing the gaudy hat was a little broader in the shoulders than Bale, but he was the perfect height. He must have been on some kind of pimp trip. The heavy, leopard fur coat the dude wore was unfortunate, but it would make a hell of a disguise.

Bale followed the pimp across another busy street. The intersection was chaos. There were no lights controlling any traffic. Cars were bumper to bumper and moving slowly in every direction. Nobody stopped for anything, not the people nor the vehicles. The crowd just moved in between the bumpers. Nobody seemed to notice or care. They just kept moving along like tightly packed salmon working their way upstream.

There was a break between the buildings half a block up. That's where he would make his move. The dude wearing Bale's future outfit hadn't interacted with anyone around him for as long as he followed him. The guy had to be on his own. Nobody seemed to notice or care about anything happening to anyone else around them. He had to take the chance.

They were three steps from the alley when Bale sped up his pace, dropped his shoulder, and drove it into the guy's side guiding him toward the darkness of the alley. The dude was big but soft. Bale didn't give him a chance to react, pushing him quickly through the crowd.

Bale tensed a bit when he heard somebody from the crowd say, "That dude just dragged that guy into the alley."

He calmed when another voice answered, "It's probably their thing.

You should mind your own business unless you want a rough threesome with the two of them."

Bale had pushed the guy about one hundred yards down the alley before tripping him and dragging him to the ground. As soon as they hit the cement, Bale began peppering the guy's head with hammer fists.

The pimp obviously wasn't a fighter. There wasn't any technique involved in his attempts to block Bale's attacks. The dude basically covered up and tried to curl himself into a ball while whimpering, "What the fuck? Please, man, I ain't into no gay shit. I've got some dudes that will do whatever you want though."

It wasn't Bale's best work. He had to hit the guy ten times to knock him out. He should have been able to get it done with one. The crying got to him. He rolled off the guy and just sat beside him looking him over for a few moments. What a shit show. Nobody is completely innocent, but this poor slob hadn't done anything to deserve the beating he got. The only small consolation for Bale was that the guy would wake up without any pain or scars to remember the event.

The fur coat was too warm, but it fit okay. The hat just made him feel silly. Even still, Bale slipped into character as he slid back onto the street and slipped back into the crowd adding a slight strut to his step. Nobody paid any attention to him. Everybody seemed to be in some kind of costume. He fit right in. As he strutted along with all the other fish swimming to whatever thing they were off to, he wondered if all the characters around him were who they had been before arriving in Perver City. Perhaps they were all what they wanted to be when they lived and breathed in whatever reality they came from. Maybe the people they became once they arrived in the afterlife were who they were always meant to be. Maybe fear kept them from being who they really wanted. Bale would never know, but it sure looked like freedom.

He only had two short blocks to contemplate if the throngs of people milling about around him were characters or if they were their true selves freed from the characters they'd played throughout their lives before he strutted past *Kill 'Em Quick*. The shop was across the street. He kept his head low so the wide brim of his hat could sufficiently obscure his face. The place was crawling with those damned demon henchmen, members of hell's army. Strolling through the front entrance wasn't an option, so he continued to the end of the street, slipped around the corner, and pulled out his GPS. He had to guess a bit at the exact coordinates. It was a small room. If he missed by even a little bit, he'd materialize smack dab in the middle of a swarm of guys he didn't want to see. He glanced around the corner and quickly estimated the distance. After more than two thousand years of educated guesses on distance, he'd gotten pretty good at it. Satisfied he'd arrive right in the middle of that beautiful room of death, he pressed the button.

His guess was good, but the scene in the armory was all wrong. A massive cross stretched to the ceiling immediately in front of him. The floor was cracked where the thing had been hammered into it. A puddle of blood surrounded it constantly fed by the poor slob who'd been nailed to it. It didn't take much speculation to figure out the poor slob was Azrael. Apparently, the undercover angel hadn't sold him out. It was a small consolation. The jig was up.

A loud *CRACK* echoed throughout the small room just before Bale noticed a decorative, steel mace head ending its swing. The spots of the thing that weren't soaked in blood shimmered in the bright light of the room. There was an odd sizzling after that, like bacon frying in grease. It sounded like Azrael's skin was burning.

Bale jumped out from behind the massive stone cross startling the demon who'd been torturing the only friend Bale had in Perver City. The guy turned to run, but Bale was on him slipping his arm around his neck before he could take one step toward the door. The mace head came dangerously close to hammering the top of Bale's head as the guy swung it wildly about. He was strong. Bale had to move quickly.

An idea about rock stars suddenly jumped into his awareness. He reached into his pocket, pulled out the baggy of Angel's Embrace, and shoved it in the demon's mouth. The stuff worked quick. The demon only struggled for a few seconds before Bale was able to lower him to the ground. Then he pulled the guy's shades off him to confirm he was sufficiently checked out. His eyes were glazed, and he was grinning like a dope.

"Enjoy the orgasm, jackass," Bale whispered before turning his attention to the bloody lump hanging from the cross.

Azrael was a mess. If there were anyone else in any reality it could have been, Bale wouldn't have recognized him. There wasn't a spot on the angel's body that wasn't covered in blood. It even dripped from his long, dark hair that had fallen out of the ponytail he wore to fit in with the demons he'd been duping for who knows how long.

Bale lifted Azrael's head as gently as he could. Despite the care he took, the action still earned a shallow groan. The poor guy was glazed over, but he was still conscious.

"I told you they were creative," Azrael almost whispered

"I see that," Bale shook his head before asking, "How did they find you?

The angel grimaced when he replied, "I don't know. They must be tracking you the same way..." Then he went limp. He was gone. Not more than a second later, he evaporated to nothing. Oblivion. Real death.

"Shit," Bale muttered under his breath.

Sudden commotion outside the closed door of the armory reminded Bale he didn't have time to lament the loss of the only soul in Perver City that was useful to him or even consider what he might have been trying to say. It was obvious he was being tracked. Figuring out how would have to wait until he figured out a way to get out of the mess he was in. Guns would help. He quickly moved to the drawer with the false bottom where Azrael had retrieved those two golden pistols with the never-ending supply of ammo, billions of years of nuclear energy condensed into a capsule no bigger than his thumb. That's what Azrael had told him anyway. When Bale opened the drawer and removed the false bottom, he found two identical pistols to the ones Azrael had given him. Hopefully, the vanquished angel knew what he was talking about.

The door to the room began sliding open just as Bale stowed the guns in his belt line. Time to go. He pulled out his GPS, spun the dials, hit the button, and he was gone.

CHAPTER 18

A NEW GAME

CITY OF GOLD

Angel Cakes sat on the same rock where she had always sat since arriving in the perfect paradise Orwell had placed her in when dad had made that deal so long ago. She was only sad when he left her. That lasted a while. After that, she was just mad at him. That lasted longer. Being alive was probably better than being dead, but she'd spent all but the first six years of her life in this beautiful prison. The longer she stayed, the more she felt like being dead might be better. At least she wouldn't be so bored all the time. They gave her mostly anything she asked for, but they would never play. They wouldn't even talk. They just stood there silently staring at nothing. What a boring life. Oftentimes, the only thing she could do to entertain herself was annoy them.

"Let's play a new game," she said as she slowly kicked her feet while staring at Michael, "One of us describes something one word at a time, and the other two try to guess what it is. The one who guesses first gets the points."

Neither of the stoic angels reacted at all. They just kept quietly staring. That wasn't any fun.

She waited a few moments hoping one of them might say something. When neither took the bait, she continued, "Okay, I'll start. Pale."

Silence.

"Nothing?" she asked. She looked back and forth from one to the other, hoping for some kind of clue they could even hear her before adding, "That's one. Keep in mind you get more points for answering with fewer clues. Any guesses? No? Okay, here is clue number two. Quiet."

The angels continued to ignore her.

She waited a few moments and asked again, "Nothing?" When she didn't get a response she added, "You guys aren't very good at this game. Those are really good clues. Oh well, here is clue number three. Stupid."

Gabriel flashed a menacing glare at her. Finally, a reaction. He still didn't say anything, but at least she could tell he was listening.

"Last clue," she smiled and added, "You know, if nobody guesses, I win the round." She glanced back at forth between them again before finishing with, "Here it is, last chance. Asshats."

The look on Michael's face as he stepped towards her was almost terrifying. She knew he was only trying to scare her. He wouldn't do anything about it. They had tried to scare her before when she pushed too far. The first couple of times had been frightening. They could make their faces do some really horrifying things, but they never laid a hand on her.

She was smiling up at Michael as he loomed over her when his face got even paler than normal. It almost looked like he wanted to run away. She only had a few seconds to think about what could scare an angel when she heard Orwell's voice.

"Leave us," he said. The command sounded a little like a threat.

Michael and Gabriel weren't scary, but Orwell was. He was creepy. It would have been best to keep quiet, but she couldn't. Instead, she looked up at Orwell in all his neatly trimmed perfection and said, "Oh great, it's the king of the asshats. Do you want to play a game?"

If being called an asshat bothered him at all, he didn't let on. He just flashed a friendly smile, sat beside her and said, "I do want to play a game. Sadly, I fear it is a game you will not much like to play."

The smile remained on his face, but his eyes changed. Something about the way he examined her made it feel like he wanted to hurt her. He didn't hurt her, but what he did might have been worse. She tensed when she felt his fingers combing through her hair like he was petting her. She didn't want to look at his eyes anymore, but she couldn't turn away no matter how hard she tried. It was like he was controlling her.

It was a relief when he finally stopped toying with her hair. What he did next was worse. It tickled slightly when he gently dragged his fingernail from her shoulder to her elbow. It was so gross. He was so gross. She tried to slide off the rock to get away from him, but she couldn't move.

"Such a pretty girl," he said, his voice barely more than a whisper.

If she could have moved, she would have gouged his eyes out. All she could do was tremble as she defiantly said, "My daddy…"

"Is failing miserably right now," the creepy look in his eyes didn't change at all as he interrupted, "He is a very stupid and frustrating man. Do you know what happens if he fails?"

She didn't want to know. It wouldn't matter anyway. He promised. "He won't," she nearly shouted, "He'll come for me, and if you hurt me…" The threat died when Orwell snapped his fingers, and her mouth vanished. She screamed as he cradled her face gently in his hands and kissed her cheek, but no sound came out.

"You talk too much, just like your father," he snarled and began petting her hair again before he added, "As I was saying, if he fails, you belong to me for eternity."

Then his eyes went white. It felt like there were hands inside her stomach ripping up her guts. She screamed and screamed and screamed, but no sound could come out. Then it felt like something was tearing at her brain, like a headache but unbearable. The light was suddenly too bright. It made her head hurt even worse. It felt like she was leaving her body, like he was ripping everything that made her who she was right out of her. The torture lasted only moments, but it seemed like forever as she sat there, frozen and unable to do anything to stop him.

Then it passed. The pain fled, and the color began to return to Orwell's eyes along with the smile on his face. He snapped his fingers, and her mouth returned. She didn't have any screams left, and though she had a million things she'd like to say at that moment, she kept them all to herself.

He looked so satisfied as he asked, "Did you like my game?" He paused for a moment as if she might respond. When she didn't, he added, "We'll play that for thousands of years or until I tire of you."

Angel tried to keep the tears in. She didn't want him to know how much he'd hurt her. She didn't want him to have that power over her, but he had broken her. All her bold defiance had fled to cower in a dark corner at the back of her mind. All she could do was slump down on the rock and cry.

"I like this game," he smiled as he strolled away and vanished into the scenery. His voice remained after he'd gone to add, "I will come visit you again soon."

She whispered, "Asshat," after him and sobbed.

She heard Michael mutter, "I can't disagree," before sleep mercifully came to drag her away.

CHAPTER 19

NO ESCAPE

PERVER CITY

The plan was gone, checked out. Bale had no idea where to go next. These were unfamiliar waters. On nearly every case he'd ever worked, his notes had been meticulous. Even when they weren't, he was the hunter. Perver City flipped the script on him. Relentless demons dressed like mafia muscle swarmed at every turn. All he could do to stay ahead of them was pop off in random directions. He had no idea where he was or where he needed to go. All he could do was stay alive.

After splitting from an alley crawling with trigger happy henchmen, he arrived in a hotel room that looked like it had been abused by a rock band. The television was hanging from the wall by cords, and the screen was cracked. Every table that hadn't been tipped over was filled with beer cans, half-empty booze bottles, and piles of pills. The desk had one small area free from cans or bottles. It looked like it had only been cleared to make room for the five lines of coke left after somebody had snorted the rest.

A loud moan dragged Bale's attention over to the bed. Two half-dressed women were going at it pretty hard. He slowed for a moment to admire the scene. It was too bad he didn't have time to see if they wanted a third. He quickened his pace and headed for the door.

He paused there and listened. There were lots of voices. It sounded like some were giving orders. They were knocking on doors. He turned the knob and slowly pulled the door open. After a deep, centering breath, he peeked his head out and stole a glance in both directions.

The place must have been pretty high end. Plush carpet and gaudy light fixtures lined the hallway. The smell didn't match. That was a mix of vomit, feces, and rotten food. Five of the leather clad demons were working the rooms at one end of the hallway. They hadn't noticed him. He had the drop on them.

Bale pulled out his golden guns and let them rip. Two of the demons vaporized immediately. Real death looked like a balloon full of glitter exploding, tiny specks of light floating for a few moments before dissipating into nothing. He kept firing as he backed down the hall, but his other three targets ducked and covered. He'd only backpedaled about ten feet before they overcame the surprise and returned fire.

The hallway filled with plaster and bits of glass as bullets tore into walls and shattered the gaudy light fixtures. There were too many of them. Bale was one hell of a marksman, but he was down six guns to two with no cover. It wasn't a winning position. He fired a couple more shots, kicked in a door, and ducked into another room.

This room was tidy and neat. He spied a circular table with a decorative lamp resting on it. It would make a perfect shield. As he hurried over toward the thing, he noticed the occupants. A boy who couldn't have been more than twelve years old knelt on the floor watching The Sound of Music playing on the television directly across from him. A priest adorned in full vestments sat on the edge of the bed gently brushing the boy's hair.

Bale paused. It was Perver City, and he knew the mantra, anything goes. But something about the way the old fucker looked at the kid wouldn't allow him to keep walking.

"Are you okay?" Bale asked the kid.

The priest stopped brushing and scolded, "How dare you interrupt our lesson! Move along now before I call security."

Bale turned his jaw up and to the left earning a crack before pointing the gun in his right hand at the priest's head and nearly growling, "I wasn't talking to you, you sick fuck." Then he shifted his attention back to the boy and asked again, "Are you okay?"

The boy's eyes grew suddenly misty as he quietly replied, "I don't like it here, but he won't let me leave."

That was all Bale needed to hear. He shifted his piercing gaze back to the defiant priest and said, "I don't have time to play with you. You have one chance. Let the boy go."

The priest's laugh was like a cackling witch from some kind of twisted fairy tale. "Do you think I haven't been shot before you dull thing?"

Bale squeezed the trigger as he replied, "You've never been shot with one of these." And the priest was dust.

He looked back down at the kid and said, "Wait until the hallway quiets down to split. Then you're free to go wherever you want."

Then Bale knocked the lamp off the table, stowed the gun in his left hand, grabbed his makeshift shield, and headed back toward the door. The firing had stopped, but he could hear them moving toward the room. The footsteps were slow and quiet. It was no doubt they all had their guns trained on the doorway just waiting for his head to pop out so they could blast it off. He took a deep breath, gathered himself, and spun into the hall.

The shield was effective, but it was disintegrating quickly as Bale held it in front of him while belching death from his golden gun. He got one of them within three steps. By that time, there wasn't much left of the table keeping him from taking any damage. He needed another option.

Everything seemed to slow down as the table he was using as a shield finally vaporized to dust. He was suddenly exposed and had to move quickly. He grabbed his GPS, spun one of the knobs, and moved his thumb to the button. A slug whistled through the air. Somehow this one was louder than the rest like it was shouting out some kind of premonition a split second before Bale's GPS exploded in his hand. All his bravado evaporated with it. That was his only way out. He popped off a quick shot at the demon who fired the unfortunate bullet, and the sucker vaporized. There was only one left, but that one had taken cover in a doorway.

"It's just you and me now," Bale shouted down the hallway feigning confidence as he tried to get a bead on the guy, "Drop your gun and walk away. You don't have to die today."

"You're trapped now, aren't you?" the demon teased. His voice was like a symphony.

If Bale were honest with himself, he'd probably admit it was jealousy, but he hated all angels, even the ones who'd fallen from Orwell's grace. They were just as perfect as they sang their threats. He hated them even more when they were right. He was trapped. That answer just wouldn't do.

"Don't kid yourself," Bale shouted down the hall. "You're trapped in here with me."

A melodic *ding* chimed at the end of the hallway. In that moment, it might have been the most beautiful sound Bale had ever heard. It sounded like salvation, an escape from the shattered cage keeping him trapped.

The elevator was only about one hundred feet away, but it looked like the hallway stretched for a mile. On top of that, it was behind the last soul on that floor trying to kill him. He'd have to run for it. With a gun in each hand blazing hot death down the hallway, he pumped his legs with every ounce of determination he could muster. Doubt squeezed him like an iron fist desperately trying to stifle his will. He had to be bigger than it. He had to push harder.

He heard the door of the elevator begin sliding open about halfway into his charge toward freedom. It wasn't that really. A small voice whispering in the back of his head kept reminding him that glorious elevator that seemed like a final goal was nothing more than a ticket to the next trap. Bale ignored it, pumping and grinding as fast as his legs could carry him, so focused on his goal that reaching out with his left hand to fire a shot at the demon hiding in the doorway was almost an afterthought. *BOOM*, and the guy was dust.

Roughly twenty feet of plush carpet littered with broken plaster and fractured glass stretched between Bale's boots and the open elevator door when two more demons stepped into the fray. Bale didn't give them a chance to get their bearings. *BOOM…BOOM…BOOM…*and nothing but sparkling bits of shimmering dust remained. There was nothing left to stop him but the damned door slowly closing as he raced toward the safety of the elevator car.

Bale dove the last five feet slipping into the car just before the door slid shut. It felt like salvation for a moment as brief as a single flap of a hummingbird's wing. He noticed B had already been pushed at the exact same time he realized he wasn't alone in the elevator. The chickenshit hid while his two compatriots had jumped into oblivion.

The guy groaned when Bale's heel connected with his gut. The kick doubled him over and sent him crashing into the wall of the car. It gave Bale the quick two seconds he needed to get to his feet, but nothing more.

The gun barrel couldn't have been more than an inch in front of Bale's face by the time he made it back to his feet. It looked like a gaping tunnel, a dark journey to hell. Instinct brought his left arm up to push the thing away from his face a split second before it erupted. The muzzle flash was blinding as the slug whistled past his ear.

Bale raised his right arm almost like an uppercut and fired, but the demon blocked it like it was a punch. Then the barrel of his opponent's gun was racing toward his face again. It felt like a boxing match, left...right...left...a trigger pull with each punch. Block...fire...block...fire. The guy was good. It was a stalemate. Bale had to try something different. For everything demons weren't, they were tireless and relentless. There was no way he could wear the guy down.

Bale feigned a jab with his left. That got the demon's arms up to block. Then he dropped his right hand low and fired. The guy's elbows shot back when his kneecap exploded exposing his chest. Bale fired again, this time with the gun in his left hand. One sizzling moment later, and he was alone in the elevator.

He took a deep breath. The basement was his only way out, but somebody else had pushed that button. It didn't take much imagination to figure out what horrors would be waiting for him when the elevator door opened again, but he didn't have another option. Jumping from a window would get him out of the building. If everything he knew about Perver City was true, he'd survive the fall, but fifty floors was a long way to plummet. He'd have a hard time getting away on broken legs.

The elevator suddenly started to slow. He didn't want to wait to find out who'd be joining him. The hatch on the ceiling looked promising. He stood on the railing, pushed it open, and climbed through. He quietly closed it back up just as the door was opening.

The elevator shaft was quiet and smooth. There was nothing holding the car up, no cables, no gears, nothing to keep the car from crashing to the basement. Oddities like that used to trouble Bale. Rules in one potentiality didn't always line up exactly with the rules in other potentialities. Up wasn't always necessarily up. The same was true for down. Perver City wasn't really a potentiality though. It was one of the anchors, the chaos to offset the order imposed by Orwell and his City of Gold. Anything was possible in this place.

Three distinct voices filtered up from the elevator car. Bale knew the names of very few angels or demons. Orwell had wanted him to learn them all, to know them and use them, be a part of one big, happy, heavenly family. Bale never gave a rat's ass about any of them. They were all just decorations no different than a chandelier or chair, characters in the reality Orwell painted. Bale thought of them as henchmen. In the City of Gold, they worked for Orwell. He had no idea who the bums in Perver City answered to. In his head, he just thought of them as numbers, Jackass 1, Jackass 2, etc. It was on odd thing, something he'd always done. He needed to know who he was killing, not because he wanted to revel in their end. It was some kind of twisted honor thing he couldn't really define in his own mind. Even still, it mattered to him that he saw them as something more than just targets to shoot at.

"The basement," Bale heard from the car below. The voice was as beautiful as any angel's voice, but there was a slight gruffness tickling its edges. This one became Jackass 1. That same voice added, "You come with me. The rest of you take the stairs."

Bale decided whoever was remaining in the car with Jackass 1 would be Jackass 2. They would be the only ones in the car when it started moving again. That would be good. Two to one were odds he could work with, especially with the element of surprise. They wouldn't know what hit them.

A voice outside the elevator with a much cleaner voice than Jackass 1 said, "Remember, Boss Yaaz wants him alive." This one would be Jackass 3.

"We'll see how that works out. It comes down to me or him..." Jackass 2 answered from inside the car.

Jackass 1 interrupted him, "We'll all mourn your loss. Let's go."

The elevator was moving again. Slipping quickly down into the depths. What Jackass 3 had said was troubling. It got him wondering if he'd still be alive if they hadn't been handicapped with a no kill clause. He'd taken a few of them out already. How many of those who remained thought like Jackass 3? Traveling down that path wouldn't help his cause, so he abandoned the journey. He had at least two more tickets to oblivion to punch sitting right beneath him.

Bale quietly lifted the hatch and peered inside. Both demons standing there beneath him were staring at the numbers changing rapidly on a panel near the ceiling on the opposite side of the car. 25...24...23... Bale didn't have much time to think about how it would go down, but the first step was surprise. He stood up and stepped through the hatch, crouching low and firing when he landed.

Poof. Headshot. That was one more down.

He wasn't sure which number he'd ended until Jackass 1 shouted, "Motherfucker," and raised his gun. There you go. Jackass 2 was toast.

Bale quickly shot his left arm out to block the gun swinging toward his head. He glanced up to see 14…13…12 peel off on the display. There had to be more of these suckers waiting in the basement. He didn't have time to go hand-to-hand with this bum. He kept the gun in his right hand low, squeezing the trigger and firing from the waist. By the time he was passing the fifth floor, Jackass 1 was a memory. Two seconds later, the car stopped. Go time.

He wouldn't have time to get back through the hatch before the elevator door opened, so he didn't try. Even if he could make it up there before the bullets started flying, he'd only be postponing the inevitable. No more running. It was time to make his stand. He raised both his guns up and started rapidly squeezing off shots toward the opening doors.

It was a bum rush. There had to be at least ten of those leather clad suckers piling into the car with him. He picked them off one by one. *BOOM…BOOM…BOOM* his hand cannons roared, belching death from shimmering gold barrels and filling the car with smoke.

Bale dove beneath the cloud and popped out in what looked like a vast, empty garage. Empty wasn't completely accurate. There were no vehicles parked in any of the multitude of spaces, but there were hundreds of leather-clad demons popping off guns in his direction. Nothing was even close. The no kill clause must have been real. It messed with his sense of fairness a little bit, but he had no plans to go wherever these suckers wanted to take him. He kept firing, punching a demon's ticket to real death with each squeeze of his trigger.

A name suddenly popped into his head, Abigor. There was something special about him. Bale knew the name, but he failed to reckon why it popped into his head as the hair on his neck stood. He only had a few seconds to ponder the mystery when a dull *CLUNK* echoed through his melon. Whatever had hit him in the back of his head was hard enough to shatter bone and swung with enough ill intent to crack a coconut. Everything went black.

CHAPTER 20

THE BIG BOSS

PERVER CITY

Darkness followed by blurry blotches of colors filled Bale's vision as he blinked several times, shaking his head a bit too rapidly. It throbbed. The act of shaking it so abruptly made his guts feel queasy. Whoever Abigor was, the guy could swing a club. Bale attempted to rub his pounding head, but all he succeeded in doing was to confirm he was tied to the chair.

Things slowly began coming into focus. He was in an office. It was a picture of modern opulence. Extravagant works of art were hung randomly about the vast walls of the place, each on gaudy golden frames. As perfect as they were on their own, not one of those frames matched another. The furniture in the place was the same. Every piece was hand-carved perfection, but no piece matched any of the other pieces in the room. It looked like the chaotic masterpiece of a designer who'd gone mad trying to craft the perfect space.

"The little prince awakes. Did you have a nice nap?" a voice too clear and perfect to be intimidating despite the effort chimed behind Bale. He decided that one would be the new Jackass 1 without bothering to look back at the owner of the perfect tone.

"It didn't do anything for my headache," Bale grunted. He groaned quietly before adding, "Come on, untie me. Let me out of here. I promise I'll play nice this time."

"Shut the fuck up," Jackass 1 replied with the slightest hint of annoyance marring the perfection of his voice.

Another equally beautiful voice added, "You're just lucky there was a no kill order on your ass."

Bale decided that second voice would be the new Jackass 2 before replying, "I kind of figured there might be one of those on me. You couldn't all be such horrible shots. I would have smoked your asses anyway."

"You'd be a memory drifting aimlessly into oblivion," Jackass 1 answered in as close to a growl as his perfect tone would allow.

Bale was about to say something cheeky to piss off his new friends when she walked in strutting like a runway model and grinning like the Chesire Cat. It was the bitch that fucked him, chucked him, and stole his guns. There was no way she was the boss. She looked like candy gliding across the floor on red pumps that appeared to be designed exclusively to break any ankle bold enough to try walking in them. Her legs were obviously up to the task. The way her calves pumped with each step made Bale forget about his headache. The tight red dress she wore ended just before those perfect calves. It was slit up the front to just below her crotch giving a brief peek at each of her smooth thighs with every slinky step she took. Bale couldn't help it. Despite everything she'd done to him, if she said she wanted to take another ride in her limo, he'd have followed her like a lost puppy. It was like a spell or something. No one else he had ever met had that effect on him.

"They're fucking professionals, Bale. With all that fire power, do you really think you'd still be breathing if I wanted you dead?" she asked as nonchalantly as any question had ever been asked in the history of queries.

Bale couldn't take his eyes off the plump, wet lips forming all those annoying words even though he didn't like what was coming out of them. He wanted to explore them, test if they were as soft as he remembered. He shook his head. Whatever trick she used to suck him in like that, he couldn't fall for it. He had a job to do. Somebody was depending on him to keep his shit together.

"I don't fucking believe this," he groaned, "You're the boss here?"

"What?" she paused adding a ditzy note to both her voice and expression, "Surprised a woman runs the show? Did you think the devil would be a big, strong man?"

"Not even a little," Bale chuckled at the act, "I've been around a long time, seen all kinds of regression and progress in all kinds of realities. The thing I don't get is, why didn't you just take care of me when you had me in your car? Why let me go if you were just going to send these fuckers out to hunt me?"

She finished her strut over to an elaborate, hand carved desk. The imagery on the thing was a hodgepodge of symbolism representing all kinds of beliefs that didn't belong in the same reality much less on the same piece of furniture. It fit perfectly with the rest of the randomness surrounding it. The top was a mess of papers and trinkets. After pouring herself some kind of alcohol out of an intricate, crystal decanter, she sat down, lit a cigar, and kicked her elegant feet up onto the desk.

After a few puffs on her cigar and a big swig of her drink, she shot a seductive glance at Bale and purred, "I had to know if everything I've heard about you was true. I needed to know if you could handle the heat."

"A test, seriously? You had your goons chase me all over hell for a test?" Bale finished with a wry chuckle drenched in disgust. He tried to scratch his head again, forgetting he was still strapped to the chair. It was obvious she needed him for something. He had to try a different tact. Slipping the cockiest grin he could muster while bound to a chair with a pounding headache, he said, "How did I do?"

After a hearty laugh, she puffed hard on her cigar, drained her glass, and said, "Well, you got caught, didn't you?"

"The odds weren't really in my favor," Bale shrugged it off, but she was right. He got caught. Assuming whatever prompted her to test him was worse than tangling with some scrub fallen angels, he probably failed the test.

His elegant captor poured herself another drink as she replied, "They weren't, but you're supposed to be the best. Still, you didn't completely disappoint."

Bale dropped the act. It wasn't getting him where he needed to be quickly enough. "Okay," he finally said, "I've got some questions. First of all, you never gave me your name. All I know now is that you appear to be the boss of Perver City. Or the mayor, or whatever the fuck you call yourself."

"I think you know who I am," she nearly hissed.

"So...should I call you Satan then? This is hell, right?" He glanced around the room dramatically before adding, "Or, at least the place that spawned all those twisted stories about eternal torture. Are you going to cast me into the lake of fire?"

Condescension dripped from the coy giggle she offered him before replying, "Don't pretend to be so simple. Satan is an imaginary character in stories littered about thousands of potentialities. I am a real being, flesh and blood when I need to be." She drained her glass again and poured another before adding, "My boys call me Boss Yaaz, but you can call me Kaye, darling."

Bale laughed earnestly for a good thirty seconds. The minute and a half longer that he dragged the laugh out was strictly for the sake of mocking drama. Once he finished with the laugh, he said, "Get the fuck out of here. You call yourself Kaye Yaaz, chaos? Really? Is that the best you could come up with? You're no better than Orwell."

Kaye's face suddenly changed. It was subtle but frightening. Maybe she would burn him for eternity in a pit of fire. Backing off the sarcasm seemed a pretty solid idea.

"You're no one to tease about adopted names. You call yourself Bale Lance. That's at least as ridiculous," she said as her expression returned to the seductive thing it had been before he pissed her off.

"Point taken," he nodded. Then he took a deep breath and asked, "So, now what?"

Kaye smiled wide as she snapped her fingers and Bale's bonds disappeared. He knew that she knew what he was thinking when he gauged the room again. He could get past her goons, but if she was anything like Orwell, that was probably a fight he couldn't win.

Her eyes invited his challenge as she puffed her cigar before saying, "Exactly. So, now what?" Then she held up the decanter and asked, "Drink?"

"Sure," he said as he stood. Realizing any move he made might be misconstrued as a planned escape, he paused, nodded toward a chair in front of Kaye's desk, and asked, "May I?"

"Please," she smiled as she set a beautiful, crystal chalice filled to the brim with whatever she was drinking on the edge of her desk in front of where he'd be sitting.

Bale gave the mystery brew a sniff—strong stuff, smelled like it was going to hurt going down—before taking his chair and asking, "What are we drinking?"

She emptied her glass with one gulp and poured another. Then she gave him that damned seductive smile that kept stealing his wits as she replied, "Real men don't need to ask. You drink it or you don't."

She was good. Bale couldn't have kept the smile from his face if he wanted to. He gingerly sipped his drink. It punched his esophagus all the way down to his gut where it exploded like a fireball. He winced as his chest suddenly felt like it was engulfed in flames.

"Too much, lover?" Kaye laughed at him.

"Nope, just the way I like it," he blasted out a quick breath before adding, "I can't feel my toes. At least my headache's gone."

"Perfect," she smiled at the lie and added, "Let's get down to business then. You are here to kidnap my son and take him to that slimy sonofabitch, Orwell."

She might as well have slapped him in the face. He took a bigger pull off his glass of firewater, wincing again as it went down, and said, "Wait. Your what?" He shook his head before adding, "And, for the record, I'm here to save my daughter's soul. The way you say it makes it sound…"

"Less than noble?" Her smile was starting to piss him off.

Kaye slammed her drink, pulled out the stopper to prepare to pour another, paused, and held the bottle out toward Bale. "Need to be topped off?" she asked.

Bale held his hand up as he sipped from his chalice. Then he shook his head and said, "I'm good for now, just developing a taste for it."

"Of course, you are," she giggled while she poured. Then she asked, "Orwell didn't tell you about us? I'm not surprised. That pompous ass likes to take credit for everything himself. Lou is *our* son."

It burned like all the fires of hell were raging in his gut when he slammed the rest of his drink. He reached it out toward Kaye for a refill before saying, "What the fuck? You and Or, really? Come on."

Kaye filled his chalice back up as she replied, "Why does that surprise you?"

Bale took another big drink, shrugged, and said, "I don't know. Looking at you, looking at him, it doesn't add up."

She rolled her eyes when she replied, "Come now, Bale. You aren't really that dense, are you? I can take absolutely any form I like. So can he. Your reaction is a perfect example of the problem with physical existence. Values become so shallow."

"No, no, no," he shook his head as he began, "It's more than just that. He's a vile cunt. You don't seem half bad. Balling my brains out and dumping me on the road was a dick move, but I've had worse things done to me."

Kaye offered a polite chuckle and said, "You know, I'm older than him, much. I came first. I created everything. Everything you have ever seen came from my twisted mind. But I was wild, out of control. Anything I wished for just happened. Do you have any idea what that was like? Some of it was good, very, very good. But some of it…" She trailed off as her gaze dropped toward the floor.

"So, big Or brought your ass in line?" Bale regretted the crass statement the moment it finished leaving his lips.

"That's one way to put it," she shrugged, "and not far from the truth. He had so much control of everything. He was so meticulous. Everything had to be just right, perfect. It was very attractive to me for a long time."

"But?" Bale prodded.

"You've met him," she sighed, "He's cruel. If things don't go exactly his way, he punishes. I suppose I don't need to tell you that. I'm sure you've witnessed it firsthand on many occasions. Your daughter, for instance."

Orwell was cruel, and Bale was grateful Kaye brought the conversation back to the reason he was there in the first place, Angel Cakes needed to get busted out of that perfect prison. He slammed his drink, made the face again, and held his chalice out for another refill.

As Kaye poured, he said, "Alright, what's the deal? You must have some kind of deal. You said you could have killed me, but I'm still here. What do you want from me?"

The coy smile left her face, chased away by the most earnest expression Bale had ever seen as she said, "I just want you to go home. Forget about Lou and leave. You know what Orwell will do to him. I'm sure you've seen it."

"Yeah, I've seen it, and that's exactly what he'll do to my daughter if I show up empty handed," Bale's head shook slowly side to side as he replied.

Kaye leaned forward in her chair, propped her elbows up on her desk, and asked, "Why not just go take her?"

That fire exploded in Bale's gut again when he drained his glass once more and held it out for another refill. He laughed as if she'd just told him the funniest joke he'd ever heard while she poured. He took another good pull before he replied, "Right. Why didn't I think of that? I could just walk in, grab her, and good old Or will just let us stroll on out." Bale's gaze drifted toward a painting of some battle he didn't recognize, but his mind travelled far past the wall the magnificent work hung from as he quietly added, "I don't even know how I'm going to get back there. One of your goons shot my GPS device. I'm dead in the water here."

"You know he was tracking you with that thing, right?" she asked.

Bale shook his head and replied, "He sees everything. Why would he need to track me?"

The laugh Kaye offered tasted less than genuine as she asked, "You really believe that?"

"I do," Bale shrugged.

"His omniscience is an illusion. He has eyes everywhere, but he can't see everything," Kaye leaned back in her chair, kicked her feet back up onto her desk, and asked, "Where do you think Odin got his ravens?"

Bale set his chalice back on Kaye's desk and sighed, "Even if he was tracking me with that thing, I don't how to get around without it."

"Look," Kaye began, "I'll make you a deal. Promise me you'll forget about Lou, and I'll send my best to help you get your daughter back."

"Or might be a cunt, but he's a known commodity. I hardly know you. Why should I trust you?" Bale leaned closer to the desk as he stared intently into her eyes.

"What choice have you got?" she asked allowing the seductive smile to return to those plump lips. Then she stretched, sat up, slipped her breast out, and began toying with her nipple as she said, "Now, come on. I have an itch you can help me scratch."

CHAPTER 21

THE MESSENGER

CITY OF GOLD

Orwell sat behind his desk with his eyes closed and tension tightening up his forehead. Things were not going to plan. Of course, Kaye had her spies, but if Bale had exercised even the slightest hint of stealth things wouldn't be spinning out of control as they were. Azrael was dead, real death. That was a loss to be sure. Hopefully, Bale had managed to keep himself alive. Sending him had been a risk, but the last time he'd waged war on Kaye, the losses were staggering. She was powerful.

The air in the room shifted as he heard the door open and close. He knew the tentative footsteps approaching belonged to Chamuel without opening his eyes. The careful cadence wasn't what gave the angel away. It was his smell. He'd given each of his minions a particular scent, some more pleasing than others. A hint of parchment mixed with oil and balsam-gum wafted from Chamuel.

Orwell snapped his eyes open as the angel began crouching to kneel before him. "Do not bother with formalities, Chamuel," he said, allowing no hint of any emotion to color his tone. After Chamuel nodded, Orwell asked, "More bad news?"

A malodorous scent of fear wafted from the angel as he replied, "Sadly, yes."

"Well, do not simply stand before me trembling. Deliver your report," Orwell commanded.

"Forgive me, lord, but we have lost sight of the collector," Chamuel's reply was quiet, barely more than a whisper.

Orwell dropped his head into his hands and let out a low groan. He did his best to avoid any emotional displays in front of his subjects, but the situation was dire. It would be difficult to imagine a more troubling turn of events. Aside from confirmation of Bale's demise, it was the worst possible news Chamuel could have delivered.

A few moments of silence to ponder would have been nice, but the angel droned on, "It appears the device we used to track him has been destroyed."

It wasn't Chamuel's fault, but someone needed to pay for the failure. Orwell's eyes grew white as he slipped his intention into the angel's consciousness. It felt like penetrating a wall, hardened brick slowly crumbling as he drilled through it exposing the soft ball of memories, feelings, and ideas that made all creatures what they were. Kaye had called them souls. Orwell had never cared enough about their composition to call them anything else, but he did use them once he realized how potent they could be. They were like food recharging him with each he consumed.

Chamuel's trembling increased to the point of convulsion as he fell to the floor and cried out his pleas in a choppy cadence, "Please...I do not write the stories...I merely recite them."

Orwell didn't care who wrote the stories. It was time for Chamuel's to end. It almost looked like smoke pouring from the angel's shaking form as he clung to all the bits that made him who he was. Orwell's muscles tensed. Angels were strong. He had made them that way for a reason. Kaye might have willed them into existence with the correct combination of characteristics to be the perfect things Orwell needed them to be, but he had honed them into the flawless creatures they were. Stripping their souls was a more difficult task than stripping the souls of any other beings.

Orwell's mouth opened, his jaw stretching and expanding until it appeared like a dark tunnel into the abyss. Chamuel was fighting him, grasping and pulling, wildly holding onto his existence. Orwell doubled his efforts, pressing deeper and deeper into the angel with force great enough to topple mountains.

Then there was a break. The resistance pushing back against his will crumbled. It was like a flood. Each memory, every feeling, and any idea Chamuel ever had poured into Orwell's consciousness as if he were experiencing those things the angel had experienced right in that moment as the angel's essence flowed into his mouth like thick smoke billowing off a dying flame doused with water.

Orwell began trembling. Every cell in his body tingled more strongly with each experience he stole from the angel. It continued to mount as Chamuel's body disintegrated to dust on the floor. Orwell tensed as the last bits of the angel filled him. Then it was like explosions erupting throughout his entire body. It felt as if each of his cells orgasmed simultaneously. He cried out as the experience reached a crescendo that left him gasping and spent in his chair.

A shiver raced through his body as he exhaled and sunk deeper into the soft leather of his seat. The corners of his mouth turned up into a satisfied smile. The sensation wouldn't last, but for the moment, he felt better. He slid the center drawer of his desk open and retrieved a cigarette. He shivered again before lighting it and dragging hard.

Then he glanced at the spot where Chamuel's existence had ended and said, "Thank you for your service, mighty angel."

CHAPTER 22

CHANGING PLANS

PERVER CITY

S tars sparkled brightly in the clear sky above. It hadn't occurred to Bale before that moment, but the bright lights of Perver City should have obscured all but the brightest stars. The sky above him looked like the twinkling brilliance nestled above a black desert. Anything goes.

He tugged at the tight tuxedo Kaye had dressed him in as she led him out of a swank high-rise. Most everybody milling about the place worked for her. The ones who didn't were just there trying to snap a picture or get a look. She was like a celebrity soaking it in, waving at her adoring fans as she strolled through throngs of people all dressed to the nines. Even the doorman was decked out like he was bound for some kind of award ceremony.

Bale leaned closer to Kaye's ear and complained, "I can't move in this fucking thing."

"Relax, lover," Kaye flashed a smile at him, "We're going to a party. You won't have to kill anything."

The doorman opened the back door of the stretched limo waiting for them at the curb. Bale slipped in behind Kaye. It was the same car she'd taken him to the first time he'd met her. The memory turned the corners of his mouth up. She was something else.

Kaye didn't waste any time getting started. She was filling a flute with champagne before the car had even pulled away from the curb. Bale just watched her move, as he tugged at the uncomfortable costume she had dressed him in. He felt more like an accessory than a companion. Every being in her life was an accessory.

She glanced over at him and offered him a flute of champagne and a frown as she said, "Loosen up. You're so tense and serious all the time. Live a little."

He took the glass and sipped it before sighing, "This just doesn't feel right. My daughter's stuck with that creepy fucker while I'm off to party it up with the devil."

A little flash of red sparked in her eyes as she laughed and said, "Calm down. She'll be fine. Orwell wouldn't do anything stupid that might risk his bargaining chip. She's the only thing he has on you."

Bale let out a wry chuckle as he shook his head and said, "You're just the other side of the same coin."

She laughed before tilting her head back and draining her glass. She gave him a dramatic pout as she poured another and said, "Ouch, baby. That hurts."

"It's true though, isn't it? Do you know what they did to Azrael?" he pressed.

She sighed and rolled her eyes before dropping the act and letting a more serious expression settle onto her face. "It's a war, Bale," she finally said, "Been going on since me and the old man split. My boys would get the same or worse if Orwell caught them. Don't get hung up about it. They're all vicious cunts."

"I can't argue with that," Bale replied with a numbness in his tone. After a healthier pull off his drink he continued, "How long are you going to play with me before you help me get my daughter back like you promised? Why am I still here?"

"You said you don't know anything about me. Well, I know everything about you. You have a big heart, but all that space is consumed by your daughter. I need to know I can trust you with my son's soul. I need to be certain you can free up a little space in that big heart for him, and I need to know that once you leave, you won't be coming back for him with an army of Orwell's angels at your back," her expression remained serious as she broke it down for him.

"I'm a man of my word," Bale argued despite knowing the effort was futile.

"We're talking about my son, Bale. No man's word would ever be enough," she replied as she slid back in her seat and stared out the window.

It was obvious the conversation was over. He must have hit a nerve.

Lou was her Achilles' heel. All the confidence she'd been oozing since he met her fled like rodents ahead of a coming storm. She was scared. He'd have to play along.

Kaye remained quiet as she stared out the window for the rest of the long ride. A couple of times Bale thought about changing the topic and maybe attempting some small talk. Something held his tongue. She didn't look like she had anything more to say. It seemed best to leave her be. It was a blessing when the car finally stopped. Kaye's demeanor changed as soon as it did. She was back in character, the mayor of Perver City, the queen of hell.

The building stretched more than a mile up into a starry sky. As Bale craned his neck to try and see its top, he was certain no structure could ever be so tall, but there it was before him stretching up to the heavens.

Kaye leaned closer to him and said, "Lou's penthouse is on the six hundred and sixty sixth floor. It was his idea. He really likes numbers, derives meaning from them. I've never been overly interested in it, but it has something to do with the number three. Anyway, that is where any reference to the number of the beast you have ever heard comes from."

Despite all the floors, the elevator ride was short. Kaye seemed to slip out of character whenever they were out of the public eye. She was afraid, but he couldn't understand why. She could end him with a thought if he tried anything.

"I never would," she responded though he hadn't said anything out loud, "I'm not the other side of Orwell's coin like you think I am. I love all my creations with my whole heart because they are precisely what I made them to be. There is no wrath or judgement. I'm not like him. He demands worship. I simply want them to experience everything they want to experience. Watching them do that is where I get my joy, and I do the same."

"Make good on our deal, and you can trust me. If you don't, I can't make any promises," Bale shrugged.

The elevator door opened before Kaye could respond. Instead, she slipped right back into character, waving and shouting to the crowd, "Mama's here, babies. Who's got goodies for me."

Bale stepped back as Kaye was swarmed by every kind of creature Bale had ever seen, and even more he hadn't. Most were naked or half-dressed as they hugged, kissed, or lay on the ground before her so she could walk over them. A vampire even bit her. She didn't flinch as he lapped up her blood. It didn't last long. There must have been something special about Kaye's blood. Bale counted three licks before the guy's cock started pulsing, and he came all over her leg. She didn't bat an eye. She just reached down and stroked the big, veiny thing to squeeze out the last few drops.

The rest of Lou's penthouse was like the after party to end all after parties. It made New Eden seem tame. Everybody in the joint was licking, fucking, or sucking something. The ones who weren't were drinking, shooting, or snorting. Except for one guy. His skin was pale red, not like a sunburn. The shade seemed too natural. He had long, black hair that shined in the dim lights oozing off all the random chandeliers dotting the ceiling in no discernable pattern. Two massive horns protruded from the front of his cranium. They were as black and shiny as obsidian. The guy was all by himself and crying while he repeatedly punched the massive cock stretching before him. Bale couldn't possibly know what that big dick had done to deserve the teary beating it was getting, but it was huge. It had to be at least a foot and a half long and as girthy as Bale's forearm.

It was all too much. Bale had been alive a long time and thought he'd seen just about everything. There wasn't much that could shock him. Lou's party succeeded in doing that. It wasn't just all the people getting into whatever freaky shit they could with whomever would entertain their random kinks. Even the décor of the place was unsettling. It was like somebody threw a mountain of cash at Timothy Corrigan and Ryan Korban and told them to fuck shit up. Then the two of them got together and went to town. There was a pool, bar, piano, and a dance floor. And that was just the foyer. None of it matched anything else. It was the most eclectic collection of shit Bale had ever seen.

Then there was that part of him that wasn't quite dead yet after centuries of hunting poor souls down and sentencing them to oblivion. He actually felt something for Kaye. It was something he didn't want to feel, but he couldn't help it. It was probably what everybody else in the joint felt for her, and she aimed to please. He tried to shake it off as he watched a werewolf all hairy and smelly slip Kaye's skirt up, bend her over the grand piano in the middle of the room, and start slamming his cock in her. She just went with it, swaying back and forth before pushing back against his thrusts. Then some red-headed broad slid across the piano and wrapped her thighs around Kaye's head. By the time the wolf man was blowing his wad in her, she was sucking on the red head's clit. Everybody was screaming and moaning. And it didn't stop. They just kept cumming.

"Kaye," he raised his voice as he shouted to her. When she just kept sucking on the red head, he shouted louder, "Kaye. I'm done with this shit. I want to get the fuck out of here."

"Okay, lover," she said to the red head as she lifted the woman's leg up higher and smacked her on the ass adding, "Mama's got work to do. We'll finish this later." Then she turned to the wolf, grabbed his cock and said, "And you. I'm not finished with you yet either."

She was still fixing her dress when Bale laid into her, "What the fuck, Kaye? Do you know how fucked up it sounds when you call yourself mama while you're fucking these freaks, like they're you're fucking kids or something?"

Kaye crossed her arms and cocked her head to one side before giving it back to him, "Whoa, big guy. Slow down. What I do with my body and who I do it with is none of your fucking business."

"I know," Bale muttered quietly, "It's just too much for me. I want to get the fuck out of here."

"How about you loosen up and have some fun, you prude," she said as she playfully smacked his ass.

"Stop it," he couldn't believe the words coming out of his mouth, but he really wanted her to stop. Then he sighed and said, "Look, you said you wanted me to meet Lou. Can I please just do that and then get the fuck out of this circus?"

Kaye looked genuinely disappointed as she shrugged and said, "Fine. I didn't think you'd break so easily." Then she turned to the biggest guy in the room—he looked like he was about to bust right out of his tux—and asked, "Where's Lou?"

The guy's voice didn't fit his build. He sounded like a choir boy as he nearly sung, "He's in the back, boss. You know, writing and shit."

Kaye rolled her eyes and said, "I swear, had that boy not squirted out of me... Why isn't he out here, living, experiencing every little pleasure of the flesh?"

The big guy just shrugged and said, "You know Lou. He's different, always up in his thoughts."

"What a waste," she sighed before grabbing Bale by the collar and saying, "He reminds me of you, all serious and sad. Come on. Let's go meet my pride and joy."

Lou's bedroom looked like a dorm for rich geniuses. Books and papers littered the floor, but the furnishings were opulent elegance. The bed was a massive stone thing with a canopy covered in vines and golden fabrics draped about it. It looked like it had never been slept in.

Lou was a sight. He made the angels look like a pack of scrubs. His dark hair was like waves on a chaotic ocean. Somehow, it just made the guy look hotter. Everything about him was perfect. His chin wasn't too sharp or too soft. His cheeks weren't too high or too low. Even the sadness haunting his eyes only served to make him more attractive. Bale couldn't stop staring at him as he sat behind a simple desk feverishly scribbling on a parchment with a quill. It wasn't quite jealousy slithering through Bale's mind, but it was probably close to it.

Before either Kaye or Bale could say anything, Lou slammed his fist on the desk and violently crumpled up the parchment he'd been writing on. Then he angrily tossed it at the ground to cavort with similar crumpled up parchments and shouted, "No, no, no...damn it! Why will you words not obey?"

Kaye glanced about the room with disgust coloring her expression. Then she smiled at Lou and asked, "Are the words misbehaving again, son?"

"Mother, please, leave me with my thoughts. I'm working," Lou snapped. His voice was even prettier than his face.

"You're always working, dear," Kaye pouted, "Take a break. I want you to meet the flavor of the day."

"More meat? Lovely. You're insatiable," Lou scoffed. Then he shot a narrow glare at Bale and asked, "Should I call this one, daddy while he's around?"

"I'm just passing through, kid," Bale shrugged.

Kaye laughed, "No, darling. He's here to kidnap you."

Lou's expression suddenly changed. Tense concentration and irritation were replaced with something that looked like sheer elation. He jumped up and ran toward Bale, fell to his knees, and grabbed his hand.

"Are you him? Could it really be? Mother's been telling me that story for eons. I thought she was simply trying to convince herself he still cared," Lou's words came so fast Bale thought he might pass out.

Bale was dumbfounded as he replied, "Well, yeah, I guess that is why I'm here. Kind of thought it would be more of a struggle."

Lou stood and hugged Bale tight. There were tears raining down his cheeks when he said, "I want to meet him. It's all I've ever wanted. Will you take me to him?"

"I don't think…" Bale began before Kaye cut him off.

"You're not going anywhere," she pointed at Lou as she interrupted.

Lou's eyes suddenly went wild with malice as he charged at Kaye as if he meant to strike her. He stopped right in front of her and shouted in her face, "Yes, I am. You can't stop me." Then he pointed at Bale and added, "Him, that man you've been telling me about for millennia, is my ticket out of here."

Kaye crossed her arms and cocked her head to the side as she sighed, "I told you that to scare you. I didn't think you'd want to go."

Bale loosened his tie and unbuttoned the top few buttons of his shirt. Then he shook his head and said, "Look, I don't want to get in the middle of a family squabble, but I don't think you get what's happening here. Your dad's not a good guy. He's a horrible cunt."

"He is cruel and heartless. He can't kill me, so he'll destroy you instead," she grabbed Lou's arm as she implored him.

It looked like honest emotion oozing from Kaye's eyes, but Bale still couldn't tell when she was being earnest and when she was playing a character. Either way, she was completely accurate. Orwell had nothing but nefarious plans for her boy.

"Pretty sure that's his plan, kid," Bale finally said.

Then Lou shifted his fiery gaze back to Bale and said, "Stop calling me, kid. Do you know how old I am?"

Bale lost an unfortunate chuckle. The guy looked like he was in his early twenties. "Sorry," he finally said, "You're just… Well, you look great for…"

"I've been stuck in this room for hundreds of thousands of years," Lou interrupted, "They come, and they come, and they come, and no one can leave without her blessing. That is, until the promise of you, my glorious savior. Will you be the hero who breaks me out of this prison?"

"He won't let you work," Kaye cried. The tears raining down her cheeks made it obvious this was a conversation she'd had more than once before, "He won't love you. He will suffocate you, destroy you."

"Oblivion," Bale nearly whispered.

Lou started pacing quickly back and forth between them, wildly waving his arms as he spoke, "She tells me stories. You tell me stories. That is all I have of him, stories. I'd like to make my own decision, write my own story."

Tears continued to rain down Kaye's cheeks as she looked over at Bale and said, "He's a great writer, my Lou. Shakespeare? That bum never had an original idea in his life. Every story he ever told was whispered into his ear from the lips of my son."

"Enough with the drama, mother," Lou shouted at Kaye as he continued pacing. Then he shifted his attention to Bale and continued, "I can't write anything. All these brilliant ideas skitter in, and I can't capture them. They're too scattered. I can only whisper them into the ears of real writers. I had hoped my father could help me organize my thoughts. Finishing something I have started, that, my friend, would be heaven to me."

"He could do that," Bale nodded, "He does like things in order, very particular. But I don't think he would."

"That is what I need, order," Lou stopped pacing and pointed toward the sky as if to say, "Eureka." He didn't say that. Instead, he turned back to Kaye and nearly growled, "You are the reason I am unable to put together a cognizant thought. You are chaos. Look at this," he waved both arms dramatically about the room, "I am drowning in your glory."

"That is enough. You sound just like him," Kaye shouted after wiping away the last of her tears. Then she turned to Bale and said, "Come, lover. Leave the genius to his work."

Bale reluctantly followed Kaye to the door. He didn't want to leave. Her plan was for him to get to know Lou. After listening to him for a few minutes, he wanted to do that. The guy was a puzzle. He had a brilliant mind, but in hundreds of thousands of years, he hadn't figured out how to escape his perfect prison.

He stopped Kaye at the door and said, "Hey, you mind if I…"

"Oh fuck," she groaned, "Fine, go ahead, get to know him, become bosom chums even. I'll go find somebody else to scratch my itch."

CHAPTER 23

THE MUSE

PERVER CITY

The world seemed to slip away. The mess of books and gaudy, unmatched furniture, even Lou reclining on an elegant chaise gazing out the window as he sipped wine disappeared as Bale sat on the floor reading parchment after parchment. It didn't feel like he was reading. He was looking at words and experiencing the meaning behind them. One moment, he felt such a deep joy he couldn't help but laugh out loud. The next moment, he was sobbing, brought to the lowest point of his life while a vast emptiness expanded in his gut. He soared through crystal skies and even to space, racing comets and rocketing past planets ominous as they loomed against the darkness. He sat next to an old woman and held her frail hand as she breathed her last. It was no one he knew, but the loss he felt at that moment ripped at his heart.

Tears rained freely down Bale's cheek as he looked up from the uncrumpled parchment and said, "Fuck, man. That's beautiful. My heart hurts."

"It's crap," Lou muttered without moving his gaze from the window.

Bale stood and fetched a decorative glass from a shelf housing a random collection of odd things that didn't fit with each other. There were a couple of wine glasses, a random smattering of books, an ornate knife with a handle that looked like a dragon's face, a bunch of crumpled up pieces of parchment, and other various odds and ends.

He walked over to Lou, held the glass out, and asked, "You mind?"

Lou obliged, filling Bale's glass to the rim before topping off his own.

Bale sat down on the floor next to Lou and sipped his wine. He swirled the glass gently as he stared into it without really seeing it. After a few moments of quiet, he asked, "Do you know what I do for a living?"

"You gather lost souls," Lou replied without looking at him.

"That makes it sound pretty nice," Bale chuckled, "It ain't that. You know the light they talk about? I suppose you probably don't."

"The light," Lou nodded, still staring out the window, "Of course, I do. Everyone here stepped into the light. I love their stories. I listen."

Bale took another sip of his wine and said, "Well, some people are supposed to go in, and some aren't. From what I hear, at that moment, they know. One way or another, they know. The ones who are supposed to go in and don't, I get their file."

"And you lead them to the light. It's quite noble really," Lou replied.

"No, it isn't," Bale scoffed, "I don't do it for them. I don't give a fuck about them. As far as I know, I'm leading the sheep to slaughter. My daughter, she's the only thing I care about. I don't give a fuck about you. You seem nice, but the way I see it, I'm here to collect you so your dad can eat you. What's that say about me?"

Lou finally turned his gaze away from the window to stare into Bale's eyes. It made him feel small. Lou's eyes were mesmerizing, somehow beautiful and terrifying all at the same time. He just stared like that for a moment before finally responding, "You love your daughter above all else. That is what it says about you. Is that not what a father is meant to do? Why are you surprised I want to meet mine?"

Bale dropped his eyes to the floor. Matching Lou's stare made him want to cry fresh rivulets of sorrow to rain down his already soaked cheeks. Once his mind settled to a place that wasn't nestled right at the edge of insanity, he said, "That's fair, but it seems like you have this fucked up, biblical idea of who your dad is. Whatever you think of him, believe me, he isn't that. What I do ain't guiding people to the light. It's more like dragging them to their doom."

Lou leaned closer, suddenly excited. "You've seen it?" he asked.

"A few times," Bale answered numbly as he stared at a wall that vanished in favor of a vivid memory he wished he could wash away, "It's something I wish could unsee. It's like he sucks their souls right out of them until there is nothing left."

"Oneness with god," Lou shrugged, "Is that not precisely what heaven is supposed to be, belonging to a consciousness greater than oneself, spiritual bliss?"

Bale scratched his head as he replied, "Maybe, I guess, but it doesn't look like that. You know, I had these two guns I got from Azrael…"

"I heard what they did to him, animals," Lou scowled as he interrupted.

"It was fucked up. But these guns, when I shot fuckers with them, it looked a lot like when your dad sets a soul free. Is it bliss? Is it oblivion? I don't know. I guess nobody does, but it doesn't look good," Bale replied.

"I'll take my chances," Lou said before sipping his wine and shifting his gaze back to the window.

Bale sipped his wine and shook his head before asking, "You really want to meet him?"

Lou rubbed his head as he continued to stare out the window. A subtle hint of annoyance slipped into his tone when he replied, "I am unable to think of way to say it more clearly. There is nothing else that I want. This is it."

"I'd love to help, but I can't get us out of here. I'm as stuck as you," Bale shrugged.

"That's easy," Lou clapped his hands and smiled as he turned back toward Bale, "I can. I designed this place."

Bale's eyebrows dipped toward his nose as he replied, "You designed Perver City?"

"No," Lou chuckled, "You can thank my mother for that. This building. There is an elevator behind the bookshelf. It leads right to my car, and Boss Yaaz knows nothing about it."

"Boss Yaaz, she's something else," Bale lost himself in thoughts about the back of her limo. Then he shook his head and added, "You may be able to get us out of this building, but I can't get us out of Perver City. Your mom's goons blew up my GPS."

"It will not be easy, but there is a way," Lou smiled.

Bale paused. Both options before him seemed like bad bets. On the one hand, he could lead Kaye's goons to Orwell's doorstep and help her fight the forever war she and the big guy had been waging against each other since the beginning of time. But could he trust she could do everything she said? Obviously, there had to be another way to get souls into Perver City. Orwell was able to get Azrael in as a spy. Kaye probably had her own spies littered about the City of Gold. She lost one battle. Bale wasn't convinced her guys would do any better with another crack at it.

On the other hand, he could help a wayward soul find the father he'd been kept from his entire life. The latter seemed vastly nobler than the former, but neither came with a guarantee of Angel Cakes' safety. Once Orwell was hip to either scam, the jig would be up. Bale shuddered at the thought of what that sick fuck would do to his little girl once he knew the contract had been breached.

Maybe it was the wine. Maybe it was the hurt he felt knowing Kaye didn't see him as anything more than a toy, a faceless scratch to whatever itch was troubling her at any given moment. Maybe he was just a sucker for sob stories. Whatever the reason, he knew he was going to help Lou.

"Alright," he finally said, "I don't think it's going to be what you expect, but I'll do whatever I can to get you to your father."

Lou jumped from the chaise, dragged Bale up from the floor by his shoulders, and hugged him. Then he sang a few words in a language Bale didn't recognize. His voice was like a choir of angels. "You are a savior from heaven," Lou finally said, his voice still as beautiful as a song, "If we succeed, I will owe you my life. If we fail, neither of us will owe anyone anything."

Bale didn't like the sound of that last bit, yet his spirit still soared. Some odd nobility stomped around his mind, like he had some purpose greater than the universe itself. It wasn't that, and this mission was anything but some universally great thing. Still, his pulse quickened with excitement as he was swept up in Lou's bold proclamation of their glorious purpose.

"We should depart straight away before my mother returns," Lou said as he released Bale from his embrace.

"Don't you need to pack anything?" Bale asked as Lou quickly guided him to the bookshelf.

"There is nothing I need but this gift you are giving me," Lou replied earnestly as he tilted a book toward him causing the bookshelf to slide left along the wall.

Then they were in. There were no buttons or markings in the car. Apparently, Lou had designed it with one destination. The car began rapidly descending as soon as the doors closed. It almost felt like a free fall. The butterflies suddenly swarming in Bale's belly reminded him of a case he'd had a few decades back. He'd found his mark on an airplane. Getting the correct coordinates to arrive on a fast-moving target had been a trick. He ended up in the bathroom. When he placed his hand on his target's shoulder, shit went sideways. The guy had surprised Bale with an elbow after he jumped up. Then he opened the emergency exit and dipped right out the door. Bale followed him. They had nearly splattered on the ground by the time Bale caught up to him and used his GPS to zap them both out of that reality ten seconds before impact. He had that same feeling in his gut while plummeting toward the ground that day.

Thankfully, the elevator began slowing down about ten seconds before it stopped. When the doors opened back up, Bale was looking at a small, private garage filled with exotic cars that all looked like sex on wheels. Bale headed straight for a shiny, black... He couldn't tell if it was a Lamborghini, a Ferrari, or something else. It didn't have any markings. Knowing Lou, it was probably some custom thing he had imagined and built for himself. Bale stood by the gorgeous car until he realized Lou had gone in a different direction.

Lou was climbing into a clunky, beige thing that looked like a Corolla when he yelled over to Bale, "Hurry up. Once mother finds us missing... What is it they say? Oh yes, all hell is going to break loose."

"Isn't this your car?" disappointment dripped from Bale's voice as he asked the question.

"Of course, they all are, but I never drive it, too pretentious. Besides, it would no doubt be best for us to avoid standing out as much as we can."

"Damn," Bale muttered as he jogged over to the unassuming, beige sedan, "I was going to ask if I could drive."

CHAPTER 24

THAT BIRD HAS FLOWN

PERVER CITY

It had been long enough. Lou's unintentional charisma should have lulled Bale into an unbreakable spell hours ago. If he wasn't convinced by this point that Lou should never meet his father, he never would be. Now Kaye just needed to pry a bit to find out if her pride and joy had been successful.

She pushed the door open and slipped into the room like fog floating over still water as she said, "I trust you boys have had plenty of time to get to know each other and discuss the minutiae of the father-son…"

She stopped dead in her tracks. The room was empty except for Lou's customary mess. Her clever boy had obviously duped Bale into helping him. The half empty wine glasses and uncrumpled parchments told the story well enough. He plied him with wine and beautiful words. She should have known better than to leave Bale alone with him. He could convince anyone of anything, persuasive little shit.

"Mammon! Berith! Get in here now," she shouted at the ceiling.

Mammon and Berith arrived so quickly it seemed they'd been waiting outside the door. That was good. The mood she was in didn't include anything close to patience. She might have done something unfortunate had they made her wait.

Both the things standing before her looked identical, save the color of their eyes and hair. She'd gotten used to the fact that Orwell had slowly changed her perfect angels over time to look the same, but it had troubled her ever since she realized what he had done. What a lack of imagination. Shouldn't perfection come with at least a little variety? Perhaps, it was just as silly that she made them all dress the same in their leather jackets and black sunglasses.

"Yeah, boss?" Mammon asked before glancing around the room and adding, "Where's Lou?"

Despite the dark shades covering the fallen angel's eyes, Kaye could see the fear in them. He knew something. She replied, "It appears he's gone on an adventure with our new guest. What do you know about that?"

"How?" Berith asked. "We've been standing outside his door all night."

Kaye offered a terrifying smile as she replied, "If I were to guess, I'd say he took his secret little elevator down to the garage."

"You know about that?" Mammon asked with a bit of shock coloring his tone. He should have kept his mouth shut.

Kaye's smile grew increasingly ominous as she asked, "Did you?"

Mammon didn't respond. He just looked at the ground and trembled beneath her horrible gaze.

She shifted her attention to Berith and asked, "What about you?"

There was no fear in Berith's eyes as he stood tall and replied, "No ma'am. I didn't know anything about any elevator until just now."

"Would you have told me if you had?" she asked without softening her piercing gaze in the slightest.

"Yes ma'am," Berith replied without hesitation.

Trust was critical. She understood her own nature well enough to know she required complete focus from her boys. Lou was good at convincing people to do things that weren't in their best interest, but she needed her crew to be stronger than that. Her mind fluttered too quickly from one thing to the next. She had to demand more from them.

Kaye continued to pierce Mammon with her stare as she said, "Hear that, Mammon? That is what loyalty sounds like. Do you remember life under Orwell? Have you forgotten all his rules and punishments?"

"Yeah boss," Mammon replied, his voice barely more than a whisper.

"What a dark time. I hated it. I much prefer the freedom we've found since chasing him off," she began as she approached him. Then she placed her hand on his shoulder and gently dragged it across his back as she circled him adding, "But, in order to enjoy these freedoms, a team needs trust. I can't trust you. Berith, kill him. Then fetch Abigor and meet me in the garage."

She kept her gaze focused on Mammon's eyes as the shot rang out. She took his hand and held it tight until he evaporated. "I am sorry, my love," she whispered as the last bits of shimmering dust blinked out of existence, "I hate to punish. Am I becoming a monster just like him?"

Abigor and Berith were already in the garage waiting by the time Kaye arrived. They stood in the empty spot where that crappy, beige sedan Lou favored any time he needed to drive should have been parked. She walked over to her favorite of his collection. It was red and sleek. It looked like it was going one thousand miles per hour even when parked.

"Why wouldn't he take this one?" Kaye asked as Abigor and Berith approached.

"Lou's smart, boss. This car sticks out like a swollen pecker in tight, white panties," Abigor replied.

Abigor was a bit larger than the rest of Kaye's boys. Though he looked identical to all his brothers, Orwell had come up with some kind of hierarchy when he'd adjusted her minions to make them his own. Kaye never cared enough to understand it. All she cared about was that Abigor was strong, vicious, and effective. He'd get the job done.

Kaye moved closer to Abigor, stretching to get as close to his ear as possible as she said, "Find my son and bring him to me."

"That's easier said than done, boss. Orwell can't track him any more like you wanted, but that means we can't either," Abigor replied without a shred of fear in his voice. That was what she needed. Most of her boys would tremble at the thought of disappointing her. Abigor feared nothing, not even oblivion.

"They're going to the well. I'm sure of it," Kaye kept her mouth close to his ear as she replied.

"Buzzard's Canyon? Perfect," Abigor smiled something wicked as he asked, "Can we finish the tourist off?"

"No," Kaye shook her head as she stepped away from him and continued, "I haven't decided what I want to do with him yet. Do your best to keep the casualties to a minimum."

Disappointment dripped from Abigor's tone as he replied, "Whatever you say, boss. I'll do my best, but it's like fighting with one hand tied behind my back."

CHAPTER 25

ROAD TRIP

PERVER CITY

It felt like every eye they passed was staring at them as Bale tried to sink as far into his seat as he could. He'd feel a bit better about things if he still had those wonderful golden pistols Azrael died for gifting him. Lou seemed unaffected by it all, loose and aloof as he slipped through heavy traffic past New Eden. He even had the radio blaring some god-awful classical nonsense. That simply wouldn't do. This was a getaway. It didn't really feel that way as calm as Lou remained, but Bale needed something with a little soul and some tempo. He reached for the dial on the radio.

"Do not dare change that station," Lou snapped without taking his eyes off the road, "This was a rare moment in your history. Eroica is possibly the finest work to come out of your potentiality. You should sit quietly and consider each glorious note, revel in the soaring and triumphant melodies as they exude steadily rising feelings of triumph. I mean, are you not filled with a complete sense of liberty? Is it not as if you could do anything your heart desired?"

"Not really," Bale shrugged and settled back into his chair wondering if he and Lou were listening to the same song as it droned on far too long. He glanced out the window at the diminishing population milling about and the sudden scarcity of buildings and asked, "So, where are we headed?"

"A place you should love," Lou raised his voice as the song still pouring loudly from the speakers reached a crescendo as if he were adding lyrics to the notes. Then he added in more measured tones, "It's reminiscent of… Give me a second. In your potentiality, it would be somewhere in the mid to late eighteen hundreds. Where were you hanging your hat in those days?"

Bale shook his head, "I learned a long time ago to never stay in the same place for too long. When everybody else gets older and you don't, they start to ask questions."

"I can see how that would be problematic," Lou nodded before adding, "It probably does not help that your job keeps you skipping from dimension to dimension to track your bounties."

"That is very true. My head has yet to rest on a worn pillow," Bale concurred.

"Has it ever rested on a pillow in the wild west?" Lou asked.

"Quite a few times," the revelation brought an unconscious smile to Bale's face, "I liked it there."

"Perfect," Lou beamed, "Buzzard's Canyon is like that. We need to hurry. The sun will be rising soon."

Bale offered a sideways glance as he asked, "What are we going to do, hide out all day?"

"In a sense. I have a room at a small inn that no one knows about. Well, I suppose it is more of a saloon with some rooms than a proper inn, but I have a good friend there who appreciates my desire to get away from time to time. He will ensure no one bothers us as we wait out the sunset," Lou shot Bale a wink as he reached down and changed the radio station to some kind of hard pounding heavy metal.

###

It looked like the wild west, and everyone there was playing the part. The men wore cowboy hats and gun belts as they walked about one long stretch of buildings, the only road in town. The women accompanying the would-be gunslingers were clad in simple blouses, long skirts, and bonnets. Abigor soaked it all in as he rolled past the wooden facades on a chopper. He fit right in with the worn leather trench coat flapping in the wind behind him, and the leather cowboy hat shading his face from the sun. The motorcycle rumbling between his legs was a different story.

He led a line of black SUVs kicking a cloud of dust high into the air like a modern gang rolling into a time warp. It wasn't the first time he'd had to lead a mission to collect Lou. Boss Yaaz's pride and joy had a habit of getting himself lost on useless adventures.

Abigor pulled his black chopper up to a weathered old joint with a long porch, a big, dirty window that had been broken more times than Abigor could remember, and a couple of double-swinging doors he liked to toss folks out of whenever he got the chance. He smiled up at the sign that read, *Earl's Last Chance Saloon.* It was his favorite spot in all of Perver City.

Abigor backed his bike up in front of a hitching post next to the handful of horses tied to it. The fact those horses didn't care much for all the rumbling out of Abigor's pipes was obvious by all the stamping and whinnying they got up to. He chuckled at them as he shut the bike down and dismounted. He'd barely gotten off the thing when some poor sucker came flying ass over tea kettle right out of his favorite café doors.

A tough looking hombre with a tight jaw, thick neck, and bushy mustache in dire need of a trim charged out the doors after the man who'd just flown through them. The latter was just getting back to his feet when old bushy face launched himself at the guy's midsection. They both toppled into the street throwing punches and elbows as they rolled over and over again. Abigor hadn't even noticed the other two guys squaring off high-noon style in the middle of the road. The two combatants from Earl's were right in the crossfire when they stood back up to continue their scuffle. Two shots rang out, and two sorry suckers hit the dirt.

His smile widened as he stretched out his arms and said, "I love this place."

He knew it wasn't real death, just part of the game. Those same two suckers had probably been having the same fight for years. Getting caught in the crossfire of somebody else's fantasy was probably a surprise, but that was the fun of it. Anything goes.

Berith approached wearing the customary leather and shades the rest of the crew wore. He was such a tight wad. He could never let go and lean into the illusion. He was all business.

"I know, I know," Abigor held up his hands, "We need to get all our pieces in position before we can have any fun, killjoy."

"Boss Yaaz is pissed. She wants Lou back right away. We don't have time to fuck around," Berith shrugged.

"Yeah, yeah," Abigor waved him off before shooting hand signals to all the guys exiting the SUVs who responded by heading off in different directions. Then he looked back at Berith and said, "See, no big deal. We're ready to roll once we find that little twirp."

Bale's head was swimming as he lounged on a lumpy mattress in the middle of a sparsely decorated room. There was one picture of some guy dressed like a sheriff and wearing a ten-gallon hat. Bale couldn't read the little plate on the bottom of the thing. He was half a bottle into some kind of booze, and his vision was a bit blurry. The rest of the décor amounted to a small nightstand, a short bureau, and a simple desk where Lou was seated writing again. The guy was always writing. This time he was using a scratch pad and a rude pencil. Whatever he was doodling away on that thing was probably brilliant.

Bale took a long pull off the bottle in his hand, then held it up toward Lou and said, "This is almost whiskey…almost. But way fucking stronger. My toes are tingling."

If Lou had heard him, he didn't let on. He just kept on scratching away with his pencil.

Bale made an attempt at sitting up. The room shifted violently when he did. Dizziness swept in to flop him off the bed. Landing hard on his back, he managed to keep the bottle upright and not spill a drop. Spilling booze was a sin.

As he lay on the dusty floor watching the ceiling spin slowly and then shift back again and again, he glanced over at Lou and said, "Hey, I thought I couldn't get drunk here."

Lou finally stopped writing long enough to shake his head, look down at Bale, and say, "What joy would there be in drinking if it left your faculties unscathed? You can get drunker than you have ever been here and not die. That is the entire point of this place, total physical bliss."

Bale giggled, attempted getting to his feet again, fell back down, and said, "I'll take that bet."

"I truly wish you would not," Lou sighed, "I need you to have some wits left when we take on that well."

It was a struggle, but Bale managed to pull himself up enough to sit with his back against the bed. Once as stable as he could hope to be in that moment, he took another long pull off the not quite whiskey he was drinking and slurred, "What is that you're writing there?"

Lou rolled his eyes as he got back to scratching away on his pad and said, "Nothing, really, just some notes about our adventure."

"What adventure?" Bale scoffed, "We drove from your building to this saloon and got a room."

Lou continued scratching away as he replied, "That is a loose approximation of a group of facts from your perspective. There is so much more to the story than that. There are reasons and feelings, emotions. We're fugitives now. That is something."

###

Abigor stood like a titan outside the doors of Earl's place and cased the joint. There was a pack of rough-looking drunks lined up at the bar pounding shots, puffing out their chests, and eyeing each other up. None of them would be an issue. There were a handful of tables hosting card games. None of the participants looked like they posed a problem for anyone except maybe somebody playing against them with one too many cards up their sleeves. A few prostitutes worked the crowd shoving their cleavage into patrons' faces, peddling their wares.

Earl was in his customary spot behind the bar. The big bald spot in the middle of his head was red from too much sun or too much whiskey, or maybe a combination of the two. The silver hair remaining along the sides of his head was stringy and wild. It flopped about while the poor guy hustled up a storm trying to keep all of them cowboys drinking and happy.

Lou was nowhere to be found.

Abigor forced a smile onto his face as he glared at Earl and said, "Hi there, Earl. It's been a while. Don't suppose you've seen Lou lately, have you?"

As soon as Earl looked up, Abigor knew he was going to lie to him. The color drained from his face faster than the cowboys he was serving were draining their shots. When the music stopped abruptly, it was just more evidence. The entire place got quiet. They were all terrified, but he knew nobody in the place would say anything unless he pushed. Why did everybody love that jackass so much?

He kept his steely gaze locked on Earl's eyes as he pushed through the saloon doors, stalked toward the bar, and said, "Don't stop the party on my account. I'm just in town looking for an old friend."

Earl picked up a glass and began nervously wiping it. His voice trembled when he replied, "Hey there, Abigor. Lou ain't been 'round these parts in…golly, I can't even say how long. It's been a stretch. Why not pull up a stool and take a load off?"

Menace danced about Abigor's smile as he looked around the room and said, "I don't know, Earl. Everybody in the place suddenly looks like somebody walked over all their graves at once, and if you ain't shit your pants yet, I'm thinking that mess can't be too far off."

It was disappointing more than anything else when Earl nervously glanced at his bar back—some pimple-faced teen who'd probably found the light trying to strangle himself while jacking off—who less than subtly hurried toward the stairs at the back of the bar. Abigor actually liked the game, the cat and mouse he had to play to get information out of folks who'd rather not share, but he couldn't stand liars who refused to give up the act even when they knew they were caught. He couldn't blame Earl for getting sucked in by Lou and trying to protect him. Everybody did. At some point, you've just got to come clean.

Abigor didn't hide his disappointment as he watched the boy go and said, "Are you telling me Lou doesn't have a room upstairs?"

For a moment, it looked like Earl might drop the act and spill the beans, but it was gone as fast as it came. Instead, the terrified barkeep stammered, "Well, now, not that I know of, but that don't mean it ain't so. I've got lots of helpers who don't always tell me everything."

The doors suddenly slammed open as Berith ran into the room and shouted, "They found Lou's car. It's parked behind the building."

It felt like heartbreak as Abigor watched the rest of the color leave Earl's face. He liked Earl, liked his bar. He really thought they were friends. The fact Earl could stand there and lie to his face to protect Lou proved he didn't feel the same way. Abigor sneered at the cowboy standing next to him and took the shot glass out of the guy's hand.

Then he looked back at Earl and said, "If there is one thing I hate more than…"

His plan was to slam the shot before finishing the statement with, babysitting, but he noticed something floating in the glass just before he shot. He set the glass down on the bar, grabbed the bottle and took a long pull.

Then he wiped his mouth and finished with, "…shit floating in my whiskey…"

"Please, Abigor, I didn't know," Earl begged as Abigor hauled a massive chrome revolver from the old, western style gun belt he was wearing.

BOOM! The hole in Earl's head barely had time to form before he evaporated into dust.

"...it's a god damned liar," Abigor finally finished his statement. Then he looked at the pimple-faced bar back who'd just returned and growled, "Boy, you tell Lou his ride is here and tell his friend there's an ass whoopin' waiting for him outside."

Then he drained the rest of the bottle and threw it against the wall smashing it into bits. He scowled at every face in the place as he stalked toward the door. He paused before exiting and said, "Y'all can go ahead and watch from the windows, but it's probably best if you stay inside."

CHAPTER 26

HIGH NOON

PERVER CITY

Bale sat on the floor leaning against the side of the bed. The frame mercilessly pressed on the middle of his back, but he didn't have the energy to do anything about it just then. Lou had gone back to writing about the adventure of an uneventful drive from one building to another. It would probably be beautiful. Everything the guy wrote was perfect. He could probably write five hundred pages describing a cantaloupe, and it would be a page turner. The words just worked for him. He could make them do things, lining them up in perfect order as if he were painting emotions on the page that were injected into your soul as soon as you read them.

Bale took another heavy pull off the near empty bottle of almost whiskey he'd been hammering. Cantaloupe was a funny word. Repeating it in his head several times got him giggling. His stomach grumbled. He could probably eat a whole cantaloupe just then.

He reached up to scratch an annoying itch on the top of his head and caught sight of his hand as it moved past his periphery. It looked funky, all loose and slippery. Focusing intently on it made him forget about the itch which sparked the movement in the first place. It seemed to vibrate as he stared at it and flipped it back and forth several times. His fingers seemed longer than he remembered. As he examined each digit, it occurred to him they were growing. That couldn't be right. He flexed them into a fist. Streaks of light followed them as they moved. It was like he was clawing through the scenery as if everything his eyes consumed was a façade loosely hiding reality. It reminded him of a time he unintentionally tried LSD. That hadn't been an identical experience, but he remembered how imaginary everything seemed, like he could rip right through it to find some kind of existential truth.

He glanced over at Lou to ask if his fingers were too long, but he was distracted by Lou's chin. It was longer than the last time he looked at him. It wobbled like a turkey's wattle every time he moved. It continued to stretch as he stared at it until it no longer resembled a turkey's wattle. The way it awkwardly bounced and jiggled it looked more like an old man's nut sack all stretched from age and dangling between his knees, flopping about with every movement. The idea got Bale giggling even harder. Lou had an old man's hairy nut sack for a chin.

Bale's giggle slowly mounted to a hearty laugh by the time Lou finally glanced over at him. His nut sack chin nearly swung all the way around his neck. That just made Bale laugh harder. He laughed so hard his head hurt. It only got worse when all the tightening of his gut from the laughter forced a fart out of him. He fell over to his side shaking with laughter.

Lou's voice sounded all slow and warbled when he sighed and said, "For the love of all that is holy, did you drink that entire bottle?"

The question barely registered with Bale. He heard and understood the words, but somehow, they got jumbled up when he tried to think about them. The only thing he could say was, "Your chin looks like a floppy, old nut sack," before the laughter took over and squeezed another fart out of him.

He barely heard Lou's slow voice say, "You had better have a nap and sleep that off. You are no good to me in this condition."

The crack of a gunshot followed by its rumbling report abruptly chased Bale's laughter away. It sounded like it went off right next to his ear. The room spun again when he looked up at Lou, ignored the nut sack dangling off his face, and slurred, "I think they found us."

"Those damned animals," Lou grunted as he stood and went to the window. "That was in the building."

The door suddenly swung open. Bale gripped the empty bottle in his hand. It occurred to him that his aim would be less than stellar, but it was the only weapon he had. He had to crawl to the edge of the bed to see who he'd be throwing it at. False alarm. It was the bar back who'd taken them to Lou's room when they arrived, but his face looked like a talking tomato.

"Lou…Abigor…" the kid was panting too hard to get a complete sentence out. He took a couple deep breaths to calm himself before adding, "Earl's dead, like real dead."

"That savage son of a bitch. That means we are caught," Lou complained before looking down at Bale and saying, "We will not be making it out of here today."

The world was still tipsy, turvy for Bale, but he was coming down fast. When the kid said, "He said to tell you your ride's here, and there's an ass whooping waiting in the street for your friend," it helped clear the cobwebs if only slightly.

Bale struggled to his feet. The room dipped one way and then shifted toward the other. It felt like he was standing on a small rowboat in rough water. He stumbled but managed to keep from falling over. The idea somebody thought they had an ass whooping for him pissed him off.

"An ass whooping, for me?" he said before stumbling a few steps along the bed. Luckily, the wall stopped his progress and prevented him from spilling himself back to the floor. Once he had his feet back under him, he added, "Who the fuck is Abigor?"

It seemed an afterthought when Lou glanced over and said, "He is mother's best, brutal and effective. According to her, he is also the one who snuck up on you and knocked you out in the garage. It seems you owe him one for that."

"Great," Bale muttered. He wasn't in any condition to fight anything. Even still, it was probably the booze talking, but he couldn't have some asshole walking around thinking he had an ass whooping waiting for him. His lack of any kind of weapon suddenly seemed troubling. He looked over at Lou and added, "I don't have a gun. Think Kaye lifted the no kill thing on me?"

"I hope not. You can barely stand much less dodge a bullet," Lou shrugged. He paced a few steps before turning, shaking his head, and adding, "No, if mother wanted you dead, Abigor would just walk in this room and shoot you. Instead, he sent this boy to lay a challenge at your feet. Either way, we are fucked."

Bale stumbled toward the window. There was a circle of people standing in the center of the road in front of the place. The jackass standing in the middle of the circle air boxing like he was getting ready for a professional fight had to be Abigor. He looked like a cosplay cowboy with his leather trench coat and silly hat.

Bale looked back at Lou and asked, "This fucking guy? Is he serious?"

"He is exceptionally morbid. He loves this place almost as much as he loves inflicting pain," Lou replied with no emotion coloring his tone, just the facts.

Bale continued to watch the guy work through his combos as he said, "It looks like he wants to have a fist fight with me, like he's got something to prove."

"He fancies himself as the best there is. There are some who suggest you hold that title. If I know Abigor as well as I think, he is greatly troubled by that. I would say he does have something to prove," Lou's tone remained flat and businesslike.

"Fuck that shit. I'm the best," Bale slurred as he stumbled a few steps away from the window.

"You are drunk," Lou cautioned.

"Very," Bale concurred. Then he looked back out the window again at all Kaye's goons circling around their champion and added, "You got my back? It doesn't look like I'm getting a fair fight out of this deal."

"I do not," Lou shook his head, "I abhor violence. However, for Abigor, this is a matter of pride. It will be one on one, and he will beat you until you give up or lose consciousness."

The sun was too bright glaring down from a cloudless sky. Bale had to shield his eyes. Closing them didn't help his equilibrium at all, so he didn't keep them shut for very long, opting to squint instead. At least he didn't have a headache. He had been equally drunk several times before, and it always felt like somebody was driving a spike into the center of his head. That would be worse. Thank Kaye for Perver City and its glorious lack of consequences.

Abigor was still shadow boxing in the center of all Kaye's goons. Bale couldn't help but chuckle. The guy looked like the king of the jackasses.

"I wasn't sure you'd come out. Thought you might be yellow without a big pistol in front of you," Abigor hollered while continuing to throw his combos at the air.

"So, what are we talking about here, to the death?" Bale asked as he attempted to stretch the drunk away. It didn't help.

Abigor's laugh sounded like oily gears grinding to a halt as he removed his trench coat and hat, handed them to one of his goons, and said, "I ain't going to kill you. You'll just wish you were dead. After I get done kicking your ass, the two of you are going back to boss Yaaz."

Bale laughed and stumbled back into Lou who somberly stood behind him. Once he righted himself, he pushed through the quietly cheering crowd until he was face to face with Abigor. Then he gritted his teeth and said, "We're not going anywhere but out of this shithole, and you're in the way."

"I hoped you'd say something stupid like that. Just say when you're ready," Abigor smiled.

Abigor was big. His swollen arms looked like they were chiseled out of stone as his muscles flexed through all his movements. His jaw was wide open. Bale tightened his fist and threw what he intended to be a tight, right hook to that jaw. It wasn't. He swung wild. Abigor easily ducked beneath it.

It felt like a mule kick when Abigor's first punch pounded against Bale's ribs. He knew what that felt like. He'd been kicked by a mule before, years ago. He woke up hung over in a barn and stumbled into the ornery beast. It kicked him right in the gut and sent him sailing. Abigor's punch hadn't sent him sailing, but it hurt just as bad. The uppercut that followed hit him right underneath his jaw and sent the memory skittering away like sand blowing over the desert. This one did send him sailing. It knocked his feet right out from under him. The hard-packed, dirt road didn't give an inch when the back of his head smacked into it.

Despite the sudden throbbing in his head, smacking it had helped a little to chase the cobwebs even further away. When he heard Abigor laugh and tell Lou, "I thought this bitch was supposed to be a bad ass," it helped even more.

Lou's response was a weak attempt at defending Bale's honor. "That is also what I have heard. I assure you that he is very drunk. He downed an entire bottle of Earl's secret recipe. Sadly, since you have killed my good friend, he will probably be the last person who ever does."

The disgust in the demon's voice when he replied, "Damn. This ain't going to be any fun. I was hoping to get him at his best," was the final straw.

It would have been easy to just give up, lay there on the ground and let Kaye's goons drag him away, but quitting wasn't an option. The sun blazing directly overhead didn't help. It was too damned bright. It kept his eyes squinted to barely more than slits. Shadows were all Bale could see, but he knew what his next move would be as soon as he heard Abigor's first heavy footfall stalking toward him. He laid there weakly groaning, playing possum, somewhat. When Abigor's big, stupid, smiling face finally loomed above him, it blocked out that bright sun. Bale unleashed. He pulled his knees in tight to his chest and fired both his feet straight up at the exact moment Abigor dropped down to pound his face with an elbow. Bale's left foot connected squarely under the big demon's chin. It was a solid hit that buckled Abigor's knees and dropped the big asshole to the ground right next to him.

That was the opening Bale needed. The world was still too swimmy and his gut too squishy from Earl's special recipe for any quick movements to be effective. A roll to the right was something he could pull off. It took way more effort than it should have, but a moment later Bale was mounted on top of Abigor with his knees pinning the demon's elbows to the ground. Then he started dropping bombs. Right, left, right, the punches weren't the crispest he'd ever thrown, but they all hit one or the other of Abigor's temples. Then Bale dropped an elbow across the bridge of the big guy's nose. Angels, even the fallen ones, were difficult to injure, but Bale put all his weight behind the blow. He felt the give and heard the crunch when he connected. That nose was broken.

Then Bale's world went sideways again. Abigor bucked beneath him, quickly raising his arms at the same moment. Stone cold sober, Bale could have ridden with it, transitioned to his back. As drunk as he was, that was never going to happen. Instead, he rolled onto his back pulling his legs up and kicking again, his two boots planted squarely against Abigor's chest and tossed the demon back onto his ass.

It was a topsy, turvy scramble, but Bale made it back to his feet in time to see a stiff left jab snapping toward his face. It wasn't head movement that saved his nose from taking the brunt of the attack. It was dizziness. He dipped hard to the right and almost lost his balance. Abigor's fist glanced off his left cheek. He'd watched the demon air boxing and working through his combos long enough before the fight to know a tight right hook would be following quickly. He leaned into the dizzy stumble and rolled back to his feet. Abigor was exposed.

It was a wild haymaker, but Bale put all his weight behind it lunging at Abigor's jaw. It was a solid connection. He barely saw the whites of Abigor's eyes as the momentum of his punch carried him past his crumbling opponent. Three seconds of internal celebration over the knockout was all he managed before he was back on the ground. His shoulder blades hit the hard packed dirt first. That was a jolt, but it was nothing compared to the big rock not completely buried in that dirt. He heard the crunch inside his head when the back of it smacked against the pointed edge of the damned thing. Then a bright flash of light blinded him a moment before everything went black.

CHAPTER 27

ESCAPE

PERVER CITY

Bale tentatively opened his eyes squinting against the hellacious hangover he expected and deserved and waited for the exploding pain of merciless throbbing to pound him into submission. It never came. He blinked a few times, raised his head and shook it. Nothing. He felt great.

He rolled onto his back and stretched. The last thing he remembered was the blazing sun blinking out above him as the whole world went black on him. An unconscious grin turned the corners of his mouth up. He beat Abigor. Knocked himself out in the process, but a win's a win.

He stretched and took stock of his situation. He was in a cell, three concrete walls, bars, a steel cot bolted to one wall, and a metal pisser that looked like it was part of the floor. What more does a guy need? He must have slept curled around that pisser, gross.

Bale had barely sat up when he heard the unmistakably angelic voice of one of Kaye's goons. They all had such glorious voices. If Bale hadn't seen so much in his life, he might have been swept up by them, filled with some heavenly feelings of hope and all that bullshit. As it was, it just made him want to punch something when that glorious voice nearly sung, "Well, look at that. The great and powerful Bale Lance survives another day."

"This place is amazing. I should be dead," Bale had to concede the fact. Then he turned his head toward the goon, grinned, and asked, "How's Abigor's jaw?"

The gorgeous voice didn't match the scowl on the demon's face when he replied, "Just be glad the boss hasn't lifted the no kill on your ass, or you would be dead."

Bale chuckled dryly at the response as he got to his feet and approached the bars. Then he grabbed hold of them and said, "That's the thing I don't get. Why the fuck am I still alive? I failed. Kaye could have killed me six times already."

Bale didn't let the emotion bleed into his expression at all, but he felt it. Angel Cakes was depending on him, and he let her down. It dragged his spirit deep into a black pit where hope melted into numbing despair. There wasn't a damn thing he could do about anything. He was trapped, stuck like a bear in a trap, just like her. He failed, and she'd have to pay for his failure.

The goon's annoying voice was a godsend dragging Bale's mind back from the pit of helpless failure to a place where he could let his rage boil instead of wallowing in hopeless melancholy. "I've learned not to question why the boss does what she does. Maybe she's torturing you, letting you think about your precious daughter and all the nasty, freaky shit Orwell's doing to her," the asshole smiled as the words slithered out of his perfect mouth.

The guy was just giving voice to the terrors tormenting Bale's mind, but it struck a nerve. His tone grew deep and threatening as he growled through clenched teeth, "Don't you dare talk about my daughter..." before the grinning asshole cut him off.

"Or you'll do what? You won't do shit," the asshole chuckled before tapping the bars and adding, "You've got nothing."

Bale just stared at him, allowing his rage to boil up to his scowl. His clenching teeth and flexing jaw couldn't hide the sinking feeling festering in his gut. The guard was right. He felt his face soften as that feeling of helplessness swam back up to the top of his awareness and dragged his rage away kicking and screaming. All he could do trapped in that cell was threaten. He dropped his head, shuffled over to the cot, and flopped down on it to stare at the gray concrete of the wall across from him defeated.

The guard laughed at him and said, "That's it? Nothing else? I heard you're full of it, always have some slick shit to say."

Bale just stared at the wall. He did have a million things to say, slick shit for the asshole goading him, but none of it would make a difference. If he could get his hands on the chuckling clown, he could show him what was what. With the guy safely on the other side of those bars, he really was just words.

"You know," the guard began pacing back and forth on the other side of the bars, pausing to lean his head in with each barb he flung. "I wish she would let me finish you off. You killed a bunch of my friends, you piece of shit. I'd like to string you up like we did Azrael, but I wouldn't let you off so easy. I'd take my time with you. Cut you up and pull all the stuff inside you out little by little."

Bale just stared. Threats had never bothered him much. The no kill was obviously still in effect. It didn't matter what the guy had to say. He was all talk too. Besides, at that moment, he didn't care what happened to him. Physical pain was a minor annoyance he'd grown used to over the years. Angel was all he could think about.

The guard must have picked up on the fact. He stopped pacing, leaned his face close to the bars, and asked, "Where do you suppose Orwell's fingers are right now?"

It was like a needle jabbing a nerve. "Fuck you," Bale growled. "You want to try me? Open this fucking cage."

The threat didn't scare the asshole at all. He just laughed and said, "There it is. Look at those eyes. Is that rage or fear? I really can't tell. I bet there's fear in your little girl's eyes right now."

"Stop," Bale warned.

"Do you think she's crying," the guard asked. "Do you think she's begging him to stop like you're begging me?"

"Knock it off," Bale grunted.

"Come on. I want to hear you say it," the guard kept pushing. "What do you think he's doing to her right now?"

"Motherfucker, I said stop!" spit fired from Bale's mouth as he shouted.

Then something changed. It started as a tingle, like electricity surged through his body. Then he was stretching. No. That wasn't it. He was being pulled apart. It was like he could feel each of his cells letting go of each other so they could spread out like a cloud or vapor, stretching like waves of sound or light, traveling along a crowded highway of color and sound. An eternity passed in an instant, and he was being put back together. Each cell reaching out to grab the cell it had just detached from. The next thing he knew, he was arriving right next to the smart-ass guard who had so much to say.

The guy's hanging jaw confirmed that the goon was just as surprised as Bale to be looking eye to eye with him minus any bars to protect him. Bale didn't give him a chance to react. He grabbed the guy's gun by the barrel and held it fast. Then he leaned back from his waist, coiling up the muscles in his back like a loaded spring, and thrust his forehead at the goon's nose with every ounce of force he could muster. That nose exploded like a crushed tomato when the dome of Bale's head connected with it and splattered both their faces with blood.

The head butt buckled the guard's knees, but it didn't knock him out. Neither did it loosen his grip on the rifle he clung to. Bale could fix that. He fired a stiff elbow at the guy's jaw and followed it up with a tight hook. That did it. He yanked the gun from the guard's loosened grip, flipped it around, and pulled the trigger. A moment later the loose-tongued cocksucker was gone with nothing but a cloud of shimmering, golden dust to prove he'd been there.

"Never talk about my daughter," Bale growled at the quickly dissipating cloud of dust. Then it was gone. A moment later, so was he.

Traveling was always a little unsettling. Distance never mattered. At least, it didn't seem to. The fact was difficult to gauge considering time didn't make any sense. It was almost like tripping on acid. The journey always seemed to take forever, but at the same time, it always seemed to be over before it began. In every instance, no time passed from departing to leaving.

Thought was strange. That never left. Despite the feeling that every shred of his being was separated into microscopic specks of cells or atoms or his soul or whatever the hell it was, he was always completely aware of everything happening. It was like reality warped to fit the experience he found himself in. Every color he'd ever seen, and even more he hadn't blasted his senses, swirling rainbows of light spinning around him as he melted through them. And the sounds, songs of unmitigated terror, unrestrained joy, and every emotion in between barking or chiming out in a celestial chorus of mixed emotion. His soul wanted to cry out with joy while weeping a hopeless lament while laughter and sobbing skipped along together as bosom chums. The pleasing scent of wildflowers laced about honey and fresh rain mingled incoherently with the rancid odor of festering rot swirling into something equal parts horror and bliss to saturate his sinuses to the point he could taste the smells. Of course, it couldn't be his sinuses. They would be as stretched out and dispersed as every other shred of his being, but that was how it seemed. All the while, it felt as if his skin had remained intact to vibrate beneath a barrage of static that shocked and tickled at the same time. Every extreme happened simultaneously.

All those things occurred as they always did when Bale traveled, and then it was done. He had arrived precisely where he wanted to be without the aid of Orwell's GPS device. Kaye must have been correct that the thing had only ever served as a means for the big guy to track his movements and ensure he was playing the good puppet. The power to travel, to rip holes right through dimensional barriers, to be wherever he wanted whenever he wanted to be there had always existed within him. The device was just a trick Orwell used to control him after convincing him he needed it to travel. Belief is a bitch.

Bale glanced around. Mark's apartment was dark enough that it took a moment for his eyes to adjust. A moan dripping with pleasure danced through the air a moment before Bale noticed Mark lying directly in front of him on the sofa. His old friend wasn't alone. A hot, half-dressed, blonde was straddling him and grinding on his waist while she lapped at his neck, tasting his blood. Vampire sex was weird.

It took a few moments for Mark's friend to notice Bale gazing down at her. Once she did, she jumped up and screamed, "What the fuck?"

Her full breasts jiggled as she quickly scurried toward the other end of the sofa. The bra barely holding them in had all it could handle to keep them from busting out, free to bounce and sway. Bale couldn't help but admire them. She was new. Lucky Mark. He'd been single for a while. Hopefully, it was more than a one-night stand.

The blonde covered herself as best she could with a small throw pillow, glaring at Bale with equal parts fear and rage. Then she dropped her gaze toward Mark and said, "Who the fuck is he? I ain't into no kinky shit."

An unfortunate and awkward chuckle fell inelegantly from Bale's mouth. He wasn't sure who was more embarrassed at that moment. Still, there was something mildly amusing about her no kinky shit policy with Mark's blood glistening around her mouth like smeared lipstick. That seemed pretty kinky, maybe not to a vampire. Maybe that was just normal shit you did before you fucked.

He should have kept quiet, but he heard the words coming out of his mouth before he could stop himself from saying, "I don't know. You're in here riding my buddy like it's the fucking rodeo while you're drinking his blood straight out of the tap. That's a bit outside the norm where I come from."

Mark finally popped his head up. A bewildered look squatted across his face as he said, "Bale? What the fuck, man? What are you doing here?" Then he shifted his attention back to his date and added, "I'm sorry, Dani. He's a friend, an uninvited friend who shouldn't fucking be here right now."

Dani, Bale latched onto the name and introduced himself, "Hi Dani. My name is Bale. Mark is quite possibly the only friend I have in any dimension, and I'm in trouble. I am sorry I startled you."

Her voice jumped at least an octave when she replied, "Startled me? Are you fucking kidding? You scared the shit out of me. Have you been watching us the whole time, you freak?"

"He hasn't," Mark interjected. "You know that little clique who hangs out at the bar on Tuesdays always talking about walking the flame?"

"The firewalkers?" Dani asked. "I can't stand them. That scent they wear is disgusting, and I swear they never wash."

"Yeah, them," Mark nodded. "Bale is like that. He can move to other dimensions, but he doesn't need to walk the flame. He has a device that…"

"Not anymore," Bale's chin dropped toward his chest as he sighed with defeat. "It's over, man. I lost. That twisted fucker is going to eat her soul."

Mark scratched his head, turned to Dani, and said, "I'm sorry, babe. I know this is our first date, but I think this is going to be a minute. Do you want me to take you home?"

Dani's head was shaking before Mark even finished. It continued shaking when she replied, "You're lucky I like you, Mark. I'm not going anywhere. I want to hear this story. Firewalkers, really? I'll get us some drinks."

Mark's smile nearly ran out of face as he watched her walk away and said, "You're the best, babe."

She smiled back as she glanced over her shoulder and said, "And you'd better not forget it." Then she strutted a couple steps closer to the kitchen and added, "He's the reason you keep that green shit in the cupboard, isn't he?"

"You know it," the dopey look remained on Mark's face as he watched her all the way into the kitchen. The smile vanished when he turned toward Bale, and said, "Alright, buddy. This must be bad. You look sober. What do you mean, you lost?"

Bale flopped down on the sofa next to Mark and sighed, "They played me. I never had a chance. They blew up my GPS. I'm fucked."

Mark's face twisted as he said, "Wait. If they blew up that little time skipping device of yours, how the fuck did you get here?"

"I don't know," Bale shrugged. "I just thought about you, and then I was here. All the same shit that normally happens when I travel happened, but I didn't use the device. It's toast. Kaye said I didn't need that thing, but I don't know how to control it. I don't know how it works without that thing."

"Kaye? Who the fuck is Kaye?" Mark asked, still looking like he was sucking on a lemon.

"Boss Yaaz," Bale shook his head. "She's like the mayor of Perver City, basically a god just like Orwell. She used to be his old lady, even."

Dani returned with drinks, O negative for Mark and the green shit for Bale. Then she sat down in the chair across from the sofa, sipped her glass, and stared intently at Bale.

"Thanks, babe," Mark smiled at her, his mind obviously traveling to the destination they'd been heading to before Bale showed up. Then he shook his head, sipped his drink, looked over at Bale, and said, "Okay, slow down. So, you don't actually need that thing to get around? Just go get your daughter then. Pop right in, grab her, and pop right out."

Bale swirled his glass as he absently stared at the floor and said, "I can't."

"Why the fuck not?" Mark scoffed. "You can go anywhere. You're like a god. Maybe you are god. Did you ever think of that? Maybe Orwell's full of shit."

"No," Bale shook his head, still staring at the floor. "No, I'm not. Orwell's god, or Kaye...or the both of them. I don't fucking know. I just know I can't beat him. I didn't stand a chance in Perver City, and Orwell's twice as bad."

Dani leaned closer to Bale and said, "Look...Bale, is it? I don't know anything about you. Mark obviously loves you like a brother, or he would have drained you by now. You must not be half bad. The thing I don't understand is, what have you got to lose?"

Mark grabbed Bale's shoulder and agreed, "She's right, man. You've got nothing to lose."

The air felt suddenly thick like it might crush him right into threads of the sofa. It was heavy, a weight pushing him down and down, deep into an abyss that he could never escape. They were both right, of course. He didn't have anything to lose, but Orwell had the ace. Orwell had the only thing in any reality that could make him feel fear. If he tried and failed, she would pay. Even thinking about the kind of tortures Orwell could concoct for his little girl was more than he could take. No way. Charging into the City of Gold on a bound to fail rescue mission would never work. On the other hand, what did he have to lose? He couldn't just hide out at Mark's. Eventually, Orwell would get hip to the fact that he would never deliver Lucifer, and that sick fuck would do whatever he was going to do to Angel Cakes anyway.

Bale slammed his drink. It burned going down, just the way he liked it. Then he wiped his mouth on his sleeve, and with less conviction in his voice than he'd hoped, said, "You're right. I'm going back."

"To Orwell?" Mark raised his glass.

"Nope," Bale shook his head. "Kaye said she'd help me if I left her son alone. I'm going to see if that offer still stands."

"And if it doesn't?" Dani asked.

Bale handed Mark his glass and answered, "What have I got to lose?"

CHAPTER 28

CHAOS

PERVER CITY

Bale was half certain it wouldn't work, but after finishing half that bottle of green shit in Mark's cupboard, he tried it anyway. He thought about Kaye, not all the stuff that could distract him from his goal. As much as he wished he had time to ponder her shimmering green eyes or her luscious, pouty lips—don't even mention that ass—he focused on the chair he'd occupied in her office the second time they'd met, after she rode him like the rodeo and dumped him like a clown. Despite his doubts, time split. He felt himself stretching across reality. He heard all the sounds, felt all the feels, tasted all the various flavors that shouldn't exist in any reality, and then he was there in the chair.

He could tell Kaye knew it immediately. Her smile gave it away. He loved the way her cheeks plumped when her lips slightly parted. Those thoughts were dangerous. She was like a drug. He had to keep reminding himself why he was there in the first place. Nothing mattered but the mission.

"I knew you'd be back," she said as she abandoned the papers she'd been fretting over to lean seductively back in her chair.

"That makes one of us," Bale replied with none of the confidence that had colored Kaye's tone. "Are you going to kill me now?"

"Why in hell would I do that?" she laughed and poured them both drinks.

"I fucked you over pretty good, shit all over your hospitality," Bale shrugged before accepting the full tumbler she handed him. After a solid pull, he added, "I bet your boys have some scary stories."

She drained her glass in one shot and poured another before saying, "Darling, you have done nothing to surprise me yet. My plans don't make much sense to most, but this one is working out just fine."

She was correct. Nothing that had happened since Bale first stepped foot in Perver City felt like any kind of plan. It was a series of incalculable events that no mind, no matter how twisted, could ever expect to happen in the precise order they happened. It probably began as a plan, but it quickly devolved into chaos. The thought gave him pause. She was chaos personified. Maybe it was a plan.

He slammed his drink and held his glass out for a refill. As Kaye poured, he asked, "Care to fill me in?"

"You're taking Lou to meet his daddy, and you're not going to let anything bad happen to him," she said, that damned smile never leaving her lips.

Bale did everything he could to keep his mind from tumbling down a hallway full of nasty thoughts that wouldn't get him any closer to his goal. It was those damned lips. Every time she dragged her tongue slowly across them, it felt like a test. He dropped his gaze to the floor and said, "You sound pretty sure of yourself."

"Of course, I am," she laughed. Then she dropped the seductive act, if only slightly, and asked, "Do you care about my son?"

A part of him wanted to storm out of her office and slam the door, leave her alone with whatever game she was playing, but a bigger part of him, the smart part that knew when to stay and when to go, knew he needed her. That part knew that she was the key to getting his little girl back. Her fate was tied directly to Lou's, and Bale knew he had to see it through if either of them were going to survive.

Bale sipped his drink and sat up a bit straighter in his chair. She was raw desire, a fucking goddess, probably just god, but he had to be stronger than that. He looked her straight in those gorgeous, green eyes and said, "I guess I do. I care about your son. He's special. You couldn't spend five minutes with the guy and not walk away wanting to be his best friend. I like him."

"Everybody does," she kept up with the game. "And because you do care about him, you will take care of him."

"I can't beat Orwell. I don't know why you'd trust me with your son's life," Bale sighed. "I'm telling you now. I like your son, and I want to protect him. But if it comes down to a choice between him and my little girl. Sister, I'm going to hand him over."

If she was at all phased by what he'd said, she didn't let on. That damned smile never left those soft lips as she said, "I would be let down if you didn't feel that way. She's your little girl. But it won't come to that. You'll take Lou and the rest of my boys to get your little girl. Then you'll take Lou to meet his daddy. What happens from there is up to you."

"You've got an answer for everything," Bale grunted. "What if I'm not as good as you think?"

Her smile finally faltered as she stood and approached him. There was an honesty in her eyes he hadn't seen before when she brushed his hair back from his forehead and said, "You are more than you think of yourself. You might not know that, but I do. I believe in you. If I'm wrong, you're all dead. It will hurt me, but life will go on."

Bale was dumbstruck. He would never think of taking a risk like that with Angel Cakes. Maybe Kaye was as desperate as he was. Whether or not that was the case, she wasn't giving him the whole story.

"That's a big fucking risk to take with your kid," Bale said as he pulled away from her, stood, and poured himself another drink.

Kaye laughed and sat down in the chair Bale had been sitting in. "I have protected him for longer than you can probably fathom. You have been around for a couple millennia. You're but a babe lost in the woods. Lou has wanted to meet his father since he was old enough to have cognizant thoughts. Now there is a way he can. I can't stand in his way anymore. His destiny is his own."

"Why don't you just go kill that cocksucker?" Bale asked as he sat down on the edge of Kaye's desk. "I mean, you're basically god, right. You said that you came first. You created everything. Why don't you just go wipe that fucker out and be done with it."

Kaye's eyes drifted toward the wall, but Bale could tell she was looking far past it. An earnestness crept into her tone when she said, "Now it seems like you have more faith in me than you should. I couldn't kill him if I wanted to. Maybe, if I could lure him here. This place is my heart and soul. This form," she glanced down at her body and waved her hands from her shoulders down to her knees as if she were displaying an object for sale, "is just a reflection of the unbridled chaos that I truly am. It is just the me I want you to see, something you can accept, even desire. If you could truly see me, you would be terrified." Her smile returned as she added, "Orwell is even worse, and equally powerful while hidden away in his orderly, little fortress."

The idea was intriguing. The alluring thing stretched out on the chair in front of Bale didn't look like it could be a reflection of anything less than perfection. She was flawless, wild and untamed, raw emotion. The idea of raw emotion got him thinking. He'd only really seen joy and indulgence from her. Perhaps what she'd shown him was just the tip of the iceberg.

"Show me," he finally said.

"Show you what?" she asked. Her coy smile was a horrible fake. It was the first time he'd really seen her crack and drop the act. She was afraid.

"You've never shown anyone your true self. Have you?" he said as he moved closer and knelt beside her. "Except Orwell, and he broke your heart. You want everyone to love you, but you settle for desire. That's why everyone is drawn to this place. You know exactly what they want, and you give it to them, so they never want to leave. That's why Orwell hates you. He's stifled by his own rules, his own restrictive order. You have no rules."

Kaye's smile had fled about halfway through Bale's observation. The expression that replaced it was something which a face shouldn't be capable of doing. Her lips twisted into something like a sneer but somehow sharper. It was like the left side of her upper lip might stretch all the way to her forehead which had morphed from being smooth and perfect to looking like deep trenches had been dug into it while her eyes squinted to horrible slits. Succeeding in drawing a different emotion out of her didn't feel like a win to Bale as he watched her melt into something more terrifying than anything he'd ever seen.

Bale didn't even realize he was moving as he stood and slowly backed away from Kaye. He wanted to look away, but his eyes were locked on her face that continued to twist through physical expressions of raw and desperate emotions. Anger, hurt, sorrow, rage, desperation, fear, and more twisted rapidly across her features like no singular feeling could find any permanence. She was a canvas, an image painted in an instant only to be washed away and replaced with another as quickly as it had arrived.

"You want to see me?" she nearly screamed; the pleasant melodic notes of her voice twisted into a horrible shriek that seemed to vibrate the very air.

It was what he'd thought he wanted only moments prior. However, at that particular moment watching her release even the loosest control on her emotions, he was most certain he did not want it at all. He was certain that what she was showing him was still yet a reflection of her truth, like an old, weathered picture, a blurry and faded recording of reality. The real her was undoubtedly far worse.

Bale was about to let his mounting terror win and beg her to release him, but he couldn't. Something stopped him. It wasn't something he could completely or accurately identify. It was almost like a feeling, some kind of twisted sense of fairness, but not quite. In her own roundabout way, she had helped him, pushed him to dig deeper into himself and find he was more than he thought. She forced him to challenge himself and finally lift the curtain on all of Orwell's lies. She made him believe he could do the impossible. She made him believe he could free his daughter from Orwell's perfect prison. He owed her.

Before he could completely shrink away from her in fear, that small but reliable voice that spoke sometimes from the back of his mind held him fast. It reminded him that he didn't scare that easily. It helped him recall that he'd spent his life chasing down all manner of monsters and beating them. It helped him remember that he actually cared about more than just his skin. He'd pushed Kaye far out of her comfort zone. It wasn't just to make a point. He did want to see her for who she truly was.

He finally stopped retreating, stood tall, and said, "I want to see you. Show me."

The world seemed to disintegrate in an instant. The walls surrounding him, the ceiling with its random and gaudy chandeliers, the unmatched furniture, even the floor he stood upon, it all cracked like aging plaster shaken by the rumbling and bucking earth vibrating from the force of a seismic quake before hurricane winds blasted it to crumbling bits to swirl into a murky cloud of debris. Flashes of color began erupting like watching lightning flash through clouds. There were no ragged and zig zagging bolts of electricity, just bright blasts of color exploding and vanishing in rapid succession. They came so quickly and in such volume that his entire line of sight was saturated with color layering itself over and over again like some kind of tempestuous light show orchestrated in a mind ruptured by a psychic break.

Something screeched a horrid note of lament like an animal being skinned alive. Beneath that terrible sound was something guttural and ominous as if the core of the earth were growling a rumbling bass that vibrated in Bale's chest. Those two distinct sounds echoed off the air and mingled with other horrifying tones, screeches and shouts, agonizing cries and pitiable howls, vicious grunts and rumbling thunder amplified beyond any sound an ear should hear. The sounds weren't all petrifying and terrible. Laced among those awful notes were pleasant tones. Soaking rain splashing over a lake, waves rushing against a sandy shore, the delicate song of a wood thrush meandering across a quiet forest, and leaves rustling in a gentle breeze. All those different sounds twisted around each other in a chorus both beautiful and terrifying.

A sudden burst of citrus filled Bale's sinuses. It was like someone was peeling an orange right beneath his nose. Then the savory scent of spiced meat roasting over an open flame danced across the top of it. He breathed deeply through his nose, drawing it all in. Something drifted in with those pleasing aromas. It was awful, like excrement soaked in sulfur and dripping vomit. More odors came, some delicate and floral, others heavy and foul. All of it blended together into a cloud of funk so thick he could taste every scent.

It suddenly occurred to him that none of the colors, sounds, or odors, or even the flavors of those things, were occurring to any of his sensory organs. It was almost like traveling, like every cell in his body was experiencing all these sensations individually and simultaneously. However, he wasn't spread out like a slowly expanding cloud of dust. His body was still intact, standing there amid the joy and terror of everything happening around him.

He was suddenly freezing. It was like no cold he had ever experienced. He felt it in his skin and every other cell in his body. At the same time, searing heat enveloped him. The impossibility of those two sensations happening concurrently was enough to twist his mind into insanity. If only they were alone in the assault. It felt like he was being tickled. At first, it made him want to laugh, but it wasn't long before he wanted to cry out. He wanted to scream for it to stop. Then every inch of his body itched. It was too much.

He couldn't tell how long this unrelenting assault on his senses lasted, but he slowly gained control of it. All these experiences continued without pause, but somehow, his deep desire to escape dimmed. He focused on Kaye. Where had she gone? Two dim spots of red began glowing in the distance. How far away, he could never estimate. The world surrounding him continued to spin out of control, every imaginable color bleeding together into one murky tone, yet still individual at the same time. It made it impossible to gauge the distance of anything.

The two spots of red glowing against the macabre backdrop continued to grow and deepen in color until they were like two stars blazing in the darkest depths of space. Bale felt small and scrutinized as he stood before them. Details began swirling within the brilliant orbs as they gained depth. They looked like faceless eyes staring at him. Though he sensed no judgement oozing off of them, he felt judged, small and vulnerable, every thought and deed he'd ever had or done laid bare before god's horrible gaze.

They didn't look like Kaye's eyes, but he knew it was her staring at him among the swirling chaos. She didn't say anything to him with her voice, but he was aware of her question as if she spoke it directly to his mind. "Is this what you wanted?" she asked.

It was. He didn't have to think about it. He knew it immediately. He wanted to see her for what she was in all her glory. He wanted to see her truth. "Yes," he attempted to say with his mouth, but no sound came out. Still, somehow, he knew she heard him.

Then a shape began forming out of the chaotic swirl of flashing light. It started as a long tube stretching across the wind, dancing on the currents of air like a noodle floating in swirling soup. It slowly gained color until it was brilliant, light-green, and glistening as if it were wet. Tiny, black diamonds suddenly began appearing in distinct patterns all over it. More details came as lines were seemingly carved into it, like wet clay being etched with a stylus. Bale realized they were scales forming all across the shape. Then one end of the tube began twisting and morphing until it resembled a snake. Triangle flaps of skin pushed up on either side of what had become a head over eyes as black as two obsidian marbles. It opened its mouth to expose long fangs. A forked tongue slithered quickly in and out between them. It was a snake, but what did it mean?

Then it wasn't a snake anymore. Six legs formed, three on either side, at regular intervals. They weren't thin like a bug's but thick and muscular, like an iguana's. It was no creature that existed in any reality that Bale knew of. It looked like some kind of snake, lizard hybrid. Then it changed again. Wings—long, wide, and leathery—stretched from the midpoint of either side of it. They grew and grew until they seemed too big for the snake's body to support. Suddenly, the currents it had been dancing across filled those massive wings and tossed the snake about, whipping it one way and then another. It was obvious the creature's body lacked the strength to control them.

The thing spun out of control long enough that Bale began to feel a deep sorrow for it. The wings never flapped. They were just yanked in one direction and then another as the thin body bent and twisted. Then it exploded in a flash of bright, white light. There was no loud report or chunks of meat and gore slopping about. One moment the snake, lizard, bat thing was spinning out of control and the next moment it was dust swirling back into the macabre tornado of colors whipping around Bale.

"What was that?" he asked. Once again, no sound came from his mouth, but he knew his question had been understood.

Kaye's reply was the same, occurring to his mind rather than his ears. She said, "It was a malformed idea. Something that might have been but never will. They all come like that. Some survive and grow into things that could exist. Millions and millions more do not."

It seemed like a small moment, but it was so much more than that. Bale suddenly realized he had just witnessed the chaos of creation, how everything had come to be. He was standing within Kaye's mind or consciousness. It wasn't quite that, her mind. She was chaos. He was within her. Regardless of whether he was in her twisted mind, or if she was a mind—some kind of swirling consciousness wherein everything that has been or will ever be exists for as long as it will—she had let him in. She had allowed him to see how reality had come to be, and she had done it all.

He loved her. It wasn't this gift she had just given him, vulnerably exposing herself to his raw scrutiny, removing every filter and protection she kept in place to prevent any being from seeing her true form. It wasn't even the faith she'd put in him by sharing her soul. Mere moments of witnessing her glory would be enough to destroy a mind. Worse for her, he thought, would be if he simply ran from her in terror.

Bale didn't break as he immersed himself in the experience of her. He wasn't afraid. He didn't run. Instead, he consumed it all, letting go of any personal desire and allowing whatever might be to be. There was no fear in his voice, only hope, when he shouted, "I see you for what you are, and I love you."

Her voice was both beautiful and terrible as she replied, "I know. You are ready."

And then it was all gone in an instant, and Bale's world went black.

CHAPTER 29

PREPARE FOR BATTLE

PERVER CITY

It was like laying on a cloud. That was the first thought Bale had when we woke in an unfamiliar room lying in a large circular bed covered in soft sheets and softer blankets. There was a pillow beneath his head and a mattress beneath his body, but it was almost as if he couldn't feel them. It truly felt like he was floating. He had no idea how he ended up in the gaudy and comfortable bed, but he must have slept well. He couldn't remember the last time he'd felt so refreshed.

The room surrounding him was as chaotic and random as every other room he'd been in while hosted by Kaye. There were three chandeliers hanging from various spots on the ceiling. One looked like decorative, old-fashioned, clear light bulbs with filaments glowing brightly inside. They were shaped like teardrops and dangled from delicate, swirling strands of diamonds. There had to be some kind of wires or cables holding them together, but they were hidden sufficiently that it appeared they just hung there in the space immediately below the ceiling. Another one hung from a golden chain. The light fixture itself was fashioned to the chain by a crystal angel, its hands clinging to the bottom loop. There were eight arms sprawling from the waist of the angel like they were legs. They stretched down at an angle away from the angel before curving out and up to support pairs of luminaires. These were crafted in such a way that the source of light was hidden, splashed about various colored crystals dangling from each of the arms and bending the light like prisms to splash rainbows all about the walls. The last one was simpler than the other two. It also hung from a golden chain, but it only consisted of six arms that looked like they were holding up candles.

There was a chair in one corner of the room and a chaise in another. Neither matched the other. The chair looked Victorian with a rich mahogany back decorated with white fabric bearing an intricate and colorful pattern of various earthy tones. The chaise was a black, neo modern piece that looked like something Mark might stick in a corner of the VooDoo Lounge. Aside from the bed and those two seats, the only furniture in the room was a small writing desk in the middle of the space with no chair that looked like someone had set it there until they could decide where to put it. None of it was terribly interesting outside of the fact that none of it fit together.

There was one interesting thing in the room. A decoratively carved bookshelf was recessed into one wall taking up the bulk of it. The shapes carved into it were a hodgepodge of horrors, everything from twisted ghouls to bored looking gargoyles to mockeries of traditional demons complete with horns, cloven hooves, and pointy tails. None of those were what made the piece so interesting. What rested on the shelves was what really grabbed Bale's attention.

These books were all intricate works of art without even considering the ideas contained between their covers, as intriguing as those ideas might be. They were all titles Bale had always believed to be mythical. One was from Potentiality 1, a place where the dominant species look just like humans only bigger. They are giants, the average man towering at ten feet tall. Bale had only ever been there once. Giants are very spiritual. They saw the light as their goal. Only one that Bale knew of had ever ignored the call into that light. His name was Agor. Bale hunted him to a cave at the edge of a vast desert. When he finally caught up to the giant, he found him emaciated and curled around a dying fire.

Bale had expected a fight. The giants of Potentiality 1 were mostly peaceful, but Agor was unique. There was no fight. Agor looked up at Bale with eyes flickering crimson in the dying flames of his fire and said, "This is where it's supposed to be. I am sorry I ignored the light. My soul is damned, but I had to know. I knew I was so close."

Bale had learned how to quell his sympathy for the souls he hunted after about one hundred cases. He had to, or he might have died of a broken heart. There was something about this one that tugged hard on his heart strings. Honesty trudged slowly about his hoarse and wavering voice. Bale sat down next to him, offered him some water to ease his throat that had to be burning, and asked, "What is it you seek? What prize led you to this place and this condition?"

"The truth," the giant replied, his weak tone suggesting Bale should have known that.

"What truth?" Bale shrugged as he asked the question.

Agor grew suddenly animated like he'd just been plugged in. He sat up, leaned closer to Bale, and with urgency in his voice said, "The book. The Choice. I've heard people whisper about it. They don't really believe it, but I know it's real. A giant wrote it, a man more than twice my size, and he did it in this cave. I have researched this my whole life. This cave is where he hid this book."

Bale recalled the sadness he'd felt for the dying man at that moment. He'd made it to the place he knew he needed to be but never found that prize. It seemed a fool's errand, but Bale heard himself say, "I'll help you find it, but you must eat. I can't have you dying on me. We'll find the book. You'll read it. And then you'll have to come with me."

Agor jumped up. The giant wore the widest smile Bale had ever seen as he trembled with excitement. He was like a child's toy whose batteries were almost dead moaning incoherent sounds that were distorted copies of the crisp tones it hoped to chirp that had its batteries replaced. The man seemed suddenly brand new. Bale couldn't help but feel a little excited about the quest himself. This random mark, his new friend, was dragging him along on this most important quest.

They searched, moving stones, shining Bale's flashlight in every crevice, nook, and cranny in the expansive, dark cave. They must have spent days looking for this book but found nothing except the random bones of critters who'd died there.

"What's so important about this book anyway?" Bale finally asked.

Agor seemed shocked at the question when he replied, "Well, it's the truth about the light, about everything. The light isn't what they tell us at the temples. That's a story made up by men who have never sought the higher learnings only accessible through opening your mind to the mysteries of reality. They only ever talk about the light as if it is the goal, the end. I promise you it is not. The light is the choice. I know this. What I do not know is what my options are. I will live with this choice for the rest of eternity. What if I make the wrong choice? The book will tell me what lies beyond. Then I can choose the correct goal for me."

All the excitement that had driven Bale on this quest to help a man find his truth fled like the air from a popped balloon as he said, "It isn't really a choice. You can find bliss, or eternal agony and damnation, torment. I'm here to take you to that place beyond the light. Believe me, that is where you want to spend eternity."

Bale honestly believed it when he told Agor that. That was before he learned what Orwell did with the souls he brought him. It was before he'd learned the truth about Perver City. After everything he'd learned, the good advice he'd given Agor felt like a lie.

They searched for a couple more days before Bale finally convinced Agor to give up on the search and accompany him to the only truth he really wanted. Standing there in front of that bookshelf, he finally knew why they couldn't find it. It was sitting there hidden among several similar books of truth from various potentialities. Bale wondered how many souls had wasted their lives on quests to find truths they would never find chasing promises that could never be fulfilled.

The heavy door of the room slamming open behind Bale startled him out of his thoughts. "Time to go, Bale," Abigor's voice rumbled across the room crushing the silence.

"I'm feeling pretty good right now," Bale said as he turned to face him. Then he grinned something sly as he asked, "Do you want to go another round?"

"No," Abigor smiled back at him. "I wanted to know. Now I do. You're worthy. And you'd better be. You know what we're walking into."

Bale's voice dropped slightly as he replied, "I do."

That sent his mind tumbling down a rough path. What the hell was he thinking? Was it false bravado to believe he could lead a small band of fallen angels against the de facto power in all reality? Maybe. Perhaps Kaye had merely convinced him of some bullshit to send him off on a mission she didn't want. That couldn't be it though. She had bared herself completely, let him see her in all her ragged and imperfect glory. Maybe Orwell wasn't the almighty. Maybe she was. None of it mattered. This was his one shot to get his little girl back. He had to take the chance.

"Alright, let's go," he finally said.

As they walked down a hall with random, ornate light fixtures scattered about at random intervals between some of the most incredible paintings Bale had ever seen encased in equally random and ornate frames—some were carved out of wood, others chiseled out of stone, others elaborately etched gold, and various other materials— Abigor filled Bale in on the plan. He said, "You're not zapping us directly into Orwell's office. We'd be sitting ducks in there. We're going in through the front door. That will draw the heat down to us, and there will be a lot of it. Once we have their attention, and every fucking angel in Orwell's tower is heading down to take us on, then you'll zap half off us up to the office. Lou can meet his daddy, and I'll help you get your little girl."

"That sounds so easy," Bale laughed. Then he asked, "How many of us are going?"

"Twenty," Abigor spat the word like he was expecting some blow back.

Bale gave it to him. "Twenty?" he nearly hissed. "Or has hundreds of thousands of angels, soldiers. No offense, but while you guys are here bathing in bliss, those motherfuckers are spending their time brutalizing each other to prepare for decimating you. We're going to be slaughtered."

"I thought you were tough," Abigor chuckled. "We've had someone on the inside studying that place for hundreds of years. A precision strike by a small force is the only way to do this. We're talking about hallways, stairways, and elevators. This isn't going to be some glorious battle in a vast, bloody field. And you know we've got the guns."

"Oblivion," Bale sighed. "We're fucked."

The rest of the group Bale would lead on the doomed mission were getting suited up and armed when he and Abigor strolled into the vast armory. Berith was there. He'd lost the black, leather jacket and shades in favor of a suit that looked like an odd mix of something space aged and something from the iron age of Potentiality 0. The base layer was black. It resembled a one-piece, zippered flight suit tucked into black, mid-ankle boots that appeared rugged enough for combat. Gold-colored greaves protected his shins and knees, mostly covering the boots he wore. The tops were shaped like dragons' heads. He wore gauntlets and pauldrons that matched exactly. The dragons' heads covered his elbows and shoulders respectively. The golden helmet he carried under his right arm had golden wings protruding slightly from it on both sides. Everyone else in the room was dressed in the same fashion.

Lou stood up from behind a table littered with weapons, shook his glorious hair out, and donned his helmet. Somehow, he looked bigger than Bale remembered standing there with his golden armor shimmering in the stark light of the armory.

"I hope you're planning on hanging back," Bale said to Lou.

"Hanging back?" Abigor laughed at him. "He's leading this little mission. I mean, I know Boss Yaaz said you'd be taking the lead, but Lou's the best of us. He'd kick your ass."

"I abhor violence, but fair Abigor is quite correct. I am expert in the ways of combat. The City of Gold boasts none who can match me, not even mighty Michael their champion," Lou smiled.

"Guy's a bum," Abigor grunted.

"He is not. He is mighty," Lou corrected before adding, "but he is no match for me."

"Well, that's just fucking great," Bale complained. "You can beat up Michael. How does that help when we're battling against hundreds of thousands of hardened, heavenly soldiers."

The smile Lou offered wasn't condescending, but Bale took it that way when he said, "Bale, my friend, you must know how very dramatic you sound. Do not fear for me. Besides, my father's army does not teem with hundreds of thousands of soldiers. There are a few hundred at best. It saddens me to think you've been taken with the stories told in all the places you visit. And, though I was too young for battle when that mythical war took place, I assure you that we won. They left. These soldiers standing before you led that fight. You should be honored to have them at your side."

It was a fair assessment. Neither Michael nor Gabriel had ever mentioned the great war. Orwell had alluded to a battle at the beginning of time but never offered any details. Lou was correct. Everything Bale believed about Orwell's army was based on religious stories he'd heard spread across a multitude of potentialities. None of the authors of those tales knew anything about what really existed beyond the light. Most of what they thought they knew were probably distortions and misunderstandings of the poetic tales Lou had whispered in their ears over time.

Bale offered a long and deep sigh before finally replying, "Okay, you're the boss, then. I don't like it, but a power struggle won't help us at all. Abigor filled me in on the plan. How are we going to pull this off?"

"Come with me," Lou said as he walked toward a square table roughly five feet long on each side. Once he was standing in front of it, he said, "Show me Orwell's tower."

The bright lights in the room dimmed slightly as a three-dimensional holographic schematic of Orwell's tower appeared over the table. The detail of the rendering was incredible. It was the tallest building Bale had ever seen aside from Lou's tower, but he'd only ever seen Orwell's office, the bar, and the prison where Orwell kept Angel Cakes, though he wasn't certain the latter was even in the building. Seeing it like that with every detail flickering in the air before him knocked his confidence down a couple pegs. The place was massive, and they had to fight their way to the top of it before they'd even get a crack at Orwell. He kept the thought to himself.

"We go in here," Lou touched the lobby of the building.

"So we're really going in right through the front, fucking door?" Bale's shock at the idea echoed in his tone despite Abigor having told him has much.

Lou's tone remained steady as he answered, "Not exactly. You will use your ability to travel across time and dimension to deposit us directly into the lobby where we will encounter two very surprised guards. We will dispatch them in loud and glorious fashion. This will attract attention and draw reinforcements to our position. Meanwhile, Abigor and Gadreel will exit the front of the building to take care of the two guards posted there."

"Who is Gadreel?" Bale asked, knowing the answer would make little difference. All angels, fallen or otherwise, were nearly identical to each other. The only differences between them were the color of their eyes, hair, and skin. There were slight variations in size between them, but it was mostly nominal. Bale was expert at putting faces with names, but it was tough when all the faces looked the same.

Lou placed his hand on the shoulder of the angel standing next to him and said, "This is Gadreel, and he is mighty. He and Abigor will have no trouble executing their tasks and returning to us. I could take the time to introduce you to everyone around this table, but I fear it won't help you tell anyone apart from anyone else."

"Right," Bale agreed. "Where do we go from there?"

"My father's forces will come down from these two banks of elevators here," Lou pointed at elevator shafts at two separate ends of the buildings. "Gadreel will lead our force in the lobby who will cut them down as they converge on his position. You will use your exceptional ability to traverse space and time to transport me to my father's office. Abigor and Berith will accompany us," he finished while pointing at a room at the very top of the building.

"And then Orwell destroys us all," Bale whispered grimly.

"That is not my expectation. I will meet my father. We will talk, and he will help me control the chaotic ideas constantly troubling my mind. I will finally be able to finish something."

"Here's hoping," Bale shook his head. It looked like a plan. It sounded like a plan. He still couldn't help but feel it was more like a death sentence.

CHAPTER 30

STORM THE CASTLE

CITY OF GOLD

Everyone was armed for battle and ready to execute their assault on the City of Gold. They all knew their roles. Confidence oozed from every face staring back at Bale. They wanted the challenge. He was less sure about it. Lou's idea of how he'd be received by Orwell was probably fancy. He was a good talker, but Orwell seldom changed his mind about anything. Lou would probably have his soul sucked right out of his body. He didn't seem to care. Abigor was tough. Hopefully, the rest of the group was equally game for the kind of scrap they'd be walking into. Even if they were, they'd still be outnumbered by more than ten to one. As much as he didn't like the odds, it was time to go.

"I've never traveled with this many before," Bale blurted the thought as it occurred to him. "I'm not sure I can."

"Everyone, circle up and hold hands," Lou raised his voice and instructed the group.

Bale chuckled as he took Abigor's hand with his left hand and some other angel he didn't know with his right hand before saying, "I'm not sure how this kumbaya moment is going to help me get us there."

"I have been thinking about your ability to skip across dimensions. It seems to be more a mental or spiritual gift than a physical one. I do not believe you need to touch a person you are transporting. However, I do believe it will give you the psychological boost you need to make that spiritual connection. If I am correct in my assumptions, you do need to make a connection with each mind who will be traveling with you. Holding each other's hands in a circle of unity is symbolic of that connection. Now you need only do what you do," Lou replied.

"I'm not really sure how it works. I never had to think about it until recently. I just had to use that device," Bale shook his head. Then he asked, "What if we don't all make the journey? What if some are lost along the way?"

"Our goals may differ, but they are clear. I have faith our desires will help you guide us to our destination," Lou's confidence was annoying.

"Alright," Bale sighed. "Here goes nothing."

Bale struggled for a few moments shifting his gaze repeatedly from one set of eyes staring back at him to another as he tried to figure out where to begin. They all looked identical to one another, Kaye's perfect creation that Orwell took credit for. Lou's eyes brimmed with hope. The rest would be screaming with vengeance if eyes could scream. They would descend on Orwell's tower, his fortress, like a disease but only if Bale could get them there.

As he stood there holding hands and looking from eye to eye with the rest of his group, a thought suddenly occurred to him. That wasn't strange. He had a million thoughts running through his mind just then. A quiet mind wasn't one of his gifts. It was always going, like a drunk friend who refuses to shut the hell up and go to sleep. The strange thing was this new thought that jumped to the front of his mind to be heard above all the rest was not his own. This new, foreign thought wondered when he was going to pull it together and get moving.

Abigor smiled when Bale glanced over at him. That had been his thought. It was obvious by the fallen angel's expression that they both realized it at the same time. Then it was like a flood. Bale's awareness was suddenly filled with Abigor's thoughts, desires, and ideas. The loudest and most immediate ones were about the coming battle. That guy had millennia of pent-up aggressions to take out on his foes. The rest were less violent. It was obvious he saw fighting as an art. He marveled at the elegance of movement and the capabilities of coordinated limbs articulating well-choreographed and practiced moves. But blood, guts, and destruction weren't the only ideas floating about his thoughts. He liked sunsets, the way the atmosphere bent the rays of the sun to paint the sky with blazing oranges and soft pinks. He liked sunrises even better. Kaye received credit for both in his mind. She was an artist as far as he was concerned. There were sad thoughts too, mingling with all the other ideas. He wished dogs had souls. The idea had never occurred to Bale, but there were no animals in either the City of Gold or Perver City. It was kind of sad. Abigor could never experience the joy of a slobbery, loyal companion happily licking his face after waiting hours by the door for his return.

More thoughts flooded in. Bale could identify the owner of each individual idea like they carried some kind of signature on them. As these random fears and desires flittered through his awareness, it occurred to him that his every thought was equally exposed to them. Every secret he'd ever kept, every dark and hopeless thought, and every moment of joy laid bare for every mind connected to his to explore. It could have been a jumble of twisted concepts, murky and incoherent like white noise, but it wasn't. They were all connected like one mind, yet they all maintained their own identities clearly and distinctly from one another. It was time.

Bale focused on the lobby of Orwell's great tower. He had never seen it from the outside, having only ever occupied two rooms in the entire structure. Knowing Orwell, it was no surprise the place would be a gaudy expression of his greatness. Unfortunately, the schematic Lou used when laying out the plan didn't help him paint a picture in his mind of their destination. The only clear images he could draw were of Orwell's office and the bar. Trapped in either of those rooms was no place any of them wanted to be. The lobby. He imagined what that might look like based on the other rooms he'd seen. Any wood would undoubtedly be the same dark and rich mahogany Orwell seemed to favor so. But what else? He knew the building was glass and the ceilings were high. Those two things together suggested massive windows bathing the room in tons of light. But how accurate could any image concocted from a square on a schematic truly be?

"Let go, Bale," Lou's lips hadn't moved despite his voice being clear in Bale's head.

Of course, Lou's suggestion was the correct one. Idly fretting about any lack of clarity or definition in Bale's imagined idea of his destination could only fail at making anything any clearer in his understanding of the place. He focused all his intent on this idea of what that place was in his mind.

It felt like it always did when he traveled. That brief moment of mind-numbing pain like needles touching every nerve in his body as his atoms split apart came and went. He felt that same fear he had felt the first time he traveled from everyone in the group but Lou. He embraced the experience, analyzing the pain in hopes of understanding its meanings and origins to understand the *why* behind it all. For everyone else, that infinitesimally small fraction of an instant was sheer terror, a natural response to something beyond their control, an uncontrollable fear that this all-consuming pain would continue forever. The relief when it subsided was a feeling Bale knew well. Then it was something like bliss, floating like a cloud, lighter than air and connected to everything in the cosmos. It was like traveling through an all-encompassing awareness while being wholly connected to it, like reality was nothing more than a vast consciousness that everything which had ever been was an aspect.

Time and distance checked out. Of course, they must have been happening, minutes, hours, or even days ticking away while miles peeled off, but Bale had no means to gauge either. No one else in the group seemed to care or notice except Lou. He was fascinated by it.

Then they were being put back together. Atoms remembered each other, reaching out, stretching to reconnect with one another and find their ways back where they belonged. They were arriving. There was no pain like he felt when departing. It was more like a tingling or a vibration like an electric current humming along a wire.

Bale was suddenly distracted by a thought, a brief hint of foreboding. It hadn't come from any of the minds connected to his. The idea was his own. What would happen to Angel Cakes if they failed? Would she be better off? Aside from the first six years of it, she had spent her entire life in a prison. As perfect as that place was, it was nothing more than a pretty cell. It wasn't any kind of life at all.

He pushed the thought down as far as he could, but it remained in the periphery nagging at him and dragging his focus away from the goal. That's when he felt the slip. The tight connection he'd made with his group of spiritual mercenaries was unraveling, falling apart like a bowlful of pasta tipped off a table. The noodles remained intertwined, loosely connected in a sprawling glob but spread out.

Blinding light filled Bale's vision as soon as he arrived outside Orwell's tower, a massive structure of glass and steel stretching up further into a clear, blue sky than anything he'd ever seen except for Lou's tower. He missed his target. He could see it through the glass. It wasn't more than one hundred feet from where he stood, but it might as well have been miles.

It took a few moments for his eyes to adjust to the glare reflecting off glass and steel. By the time they had, the building's lobby was ablaze with gunfire. Most of his group was already inside. The blazing sun reflecting off the mirrored glass made it impossible to know if they were winning or losing. Hopefully, the shock of a bunch of demons decked out for spiritual combat had been enough to give them an edge. He had to get in there.

Bale drew a split second too late. Worrying over his lost flock, that group of soldiers he failed to deliver to their precise destination, he had failed to clock the two guards posted at the front door. They both wore impeccable, white suits. Their long, perfect hair splashed over their broad shoulders like blonde water gushing over white stone. Their features were identical to Michael's or Gabriel's, Orwell's perfect eye candy, creep. None of that mattered much in the moment, just another distraction. What did matter were the guns those two perfect creatures aimed at him.

Bale had only raised his gun about forty-five degrees when he heard two shots ring out. They were louder than the chaotic cacophony of shouts, gunshots, and an annoying alarm that had just started clanging away, a digital copy of the sound of a bell being struck that failed miserably at matching the clarity of the thing it mocked.

The world slowed in that moment as his arm failed to move fast enough to bring his barrel in line with either of the targets who already had their guns trained on him. Despite the faith Kaye and Lou both had in him, he had failed. He'd never even make it inside. Hopefully, the rest of the crew could get the job done. Hopefully, Lou would take care of his little girl. He would never know. In a moment he'd be nothing but dust slowly falling to the ground.

The hits never came. He expected his skin to be sizzling by then, the fury of a million suns tearing across his body and vaporizing every cell. He wondered what that would sound like. It happened so fast every time he'd seen it happen that there was only a brief explosion, like a balloon filled with wet muck exploding. As slow as the world was moving for him just then, it might sound different when it happened to him.

The world sped up again when he watched both guards vaporize before his eyes. There was no sizzling, just a quick flash of light, and then two clouds of dust slowly falling to the ground.

"You fucked up, Bale," Abigor's voice bellowing across the

courtyard might have been the sweetest sound Bale had ever heard. The demon had obviously gotten his bearings and sprang into action more quickly than Bale had. Thank the Universe for that.

"I did," Bale shouted back. "It looks like everyone else is inside. We need to get in there."

Bale reached the door just as Abigor was grabbing the handle to tug it open. "It's locked," the demon grunted a moment before stepping back and kicking it.

It's a damn good thing those perfect creatures Kaye had created first were more durable than anything she created after. If a man's knee buckled the way Abigor's did when it connected with the thick glass of Orwell's tower, it would have cracked under the force of the blow. The raging demon just yelled, "Fuck," and smashed the door with an equally ineffective elbow.

Bale was about to grab Abigor's hand and will them inside the lobby when he heard the crystal clarity of Lou's voice in his ear, "We're losing, Bale. Get us inside."

The sound of Lou's voice was surprising. Bale had been so focused on the two guards he hadn't noticed Lou crawling out from under a row of perfectly manicured hedges. It was too perfect. The rest of the group was already inside drawing the heat down to them and away from the goal. He could just transport them directly to Orwell's office.

Bale wasn't sure if Lou was still somehow connected to his mind, or if it was just intuition when the damned perfect creature answered the thought with, "Stick to the plan, Bale. We need to give my father's minions time to reach the lobby."

Bale knew Lou was right, so he didn't argue. If everyone else died, there would be no need for heat. They needed to get inside and shore up their defenses. This time when Bale focused on being inside that room with his two travelers, nothing distracted him from it. He couldn't be sure if it was the sense of duty he felt at giving the soldiers who had put their faith in him to safely transport them to their goal a fighting chance, the fact that he could clearly see where he wanted to be, or simply the adrenaline coursing through him like water pumping through a pipe at full pressure that made this trip different. Whatever it was, it did the trick. One moment he was standing outside with Lou and Abigor helplessly peering at the battle through thick glass and the next moment all three of them were smack dab in the middle of it belching sunshine from the barrels of their glorious guns.

Bale only counted twelve on his team besides him and his two travelers. That meant five had already fallen, blasted to oblivion to do whatever a soul does when it ceases to exist within reality. None of Or's angels or Kaye's demons could know what really happened when they blasted somebody with their special guns. He wasn't even sure if the two of them could know. They both acted like they knew everything, but oblivion—that limbo advertised as nothingness, absolute separation from everything—seemed to be something outside even their control or understanding. Kaye might tell the truth about it, but Orwell never would. Somehow, not knowing if it was a place, some kind of prison where a banished soul served out a pitiable sentence for all eternity, made it worse. It made him think of Angel Cakes. That was the riskiest part. If anything he had done or planned to do sentenced her to that place, he could never know if she would be freed from her prison or sentenced to a worse one. As gunfire echoed all around him, he decided knowing was better. The mission could not fail.

Bale's consciousness checked out. Feelings like empathy and compassion were wrapped up and tucked into a deep, dark hole. He'd been there before. Elaborate thoughts were great for planning. Once you're in the thick of it, they become a hindrance. Instincts rule the battlefield. His mind became clear and empty as his body did what it needed to do. His muzzle flashed three times in rapid succession, and three furious angels were reduced to ash slowly floating on the delicate currents gently swirling through the lobby.

"On me," Lou's voice rang out with an authority Bale hadn't heard from the son of creation prior to that point. It was like he'd morphed from a thoughtful, creative soul, some kind of heavenly hippy, into a battle-hardened field sergeant the moment they had arrived in the middle of the melee.

Bale couldn't help but obey the simple command. As difficult as it was to believe the boasts Abigor had made about Lou, he suddenly felt like he'd follow the guy anywhere. The change wasn't subtle. The guy crouching behind an overturned leather sofa belching sunshine from the barrel of his oblivion gun and barking orders bared little resemblance to the melancholy poet he'd shared drinks with only a day or two earlier.

Two more demons fell as they executed Lou's command and took cover near his position. Bale felt their pain as they vaporized. It wasn't as bad as he expected it would be. It almost felt like relief, long sought after freedom from existing for longer than a conscious mind should. Twisted up with that feeling was undeniable regret fueled by a deep sense of duty. They had failed to see Lou to his goal. Bale almost felt jealous at the love these guys felt for him.

The thirteen who remained were finally locked in and safely behind cover. That was good. The fact nothing up to that point had gone to plan wasn't. There had to be forty angels belching what looked like bolts of sunshine at them. Bale kept mowing them down, but they just kept coming. It was like every time he dropped one, two more popped out from behind a chair or a corner or some other damn place. It wasn't working.

Abigor must have been thinking the same thing when he turned to Bale and shouted, "We're not winning this fight. You need to get Lou to his old man."

"No one leaves this spot until we've gained an advantage for those who remain to cover our exit," Lou's voice echoed loudly in everyone's head.

Bale latched onto Lou's awareness. Though it was solely a mental exercise, his body felt like it was moving. It wasn't. His body was planted firmly behind a makeshift barricade as he fired off shot after shot at the seemingly never-ending supply of angels, but that wasn't the movement he felt. His mind was on a mission. It felt like he was walking or running. He'd never experienced anything quite like it. He remained engaged in the moment, active in the battle. Yet, he was suddenly seated at a simple, steel table, the kind where the legs fold up and you can throw it in a closet to hide out until the next poker night. Lou sat across from him. It was crazy. He was still seeing and responding to everything happening in the lobby of Orwell's tower, but there he was at the same time holding Lou's hands in his own and imploring him to leave his demons behind to cover his exit like they'd planned.

"Do not waste any air pouring the words I know you are going to say into the world," Lou sighed.

The argument Bale planned to make was right there at the front of his mind, but they weren't the words that came out of his mouth when he gasped, "How the fuck are we sitting here talking while we're still fighting, and I can see, hear, and experience everything in both places at the same time? I can feel your hands in mine, and you must be ten feet away from me right now."

"How should I know? It was you who dragged me to this place. Maybe you reached out to me with your subconscious mind or something. No matter how much we learn about how the mind works the more mysterious it seems. Mind you, I am not talking about the brain rather the machine within the machine," Lou replied quietly. Even tainted with frustration, his tone was as pleasing as a song when he added, "What does it matter anyway? We are here regardless how you made it so."

"You're right," Bale conceded. "It doesn't matter. Hell, it's probably only the tenth most amazing thing I've seen in my long life."

Lou's eyes grew intense as he asked, "So then, what do you hope to gain with this distraction?"

"We need to leave," Bale shrugged. "You get no closer to your goal pinned down in that lobby."

"I will not leave them to die," Lou remained defiant.

"Then we'll die with them, and this mission will have been a waste. They all love you. No. They adore you. I saw everyone's thoughts while we traveled. They all signed up for this mission for two reasons: to get you an audience with your father and to waste some angels along the way. They are holding up their end of the bargain. You need to hold up yours."

"I let them down," Lou's gaze dipped toward the table as he replied.

"No," Bale shook his head. "I fucked up. This is on me. I'm sorry for that, but my failure doesn't change the mission."

It looked like defeat in Lou's eyes when he whispered, "Fine."

The room, the card table, and Lou sitting across from him were all suddenly gone. A lobby full of furious angels was all that remained. Bale fired off three quick shots before diving toward Lou's position. Abigor had done the same.

"Do your thing, Bale. Get him up there. We've got this locked down," Berith shouted.

"The plan was for you to join us," Lou snapped.

"The plan was to steamroll these punks and draw the rest to us. That didn't happen, and now we're shorthanded. Take Abigor. I've got this," Berith never stopped firing as he replied.

Bale didn't wait for the argument to continue. He allowed his awareness to slither into both Lou's and Abigor's minds. The push was rough, crude almost, but it worked. It felt like he was firmly gripping their hands, though no one physically touched anyone. Focus was critical. He couldn't fail this time. Once he was firmly latched to his two companions, he allowed the image of Orwell's office to fill his mind. It wasn't long before it was the only thing he could see.

A moment later, the three of them were crouching in that same office in the exact same positions they'd been in down in the lobby. There was no pain. In fact, it didn't feel like they had traveled at all. One moment they were pinned down in the lobby, and the next Bale was looking up at the shocked expression painted across Michael's face.

Nothing else in the room mattered at that moment. Bale had waited centuries to go toe to toe with Orwell's favorite, the fair-haired Michael. It was finally time.

The elbow Bale pounded into the side of Michael's jaw should have dropped the angel to the ground. It only earned a pompous smile from the self-righteous prick. Bale only had a moment to consider how badly he'd underestimated Orwell's little pet before a heel connected with his sternum. Michael hadn't moved. Bale had been so focused on him that he failed to see Gabriel jump up from the chair he'd been lounging in to deliver the blow. It was like getting hit by a car. The assault tossed him ten feet across the room to slam into the wall.

Before Bale could get back to his feet, Abigor's knee was flying toward Michael's chin with the big demon racing up behind it. Then Michael was flying through the air to smack into the wall. Abigor's feet had barely touched the ground when he fired his foot back toward Gabriel to plant a heel in his chest. The kick sent the fire-haired angel tumbling over a chair.

"Quit fucking around," Abigor shouted to Bale before charging after Gabriel.

Abigor was right. Bale needed to be stronger. The physiology of angels was completely different than any of the creatures he'd ever faced. Werewolves and vampires were built tougher than men, but they were still skin and bones. Their skin could be split and their bones broken. Angels were different. Bale focused on his fists. He needed his knuckles to be harder, denser. He needed bricks hanging from his wrists. No. He needed wrecking balls to smash that asshole's perfect face in.

Bale jumped back to his feet and charged at Michael. He stopped just short of him and fired a tight, right hook at the angel's jaw. His clenched fist felt strong racing toward its target. Unfortunately, it had only moved about six inches toward it before Bale was sailing through the air again looking up at his feet. He had no idea what Michael had hit him with, but his cheek throbbed like it had been hit by a bat. He needed to be faster.

"Let me know if you need me to take him for you," Lou chuckled as he lounged behind Orwell's desk enjoying the show.

"I've got this," Bale grunted as he scrambled back to his feet.

It was a lie. Lou probably knew that, but Bale wasn't ready to throw in the towel just yet. He owed Michael an ass whooping, and he had no intention of letting someone else pay his debt. The idea barely had a chance to manifest in his mind when Michael's smug face was directly in front of him again. Damn, he was fast.

This time Bale saw it coming. It was a jab. He'd never seen anything move that fast. It was like a bullet racing toward his nose. There is no reality where he should have seen it coming, but he did. Whatever his mind was doing was working. He did feel stronger. His fists felt heavier. When he slipped his head to the right to dodge the blow, it sailed past his face a solid inch from his cheek. This time the right hook he fired at Michael's jaw connected hard enough to stagger the angel.

"That's right," Lou coached from behind the desk, "Get out of your own way and be what you were meant to be."

Bale had no idea what Lou was getting at, and there was no time to think about it. As soon as Michael had steadied himself, he threw a lazy, looping kick toward Bale's head. It was easy to avoid, too easy. The straight low kick that connected with Bale's knee hard enough to buckle it and ruin his balance was the real attack. It worked. Bale nearly ended up on his ass while retreating several feet to avoid whatever Michael planned to follow up with.

After adding enough distance to give himself a moment to recover, Bale flexed his left knee. It wasn't broken or dislocated, but it would be sore for a while. That was all the time Michael gave him before unleashing his next attack...jab, hook, knee, the combo was quick and crisp, but Bale was ready for it. He slipped the jab, blocked the hook, and swayed back a step to avoid the knee.

For that brief moment, Michael stood wide open and exposed. That was the opening Bale was waiting for. He didn't bother setting up a combo, some elaborate series of moves to soften his opponent up. He went all in and fired a crushing overhand right. The angel seemed to crumble when Bale's fist connected with his cheek just next to his nose.

The cocky smile that asshole always wore finally left his face as he stumbled backward.

Bale wasn't finished. He stayed with him step for step and rocked him with an uppercut that connected solidly with the bottom of his chin. This one lifted the angel right off his feet dropping him on his ass about five feet away. Then he jumped on his chest to rain bombs down on his head.

The first blow was an inch from Michael's nose when Bale's vision went completely white. It was like staring at the desert sun. There were no shapes or shadows just blazing light filling everything.

"How dare you!" Orwell's voice rumbled across the shapeless, white expanse.

He heard Abigor groan, "Motherfucker," and then he felt him die. It was real death. An odd mix of emotions twisted up his awareness. The feelings weren't his own. They belonged to Abigor. It was equal parts rage, sorrow, helplessness, and elation. Hovering underneath it all was a subtle satisfaction that he'd sent that prick Gabriel to oblivion before Orwell wiped him out.

Several moments passed before Bale could make out any shapes. There was no vast expanse. It was Orwell's office. That had been obvious when his back crashed into the bookshelf, and he flopped onto the floor. Despite a loud whistling that left his ears ringing, Bale was able to make out Lou's ecstatic reaction to finally meeting his father.

"I have waited my entire life for this moment," Lou gushed like a child, his normally elegant voice vibrating with excitement.

"Of course, you have," Orwell responded as aloof and uncaring as ever. "It was wise for you to come to me. I thought I might never see the day with the way your mother meddles."

"She said she was protecting me. I am convinced she believed it, but I never did. There are so many things I yearn to learn," Lou continued in a rapid cadence.

"And I have much to teach you," Orwell's tone dropped and deepened as he replied. Bale recognized the ominous change immediately. He'd heard the shift a million times before. The god was about to feed. His next words were no surprise, "But first, we must become one. I cannot share the things I need to share with you until you are within me."

Lou's silence conveyed more meaning than any words he might

have spoken in that moment. Bale was there with him. Their minds were connected as if they were both part of the same network of neurons. Any idea or feeling sprouting up in Lou's mind occurred in Bale's as if it were his own. He felt Lou's pain as the poor soul's spirit shrunk like a spent balloon. Bale expected the moment Lou met Orwell to go exactly as it was. Lou's expectations were different. He'd always thought his mother was overreacting, responding to her own scars earned long before Lou had been born. Finally seeing how right she'd been all but crushed him.

Then it came. The physical pain. After witnessing Orwell feeding, hearing his victim's screams of agony, he'd assumed having your soul ripped from your body was painful. As connected as he was with Lou just then, he felt everything. It started as a pin prick, just a poke. It felt like a needle breaking the skin right between Lou's eyes. That was only the beginning. Pressure quickly mounted as the poke became a crushing force boring deep into Lou's head until it felt like it might explode at any moment. The pain was greater than the worst migraine Bale could remember. It didn't throb. It just continued to grow stronger, each moment feeling like it couldn't get any worse. Yet, it did.

Then finally, there was relief. Like someone had opened a valve to relieve all the mounting pressure. It only lasted for a moment. It was like Orwell had forced his consciousness into Lou filling up every tiny crevice of his being to latch onto every bit of him, grabbing hold of everything that made Lou who he was to rip it out of him. Then the pulling, yanking, and tearing started. There was nothing methodical about the process. It was all brute force.

Despite the pain tearing through Lou's body, it wasn't what hurt him the most. The man's heart was broken, cracked like a mountain twisted by a cataclysmic earthquake. Lou truly believed his father would rejoice at his presence. Not because he presented a vehicle for increasing his vast power, but because he could finally spend time getting to know his creation. Lou finally understood the naivety of the idea, an abandoned child's dream. The knowledge did nothing to dampen the hurt. Bale felt it all right along with him as if it were his own pain.

All the remnants of the blazing light Orwell had filled the room with when he arrived had finally faded away, and Bale could see clearly. Orwell's mouth hung wide as Lou trembled before him. Lou's soul, his essence, or whatever it was, looked like thick, white smoke billowing off his body and curling its way into the gaping, black pit at the center of Orwell's face. In moments, that brilliant and beautiful mind would be lost for eternity, trapped in a prison to mingle with every other lost soul Orwell had called home. Bale couldn't let that happen.

An idea occurred to him as he stared into the cavernous pit Orwell's mouth had stretched to become. It bared no resemblance to a mouth at all. It looked like a corridor, dark and ominous, but an entryway to someplace else. Bale knew he couldn't stop Orwell from feeding while he slumped there on the floor like trash waiting to be swept away. What if he went inside?

He jumped. There might have been a moment of regret the instant he entered Orwell's mouth, but he couldn't imagine making a different choice if given the chance. Orwell would not have Lou's soul. Not if Bale had anything to say about it.

CHAPTER 31

HEAVEN OR HELL

CITY OF GOLD

It was just like traveling. Bale felt it as soon as he touched the darkness swirling in the vast void Orwell's mouth had become. It wasn't subtle but immediate. His cells ripped apart from one another stretching like a cloud and racing toward some destination. The difference was that he had no idea where he was going. What did it mean to be one with god? Would he simply become a part of it, or a part of him, whatever Orwell was? Bale had always known the character who referred to himself as Orwell who he had interacted with wasn't the real being controlling every aspect of every reality he'd ever visited. However, prior to racing toward the center of that thing, he'd never had a reason to think too deeply about it. All of a sudden, what it was seemed monumentally important. Was it doom? Paradise? Something in between?

The need for asking answerless questions quickly evaporated. He was arriving. Bale's cells were finding their ways back to where they belonged, remembering each cell they had touched before tearing away from one another and finding their ways home.

At first, it seemed there was nothing but a vast expanse of blazing white with no color or shadow to give anything any shape. As Bale's eyes slowly grew accustomed to the bright light, he realized it wasn't that. The light was energy. It was alive. A dull hum surrounded everything as Bale finally saw Orwell for the first time. Not the puppet who walked about offering condescending quips about this or that, but his true form. He looked like a god. At least, he looked like Bale's idea of how a god might appear. Of course, the image was based on stories told in every reality he'd ever visited. Somehow, these almighty and omniscient beings so enlightened to have created everything in every reality always ended up resembling their creation. Of course it was ego, but Bale had never really questioned why anyone thought some multi-dimensional intelligence would look like any other man. As he gazed upon this thing who looked like a god should based on anything he'd ever read or learned about what a god was, he wondered if Orwell actually was god.

This aspect of Orwell was giant, a massive, thickly muscled man loosely covered with strips of cloth that might be some kind of robe and seated upon an ornate and gaudy, golden throne. His white hair was wild like energy coursed through it. The thick beard covering his jaw and draping down to his waist was the same. His eyes were colorless and horrible, like two pits of such depth no light could penetrate.

As this massive thing Orwell was lounged upon his gaudy throne, he was anything but idle. His body trembled almost to the point of convulsion while his lips curled in unnatural ways. The odd contortions of his face looked like a man perched on the precipice of orgasm when every muscle in the body tenses before exploding in the sweetest release, but the apex, that glorious crescendo never came. Bale wondered if that's what he was looking for in Lou's soul. Perched on the edge of some kind of spiritual orgasm for millennia, was he hoping a soul as pure and powerful as his son's would be the one that pushed him off that ledge to total release?

"I always knew you were a twisted fuck, but damn," Bale shouted to be heard above the loud hum, "Using your own son's soul to get off is a special kind of depravity."

"You are a simple creature, Bale Lance, a waste, unrealized potential," Orwell's voice peeled like thunder as it vibrated the air. "You could never comprehend the mysteries of my creation. This renders your perception of events as meaningless as your existence. You are nothing. You are powerless. Leave me to my work and save yourself my wrath."

"I won't let you have him. His precious spirit belongs to all," Bale replied in a quieter tone suddenly knowing he'd be heard. Somehow, as he said the words, he also knew Orwell's threat had been empty. It wasn't confidence or some innate belief. He knew in that moment that this supposed god had never had any power over him.

Orwell must have realized it the moment Bale became aware. It was the same moment he released his grip on Lou's soul. Bale couldn't see him, but he could feel the relief as the pain Lou experienced while Orwell ripped his essence away from him fled. Orwell's attention was suddenly focused on Bale.

The pulling and tearing and ripping he'd expected when Orwell's horrible gaze fell upon him was absent. What he felt was nothing like what Lou went through. This was a push not a pull. Like a wave crashing against a rocky bluff. The force was there, the energy, with enough momentum to blast him into space or whatever the white expanse surrounding him was, but Bale didn't move. The attack had no effect on him. He stood there, defiant, and latched onto the energy pummeling his entire form.

That's when everything shifted. There was no giant man seated on some gaudy throne surrounded by some kind of holy light. There was only light, a massive, glowing ball like a star floating in the center of a void and burning with white heat, pure energy. He felt a tug. Orwell was retreating from him. Bale held fast, clinging to his awareness as if he were squeezing a mind. Then he pushed harder and harder, forcing his will into Orwell's awareness, drilling into it as if it were some kind of skull.

As Bale pushed, he became more and more aware of his surroundings. Everything was happening at that precise moment. Time was an illusion. Every reality which existed, every place he'd visited had been right here in this one spot within Orwell who wasn't any kind of man at all. He was an intelligence of some kind to be sure, but not any form of physical being in any sense of the word Bale had ever understood. He was thought itself. Everything Bale had ever experienced was merely an aspect of that. Kaye had been that in the beginning. She and Orwell had been equal, but Orwell had somehow absorbed her. That was why she couldn't protect Lou from him. She'd become a part of him, hidden deep in the darkest depths of some cosmic subconscious he couldn't find or actively access. He could send his minions to Perver City, but he couldn't get to her.

As Bale drilled deeper into this vast awareness, the expanse surrounding him gained clarity. It wasn't just a wide and empty space filled with light glowing from some giant orb. Gray smudges filled it. They were blurry but dully glowing in their own way. It seemed they were trapped behind invisible walls unable to move or unaware they could. They all fed Orwell with energy, before and after they finished their imaginary journeys through some imagined physical existence. He suddenly wondered why Orwell needed to feed on their souls at all if they were already a part of him.

Then it occurred to him. It was different than the relationship between the subconscious mind and the conscious mind, but the connection was similar enough. Every being who ever existed lived out what appeared to be some kind of physicality completely outside of Orwell's awareness. It must have been quite a trick when he'd figured that out. He couldn't realize them until they passed on from their supposed physical existences. The light they saw at the end was his way to guide them home. When they went into that light, he could feed off the energy they'd accumulated through experiences. It was quite a system, but it was time for it to end.

"Petulant, impotent child, how dare you!" Orwell's voice continued to rumble like thunder, but all the authority it had carried was gone. Fear saturated the words in its place.

"I exist outside of you," Bale finally said. "You can't control me, because I don't belong to you."

The loud humming that had been vibrating all around Bale suddenly increased in both volume and intensity as Orwell quietly commented, "You fool. You have ruined everything I have built."

The light surrounding Bale blazed even more brilliantly than it had been for a moment then quickly began to dim. Bale shook his head and said, "You don't exist in my reality."

Kaye lounged on an elegant chaise in her office sipping bourbon as she absently twitched while a satyr rapidly flicked her bean with his tongue. He was doing a fine job, but it was just a distraction. Her mind was elsewhere. Her baby boy was off to see the wizard, and that bastard would probably suck the soul right out of him. Hopefully, Bale would figure out who he was in time to prevent that. Things were going to end for them both either way. The only question was how that ending would go. Everything would change for the better if Bale were successful. If not, Orwell would finally have the power to destroy her. Perver City would be no more. That would be a shame. All the souls she loved so much would be sucked into that twisted fucker's demented awareness where he could torment them until the end of time.

The satyr's teeth scraping her clitoris a bit too roughly brought her mind back into the moment as she grabbed a hold of one of his horns and said, "Take it easy down there, you fucking animal." She was done with it. She threw her glass along with her last sip of bourbon across the room, lifted the satyr's head up and said, "No, you know what? I'm done with you. Get the fuck out of here."

Then she felt the shift. It wasn't a physical shift. It was in her mind. Things were slipping out of her control. It was as if she'd been holding Perver City in her arms for all those millennia, and someone had grabbed her wrists to begin prying them away. The walls suddenly rumbled around her as plaster cracked and all her paintings in their mismatched frames began falling off the walls. She smiled. It wasn't Orwell stealing her world. It was Bale destroying it. All those souls would finally be free.

Kaye looked back down at the satyr dumbly staring back at her from between her legs and said, "Change of plans, get back in there. Quit fucking around and finish the job. I want to go out with a bang."

CHAPTER 32

THE BEGINNING

A NEW REALITY

It was cold at first, freezing, that kind of bone chilling cold that overwhelms you and sends your body into shivers so violent they border on convulsion. Then it was melt the flesh from your bones hot. Luckily, both happened so quickly that Bale had neither the time to freeze solid nor melt into a pile of sloppy goo. Then it was comfortable.

Everything was black for a moment. Not just dark, it was the complete absence of light. At the same time smells of sulfur and ozone wafted about despite a complete lack of any kind of breeze. Nothing moved. Total silence surrounded everything.

Then there was light. Bale stood alone surrounded by white, a blank canvas for him to fill. He was like Orwell had been, but he didn't want to be in that place. He didn't want to be some kind of parasite feeding off imaginary experiences in his own mind. His reality would be different.

The first thing that popped into his mind was Angel Cakes. As soon as the image of her face occurred to him, there she was standing before him, gazing up at him with those deep, blue eyes so full of innocence that he'd missed so much.

"Daddy," she screamed as she jumped into his arms.

The tears he'd been holding back from her for more than two-thousand years poured down his cheeks. He didn't need to stop them anymore. There would be no lie this time. He would never again have to tell her everything was going to be alright when he knew it wasn't.

Everything was going to be alright forever.

"Angel Cakes," he gushed as he held her close and spun them both around before falling to the ground. It was softer than he'd expected it would be.

She lifted her head from his chest, looked around, and asked, "Is this home now?"

"It is, Angel Cakes," he replied as he sat up, "and it is going to be whatever you want it to be."

Her face twisted up like she'd just tasted something sour. "Whatever I want it to be?" she asked.

"That's right," he smiled as he hugged her tight.

She grabbed her chin as she looked up toward the vast expanse of nothing surrounding them and said, "Okay, first things first then. I don't want to be Angel Cakes anymore. That sounds like a baby's name. What was my name before? I can't even remember it."

"I called you Eirini when you were born," he replied. "It means peace."

"That's pretty, but," she trailed off.

"But what?" he asked.

"But I want to be Martha," she said with the most conviction he'd ever heard in her voice.

Bale suppressed a chuckle as he asked, "Where did you come up with that name?"

"I don't know," she shrugged, "Probably from one of the asshats, but I like it. I want to be Martha."

"Okay, you can be Martha then," he shrugged back at her. "So, Martha, what else do you want?"

She thought for a moment and then asked, "How old am I?"

"That's a tough one. You were six years old when Orwell took you, and you haven't aged since then. Two thousand three hundred and eighty-one years have passed since you were born in the reality you were born into. That would make you very, very old. How old do you want to be?"

"I want to be how old I am, but not forever," she replied.

"Okay, you'll naturally grow older until you don't want to anymore," Bale shrugged. "This is all pretty easy, so far. What else do you want? What do you want your world to look like?"

"Well, there is one thing," she began, "Gabriel was teasing me once, and he told me about candy. He said it was sweet and tasted so delicious. He said little girls like me love candy, but I'd never get to have any. I want candy to be everywhere."

"As you wish," Bale smiled.

Dirt began to flow out from where they sat. It was just dirt, at first, but it wasn't long before licorice whips began growing up from the ground like tall, red grass. Then trees began sprouting up here and there. They looked very much like any normal tree, but the bark of their trunks and branches were chocolate, and gumdrops grew where leaves should have been. Shrubs and mushrooms and flowers sprouted up here and there, all of it bright and colorful and totally edible. It stretched and stretched for miles until they could no longer see past it.

"There you go, a world full of candy," he finally said. "Go ahead, try a blade of that grass. It's red licorice, cherry. You'll like it."

Her eyes lit up as she did as he had instructed, plucking a long whip from the ground and biting into it. "This is amazing," she mumbled as she chewed.

"That was still pretty easy," Bale mussed her hair and offered a beaming smile. "What about animals or people?"

She stopped chewing for a moment as she thought about it. Then she swallowed and said, "There were unicorns by that lake sometimes. I liked them. We should have unicorns here."

"That is a wonderful idea," Bale agreed.

As soon as the words left his mouth, a pink unicorn snorted behind them. It startled them and left them both reeling with a mad fit of giggles. Another blinked into existence. This one was pale green and immediately stooped to chew on the licorice grass. More and more came. They were purple and blue and orange and yellow. There were thousands of them all glowing and majestic with long twisted horns jutting from the centers of their heads.

"They are so beautiful," Martha gasped as she stood to scratch the neck of the pink one who'd startled them.

"Come on. Let's explore this world we're creating," Bale said as he stood and stretched. "We have lots to do. We should probably have more animals, and probably rivers and mountains and lakes, and clouds too."

They strolled along with the pink unicorn who seemed quite smitten with Martha. As they walked, Martha would shoot out random ideas of things she'd like in her world. A moment later they'd be there. Monkeys swung from the candy trees as mountains stretched up from the ground. She finally asked for people to exist, and then they did. They were naked at first. She thought it might be embarrassing for them, so she suggested they have clothes, long colorful robes and jewelry to wear about their necks and wrists. They seemed to like the candy too.

Martha suddenly stopped, tugged on Bale's hand, and said, "What about mama? Shouldn't she be with us?"

"I thought about that," Bale frowned. "It's been a long time. Neither of us are the same people she knew when she was alive. I'm sure she'd love you anyway. Mothers never stop loving their children. I'm not so sure how she'd feel about me. I've done things I can't forgive myself for. I wouldn't expect her to either."

"I'd like to know her," Martha replied.

"And you should," Bale nodded his agreement.

Then Alexandra was there, standing in front of them. Her long brown hair cascaded over her shoulders in loose, careless curls. She was as beautiful as Bale remembered, but sadness lingered in her soft, blue eyes. "What is this place?" she gasped with a hint of fear coloring her tone.

"It's a brand-new world, my love," Bale replied with sadness lingering about in his smile.

Martha didn't hesitate. She shouted, "Mama," ran to Alexandra, and wrapped her arms around her legs.

Alexandra picked her up and held her tight. Her eyes narrowed as she looked at Bale and asked, "Who are you?"

"It's daddy," Martha said, as she looked up at Alexandra. "Don't you remember him?"

"Bale?" she asked as she continued to examine him, "Could it really be you?"

Bale lost the tear that had been teetering on the edge of his eyelid. It tickled his cheek while slowly meandering toward his chin. "It's me," he finally said. After a few more tears, he added, "I wasn't strong enough to save you."

Alexandra's gaze dropped toward the ground, "Those men hurt me. They took things from me. What they did was nothing compared to what happened after that. There was a light. I was drawn to it, like a flowing river whose current was too strong to swim against. I found myself before Zeus. He was both beautiful and terrifying to behold. He ripped everything away from me, everything I loved and everything

I feared. I was nothing when he finished with me. Knowing that was worse than the pain it caused while he took it all from me. Then I wasn't anything at all, aware but empty. All this time, it was like I was floating, feeling nothing and knowing nothing until this very moment. I never blamed you for any of that. How long has it been?"

"Dad said I was two thousand three hundred and eighty-one years old. If you died when I was six, that would mean you were stuck there for two thousand three hundred and seventy-five years," Martha blurted.

"I had been on the earth for twenty-eight years at that time," Alexandra shook her head. "I can't even fathom how much time that is, how much I lost. How is it that both of you have lived so long? Are you a god, Bale? Could you have stopped Zeus from taking everything from me?"

The lie was there. It would have been easier, but he owed her honesty. He scratched his head and replied, "I guess I am in this place. I didn't know what I was then. I could have stopped him had I known."

She hugged Martha tighter as a slightly maniacal smile danced across her face before she said, "I felt the moment when I ceased to be anything at all. I can't explain it. I was already nothing. Then I just wasn't until you brought me here. That moment was a relief. You could have left me. I would have never known all this. I wouldn't have to remember. I don't blame you for anything that happened before that point, but I blame you for the way I feel right now."

"It was me, mama," Martha said as she raised her head to look in Alexandra's eyes. "I wanted you back. I'm sorry for that."

Alexandra offered her daughter a warm smile as she set her down and knelt before her. Then she mussed her brown locks and said, "I am happy to be here. I just need some time." Then she looked over at Bale and added, "I am uncertain if I will ever feel like I did for you."

"I know," Bale frowned. "I'll be here if you ever do."

Then Martha held Alexandra's face in both of her hands and said, "We have lots to do. We have to make this whole world."

"We?" Alexandra asked.

"Yep," Martha began, "Well, daddy has to make everything. We just have to tell him what we want."

"What do you want?" Alexandra asked.

"I don't know," Martha chewed her bottom lip. "I feel like I have everything I want."

"Have you ever had a cheeseburger?" Bale asked.

"What's a cheeseburger?" Martha asked.

"Heaven in your mouth," Bale smiled back at her. "Come on. Let's make a diner that grills up the best cheeseburgers of all time. Milkshakes too. You'll love it."

"I can't wait to see what a diner is," Martha said as she led Alexandra over to him, skipping all the way.

Bale paused and said, "There is one other thing I need to do. I made a promise to someone who helped me get you out of that place Orwell had you trapped in with the two asshats."

EPILOGUE

PROMISES KEPT

A NEW REALITY

Bale sat at the bar at Club despair sipping the green shit he'd always drank there back when Orwell ran the show. The scene was a bit different. None of the vampires in the place wanted to drain him or turn him. The music was the same, that eerie violin dancing across the top of a hard-pounding techno beat. Martha sat next to him. She seemed to like the music. Her head bobbed along with the rhythm. Alexandra sat on the other side of Martha sipping wine and seemingly enjoying the tune as much as her little girl.

"I can't believe you did it, Bale. I can't believe you killed Orwell," Mark chuckled as he poured Bale another drink. Then he shook his head and added, "I'm not praying to you or anything."

Bale laughed at him and replied, "Nobody is praying to me. I don't need that. I just want to live my life with everybody else."

Then Mark looked over at Alexandra and said, "I feel like I know you with everything Bale told me about you. It broke his heart that you were gone. Most of my booze went to trying to deaden the pain."

Alexandra smiled and said, "Perhaps one day I will help him heal it. I am not ready for that yet."

"He's a good guy," Mark said as he refilled her glass. "A little rough around the edges, but he has a good heart."

It hurt Bale a bit when she offered only a shallow smile and a slight nod as a response to Mark, but he understood. It was going better than he expected it might. At least she lived with him, and he didn't have to go through some pain in the ass visitation with Martha. They were all together in the house they had occupied before Orwell destroyed their lives.

Bale turned his attention back to Mark and said, "So, I kept my promise and delivered that little shit to you. Tell me about it. How did the nicest guy I've ever known torture tr0Gmortem69?"

If Mark were human, he might have blushed when he said, "That little fucker had it coming. I made a promise to him you know."

"I remember," Bale shook his head. "You told him you were going to drain his parents and teabag them while he watched. That's pretty fucked up, Mark"

"I know. I know," Mark shrugged. "I can't explain it in a way that would make sense to you, but that kid really fucking gets to me. Well, he did. Now I feed the little fucker steaks, and my patrons happily sip his blood."

"What about his parents?" Bale asked.

Mark's expression tightened as his tone grew serious, "Just what I told him I was going to do. I dragged them into his room. He was fast asleep. Looked like a little cherub, all sweet and innocent. I sang in his ear El-ee-ot, El-ee-ot. It took a few minutes, but he finally woke up. You should have seen that little fucker's face when I punched my fangs into his mom's throat and splattered his cheeks with her blood."

"Really?" shock colored Bale's expression. "That's fucked up, man."

The tension in Mark's jaw fled as a dopey smile crawled onto his face, and he said, "No, not really. That was totally my plan, but I couldn't do it. They were all so fucking scared. I felt bad. Elliot's actually a really nice kid. He just likes talking shit, and he's really good at that fucking game. I'm teaching him how to work the farm. He's a twisted little fucker, kind of like my creepy, little apprentice."

"See? The nicest guy I know," Bale smiled, drained his glass and set it down on the bar.

Mark grabbed the bottle of green shit and asked, "Fill her up?"

Bale moved his hand over the glass, shook his head, and said, "Nope. I'm good. Everything I need is sitting right here at this bar."

The End

ABOUT THE AUTHOR

E. Michael Mettille is the author of the Lake of Dragons series, Fleeing from Light, and Hell and the Hunger (as Mike Reynolds). He has also written numerous short stories and poems. Mike has spent the last thirty years in direct marketing, print, and communication. He is fascinated by history, belief systems, the human condition and how all of those things work together to define who we are as a people. The world is a wonder and, based on the history of us, it is a wonder we have a world left to wonder about. Mike lives in Franklin, WI with his wife, Shelia, and their four dogs, Ziggy Stardust, Lady Stardust, Major Tom, and Bowie, The Spiders from Mars.

www.ingramcontent.com/pod-product-compliance
Lightning Source LLC
Chambersburg PA
CBHW050314110726
47899CB00007B/2238